G000167601

This book is dedicated to former soldier and police sergeant, Dennis Chopping, who not only inspired this story but was also a tireless supporter of child welfare and the last of the 'Old time Coppers'.

Like Sinatra, he did it his way.

Cliff Comber

Running For His Lives

An Explosive Story of Love, Myth and Ultimate Retribution

AUSTIN MACAULEY PUBLISHERS™

LONDON • CAMBRIDGE • NEW YORK • SHARJAH

A CIP catalogue record for this title is available from the British Library.

This is a work of fiction. Any references to real people, living or dead, real events, business, organisations and localities are intended only to give the fiction a sense of reality and authenticity. Many names, characters, places and incidents referred to are real, others are the product of the author's imagination. The real-life characters mentioned have given their express permission to be fictionalised in this volume. All behaviour, history, and character traits assigned to their fictional representation have been designed to serve the needs of the narrative and do not necessarily bear any resemblance to the real person.

ISBN 9781788481731 (Paperback)
ISBN 9781788481748 (Hardback)
ISBN 9781788481755 (E-Book)

www.austinmacauley.com
First Published (2018)
Austin Macauley Publishers Ltd™
25 Canada Square
Canary Wharf
London
E14 5LQ

Acknowledgements

Although the crimes committed in this novel are fiction, many of the people and places mentioned are real, which enabled me to put myself there, on the spot, hopefully supplying a touch of realism to particular scenes.

My utmost gratitude goes to Sarah for encouragement and sharing her grammatical and literacy knowledge with me. Her enthusiastic support and vision greatly assisted my story on these pages.

Special thanks also to my wife, Carla, who had to endure all my rants when things didn't go as planned and for the continual running up and down the stairs to the office to assist this wannabe author and technophobe as I wrestled with a computer that I had little understanding of.

I am also grateful to the following for their contribution or advice on various aspects: radio and TV presenter, 'Diddy' David Hamilton; Detective Chief Inspector, Pierre Serra; Fire Safety and Fire Investigation Officer, Lee Spencer-Smith; Armed Forces Recruiting Office Brighton; DVLA, Swansea; Martin Read, local journalist; Victor from Venezuela now resident in the UK; Ross Beare of Holmbush Events; all my family, friends and ex colleagues who, with them in mind, allowed me to bring this fictional story to life.

My thanks also go to Austin Macauley Publishers, who showed faith in me and provided friendly professional help to make my dream come true.

Throughout the formation of this novel there have been many reasons for me to question some form of spiritual assistance, so just in case I thank them also.

Finally, my thoughts and gratitude go out to my good friend Dennis Chopping, who, being one of the characters who inspired this story, remains severely physically handicapped following a stroke some years ago. Despite this misfortune, his mind and wit are as sharp as ever. They say behind every good man is a good woman, and his wife, Cynthia, has been his rock and remains so to this day.

Tybalt: "What wouldst thou have with me?"
Mercutio: "Good king of cats, nothing but one of your nine lives."

Romeo and Juliet
William Shakespeare

Foreword

Music is all about memories. You hear a certain song and it can take you back to a special time in your life. It could remind you of a place—the long and winding road that leads to your door. It may remind you of a special relationship with someone you've loved or perhaps with your parents.

Music can remind you of happy times and sad ones, too. It can bring back the days of your teenage years, when you were full of youthful enthusiasm or memories of a birthday or the first dance on your wedding day.

How grateful we are to the song writers, who have crafted these gems down the years that have raised our emotions in one way or another. Like John Miles who wrote:

> *"To live without my music would be impossible to do...*
> *In this world of troubles, my music pulls me through."*

David Hamilton
Sussex, England
March, 2017

Radio and TV personality with a career spanning over five decades during which time, he presented over 12,000 radio shows and over 1,000 TV shows including BBC's *Top of the Pops*.

The only thing necessary for the triumph of evil is for good men to do nothing.

Edmund Burke

Chapter 1
Airport (1978)
Artists: The Motors   Writer: Andy McMaster

The deeply dreaming English passenger was abruptly awoken by an authoritative female voice speaking rapidly over an intercom, in what he believed to be Spanish; dazed and confused as to where he was and what he was doing there, the same voice repeated in English, "Ladies and gentlemen, we are now making our final approach into La Chinita, Maracaibo. Please ensure that all of your luggage is stowed away in the overhead lockers and your seat belts are fastened. The weather in Maracaibo is fine with a ground temperature of 33 degrees but a chance of rain expected later. On behalf of the captain and crew, we wish to thank you for flying with Lufthansa and look forward to travelling with you again in the future."

Dennis 'Dutch' French finally woke up from his 14-hour journey, sufficiently enough to gather his thoughts. It was no wonder that he was so dog tired, his past seven weeks had been far from anything resembling the normal pattern of everyday life, taking its toll on even his physical and mental endurance.

Whilst attempting to regain some sensation in the lower half of his cramped body and continuing to awaken from his slumbers, he could now feel a new calmness within himself; a calmness that he had not experienced since the initial event that first triggered the intense anger within. He realised that as devastating and life changing his actions had since been, he now felt a sense of release from the torment that had consumed him.

One of the last passengers to disembark, he wearily made his way from the jetliner, yawning and rubbing his eyes, and joined the line of new arrivals in the immigration hall, taking the opportunity to adjust his watch to the five-hour time difference. Having finally shuffled forwards to the appropriate desk, he passed his passport and papers, and following a brief examination of them, the plain-clothes official turned and nodded to a military clad man standing close by. The uniformed officer, who was armed with an assault rifle strapped around his neck, approached Dutch and gestured him into a nearby room. He was unnerved at this, but feigned indifference; as of all the other passengers on the same flight had passed through the controlled area before him, he had been the only one that had been singled out. A distinct feeling of unease swept over him, though he remained composed and tried to give no outward sign of his sense of foreboding, but he couldn't help but wonder whether the authorities here had received some form of advance communication from the UK.

The late morning temperature was tipping 35 degrees inside the small immigration office interview room in the Venezuelan airport.

After what seemed an eternity of waiting in the oppressive heat of the oxygen-starved room, a man entered; an official, smartly dressed in a white shirt and navy slacks with a loosened tie around his neck, making Dutch feel underdressed in his now creased shorts and t-shirt, and the man too, was not impervious to the heat, judging by the damp patches on his shirt. With his jet-black well-groomed hair, clear olive skin, shaven appearance and lean good looks, he could have easily been mistaken for a Latino pop or film star.

A moment later, another man entered and walked straight to the back of the room, where he sank down heavily onto a cheap-looking, brown metal and plastic chair which, like the matching table, was bolted to the floor. He appeared to be a similar weight and height to Dutch, though he looked to be not far off retirement, and his dishevelled look suggested someone who had not long got out of bed: he was dressed in military-type attire of green shirt, green baggy trousers and black lace-up boots, one lace untied, with a green peaked combat cap perched on the back of his unkempt hair; he had a swarthy, moustachioed appearance and silent, hostile countenance. On his wide, black leather belt, he carried a pistol contained in a holster. Dutch became distracted from the situation, trying to establish the make and model of the weapon at the same time, thinking to himself that as the man was presumably part of the National Guard, if he had been a recruit under his command, he would have described him as looking like a sack of shit tied up in the middle by a belt.

At first glance, the official appeared to look relaxed, not at all what Dennis was expecting in what he understood to be a high-risk corner of the globe, though the other man matched his expectations: put a cheroot in the side of his mouth and he'd have been the image of a Mexican bandit, straight off the set of a spaghetti western; Dutch mentally dubbed him 'Pancho', appertaining to the notorious Mexican revolutionary general, Pancho Villa. The two were such opposites, he wondered if he was about to experience the 'good cop, bad cop' routine.

The official, whom Dutch estimated was in his mid-thirties, introduced himself in almost perfect English with a heavily Spanish accent. Dutch was apprehensive as to why he had been singled out for interview but pleased that this man spoke so clearly because foreign languages were not his forte. When he first chose this destination, he had intended to learn some basic Spanish, but his meticulous planning and actions, he deemed necessary before his departure, had not afforded him the time for such study.

The man sat down on the opposite side of the functional office table and after a cursory examination of his passport, asked him the purpose of his visit to this country.

"I'm here to work a three-year contract as a security operative."

"Security guard or bodyguard?"

Dutch hesitated, not altogether sure that he really knew the answer to this.

"Both probably, I'll be heading up a team, looking after an oil company executive."

The security official glanced back down at the passport and then back up at him.

"Who will you be working for?"

"Not sure. I only know that he's the head of a large oil company."

Dutch felt a stab of apprehension about the vagueness of his answers. He wondered whether his physical discomfort with the heat in the room and his jaded and dishevelled appearance after the long flight would make him appear disproportionately uneasy. He cleared his throat and sat up a little straighter in his seat.

"I applied for the job through a US agency, via a military magazine. My new employer should be sending someone to meet me here."

The official merely nodded briefly and said,

"Can I see your work permit?"

Dutch reached into the small zipped folder he had resting on his lap and retrieved the permit. He unfolded the document and laid it on

13

the table in front of the official; as he did so, he was distracted by the insistent buzzing of a large fly, crawling across the face of a wall clock mounted on wall to the left of the official's desk. As his eyes traced the fly's noisy progress across the glass casing, he noticed the time displayed, and he was taken by surprise; how could he have got the time adjustment so wrong? He then realised that the second hand was not moving, and the clock had stopped. Dutch then glanced down at his own wristwatch and as he did so, a bead of sweat ran into his eye, causing a stinging sensation; he hadn't experienced such heat since his last tour of the Middle East some seven years ago.

"Do you know of what happened to the, hombre, err, man who was doing this work before?"

The question immediately refocussed his attention.

"I can guess a vacancy in this type of work only occurs for one or two reasons, and I'm aware of the risks."

"Risks, si. You will know the murder rate here is one of the highest in the world, and your employers will be…err, target for armed kidnappers?" He glanced up at Dutch.

"Kidnappers," he repeated, "there are many here."

The official was now looking at him quite intently and appeared to be carefully gauging his reaction as he asked,

"You not concerned about the danger of this type of job? There are some very dangerous gangs out there…"

Before he could finish, Pancho, who had been staring at him intently throughout, interjected in broken English,

"Bad men, si, many bad hombres here."

As he spoke, a slow smile snaked out onto his lips and it seemed as if he was about to say more, but instead, he merely gave Dutch an enquiring look, prompting him to reply.

"I wouldn't be here if I were. I'm used to this kind of work; circumstances have forced me to do what I know best."

The official said, "Circumstances…what circumstances? Are you running away from the police or other authority?"

Dutch's eyes snapped back to the official, as he too was obviously aware that there was no extradition arrangement with the United Kingdom.

"No," he replied firmly and truthfully, as at this present time, he knew nothing to the contrary.

The official gave the briefest nod of acknowledgement and enquired,

"Your employers will need to sponsor you to possess a gun; I assume have you used one before?"

As he went to answer, Pancho interrupted again with,

"Guns, you know guns?" tapping his holster.

Dutch looked between the two men and noticed the plain clothes official roll his eyes, clearly aggravated by the other man's interruption. Dutch replied,

"Yes, I was in the British Army for a long time."

Raising his eyebrows, the official said,

"That is unusual. Most of the security workers here are either local or American."

"I imagine my British Army training and experience are the primary reasons that I was selected."

The man appeared to consider this answer carefully.

Dutch glanced up at the clock again and wondered as to why, as he knew, it wasn't working, then realised that it was the only focal point in the barren, non-descript room. This was beginning to remind him of an operational briefing that he had once been given regarding procedure should he be captured in enemy territory.

"Why are you taking such risks?"

"It's a three-year contract and if I'm successful, I will earn enough money to set me up for the rest of my life. It seems worth the risk to me."

"And you are a married man?"

"Yes, my wife is joining me here soon; she's been promised a job within the secure home of my new employers."

"What work will she be doing here?"

"She's a nursery school teacher, she will be teaching my new employer's young children."

"Have you any ninos, err, children, of your own?"

Dutch shook his head, "No, no children."

The man leaned back in his chair; crossing his arms loosely, he inhaled deeply,

"Do you think that she will be happy here, in a, err, lonely place, in an unfamiliar country?"

Dutch noted the unmistakeable note of scepticism in his voice but answered calmly,

"I have been assured that we will be living in a comfortable, secure home within our employer's grounds. She has done her own research and understands what it is like here, but she..." he hesitated momentarily, "she just feels the need to get away from her present situation for a while."

The man gave the slightest suggestion of a smile, then sat upright, promptly gathered Dutch's papers together and handed them across the table to him, which he picked up and zipped securely back into his folder.

The interview appeared to be over, prompting Dutch to say, "Can I ask why I was singled out for this interview?"

He replied, "How you say, just routine."

Dutch didn't believe him, it appeared they had been expecting his arrival, or was he being paranoid?

The official stood and said,

"Gracias, all appears in order and I wish you luck in your work," and began to cross the room towards the door.

As he began to leave, Dutch said, "Thanks, I'll be fine. I'm a survivor and anyway, I've got a few lives left yet."

The official paused, his hand resting on the door handle, and looked at him directly, "What do you mean?"

"Oh, take no notice, it's just a personal joke of mine."

The official continued to hold his gaze.

"Let's just say that I have had more than a few lucky escapes in my time."

Looking slightly puzzled, the official followed Dutch out to the outer lobby and promptly disappeared behind an unmarked, white door. Pancho also followed them out and appeared to wait for the official to leave, then menacingly approached Dutch and, almost nose to nose, looked straight in his eyes and in broken English, uttered,

"Si, Senor French, you will need many luck here."

The foul odour of the man's breath was almost enough to render Dutch speechless and caused him to turn his head away, and before he could reply, the man strode off leaving him to get his bearings. Dutch couldn't help but think that if this was one of the 'good guys', the 'many bad men', he had warned him about, must be real charmers.

· Dutch decided to take the comment to be a gypsy's warning from someone he estimated to be a highly suspect individual, who seemed to have taken an instant disliking to Dutch and the feeling was mutual.

He made his way towards the baggage reclaim, noting that the light, airy walkways of the airport building were not really what he had imagined when he pictured all this back on UK soil. He followed the signs to the row of baggage carousels and locating his flight number, prepared to wait for his bags; this was the last hurdle before exiting the 'Arrivals' building and meeting his contact from the oil company.

It was a lengthy wait, and he began to wonder if his luggage had become another casualty of the reputedly unreliable and theft-prone baggage handling system. He knew it to be a country both rich in natural resources such as diamonds and oil but hindered in so many ways by a potent cocktail of inept politicians, corruption and crime.

The carousel finally jerked and chugged into life, and his well-worn bulky rucksack and suit case, with its equally battered exterior, one of the few items inherited from his late father, whom without foresight had conveniently embossed his initial and surname on the lid, rumbled down the belt towards him. Reunited with his belongings, he made his way towards the exit boundary.

Waiting on the other side of the transparent screens, many armed with name boards, were a multitude of people—mostly men. Dutch rapidly scanned the boards, searching out his own name.

Finally, his eyes came to rest on a huge man, black with a completely shaved head that reflected the overhead spotlights. He was about 6' 4" and muscular with the look of a weight trainer, though, judging by his waistline, it had been some time since he had been putting the road work in. His expression was impassive but he had the stereotypical 'boxer's nose', which had clearly been subjected to a break or two in its time. Around his huge frame, he was wearing a khaki, safari style gilet, which was straining at the zipper; a red, short-sleeve t-shirt; black, cargo trousers and black trainers. The makeshift cardboard sign he was holding, bearing the name 'French', looked minute in comparison.

Dutch walked up to the man and held out his hand, pointing to the sign and saying,

"Hi, I'm Dennis, although everyone calls me Dutch as my last name is French."

The black man gripped his hand firmly and looked him in the eye; when he spoke, it was in a deep southern American accent,

"French, Dutch, yeah, I get it, Dutch." He gave a small laugh and shook his head.

"People call me Big George, cause of my resemblance to George Foreman, y'know?"

Dutch instantly recognised the similarity to the boxer due to his keen interest in the sport and the celebrity who endorsed a universally known product.

"S'better than my real name, anyhow," said Big George smiling, though it was clear that he wasn't in any hurry to share that particular information, and Dutch suspected that might be the case for many visitors to this country.

Reaching over and easily lifting the heavy rucksack, the huge man set it upon his shoulder saying,

"Okay, Dutch, time to make a move outta here."

Dutch then noticed the feint tattoo of the US flag and eagle on his exposed right forearm, indicating to him that he had most probably once been a member of the US military. Dutch had no wish to be tattooed, neither was he a fan of any kind of jewellery; he didn't even wear his wedding ring, he felt that you enter the world naked and that's the form you should leave it in. He wore only a cheap running sports watch and his dog tags for identification and his blood group, should he be badly injured or killed, should his lives finally run out.

He turned and strode off in the direction of the outer sliding doors, glancing over his shoulder from time to time as they stepped out of the airport building. The heat and humidity felt more intense than it had been when he had first stepped off the plane that morning.

The midday sun glinted behind a hazy wisp of cloud, and Dutch retrieved his sunglasses from his shirt pocket, although there was a heaviness to the air which suggested that rain was on its way.

"So, what brings you out here then, Dutch?"

"Money mostly and the need to get away for a while."

"Touche," called Big George in a loud jovial voice, clearly not caring if he was overheard. "Me too, man; it seems we have something in common already. But then, I can't think of any other good reason for coming to this god forsaken place."

Dutch smiled to himself as he followed his new-found associate to the waiting vehicle; he had taken an immediate liking to this man, who on the surface appeared to be a gentle giant.

They walked a short distance in the bright sunlight until they stopped in front of a shiny, black Chevy SUV fitted with a stainless-steel bull bar and tinted windows. Big George motioned for him to open the rear passenger door, whilst he took his bags and stowed them in the back of the vehicle. Dutch instantly recognised the tell-tale weight of armour plating as the door swung open, heavy and solid, and guessed, correctly, that the windows were made from bulletproof glass and the doors of reinforced steel.

Sitting in the driver's seat was a short, stocky man with long rather straggly black hair, wearing an identical gilet, and it occurred to Dutch that the purpose of these garments in this heat must be for weapon concealment. At that moment, the front passenger door swung open and Big George jumped up into the seat; as robust as the vehicle was, it still rocked as George's huge frame hit the upholstery. He waved a giant hand towards the shorter man,

"This excuse for a human is Cesar Rodriguez, our trusted local member and guide, but I call him Bo because just like Mr Bo Jangles, he is scruffy, likes to dance and drinks a bit, but he's trustworthy, a good shot and knows his way around." Big George laughed at his own joke and whilst Dutch was familiar with the song, he wasn't sure how much his colleague understood the reference, but his thought was immediately answered when Cesar turned to Big George, smiled good naturedly and said,

"Fuck you, bastardo. You, you big, black lump of Yankee Buddha-looking shit."

Big George, smiling too, looked at Dutch, theatrically displaying a gaping mouth pose, and said loudly,

"Wow man, that's magnificent, real impressive. Now stop showing off your wide English vocabulary to our new friend and if possible, politely introduce yourself."

Both men laughed and raised an arm and high-fived.

Cesar then turned, reached over the seat with his left outstretched hand and half-faced Dutch, saying,

"Bienvenido, you can also call me Bo, it is easy."

Both men shook hands.

"Good to meet you, Bo. Everyone calls me Dutch."

"Dutch? OK, whatever you want."

"Do you speak any Spanish?" said George.

"No, but my wife and I have been attempting to learn some basic words, but at the moment, I would be hesitant to try them, but I have come armed with a Spanish dictionary." He said, tapping loudly on the pocket size book in his shorts.

"Don't worry. Where we are, it's only the domestics that use it; they do speak a little English and sign language does the rest."

"There's a welcome relief," said Dutch.

"That's that all sorted then," chipped in George, "that's our team complete again, ready to kick ass."

Dutch smiled ruefully to himself as he considered that the three of them were, here together, all operating under aliases and yet, relying on one another for their mutual wellbeing; the camaraderie and verbal sparring almost made him feel as if he was back in the mob again.

"What happened to the guy before me?" Dutch ventured, not entirely sure that he should ask now.

The two men in the front of the car exchanged a quick glance and then Big George replied hesitantly,

"The boss will tell you all you need to know when we get to the compound; let's just say there was an incident."

'An incident,' thought Dutch; he was only too familiar with 'incidents' and as his new associates, who despite their exchange of insulting remarks had now lapsed into friendly banter over the quickest route back to their destination, he sat back in his seat and turned his mind towards the series of incidents that had bought him here—thousands of miles from home to be sitting in an armoured vehicle with two complete strangers, heading for an unknown destination that could possibly be home for Melanie and himself for the next three years.

Speckles of rain had begun to obscure the tinted window of the vehicle; just like home, he thought, though not entirely unexpected as he had done his homework on this district of Venezuela and knew that it was now the rainy season with extremely high humidity and in the summer had annual higher temperatures than anywhere else on the continent. As he watched the progress of the tiny rivulets making their way down the pane, it took his mind back to very different circumstances and altogether, a more settled time.

Bo drove out of the airport complex and through the suburbs of Maracaibo, Venezuela's second city and also its oil capital and a major port. On leaving the city limits, they crossed the impressive 5 mile-long General Rafael Urdaneta Bridge, spanning the wide sea inlet of Lake Maracaibo, which Dutch knew to be one of the longest concrete spans in the world. The murky waters of the lake reflected none of the sapphire beauty of the Caribbean Ocean. He had not long flown over to reach this unfamiliar country and the immense lake was peppered with large oil tankers floating near the distinctive sight of the derricks and white storage tanks of a massive sprawling oil refinery.

It wasn't long before the lake disappeared from sight as they headed off to join what appeared to be a major two-lane highway. From the elevated position on the highway, the road cut its way through wide expanses of contrasting landscapes, from lush green fields and verdant undergrowth with rivers and bridges to barren plains bearing cheerless cactuses and tortured shrubs passing through small farm settlements and ranches. Throughout the journey, there were a number of churches, one no more than a ruin of artfully stacked stones and a long-redundant bell hanging mournfully in a skeletal tower, colourfully painted, shanty-like homesteads, some derelict and abandoned, and roadside stalls and small shops selling all manner of goods.

They stopped twice on their journey, not for coffee or a cold welcoming beer with his new buddies at one of the roadside bars or cantinas but to abandon the car to escape George's flatulence as he passed the most noxious of gases. Bo rebuked George vehemently as to his conduct in front of their new colleague, but George just laughed, apologised and blamed the eruptions on the stronger than usual chilli dish that he consumed the night before. Dutch just smiled, realising that he was back in an army-type environment again with all that entailed and made a mental note that it was clearly a meal best avoided.

After over two hours on the road, Dutch was coming to the conclusion that life was very tough for the residents in the rural areas that he had seen. He also became aware that many of cars that he was seeing were old American gas-guzzling road cruisers, most looked far from roadworthy including the numerous taxis which he put down to the countries limited railway system. Such monsters were very prevalent outside of the numerous roadside cafés and restaurants throughout the journey. He presumed that the viability of keeping such vehicles on the road was only possible due to the abundance of the region's oil and petrol reserves.

It had stopped raining when George pointed in front, bellowing out, "There she is, sweet home Alabama."

In the distance, he could see a huge, brilliant white-painted, stone fortress-like building set high on a ridge and encompassed by white grille fencing, softened in appearance with palm trees and tall ornamental grasses.

"Wow, that's impressive," said Dutch.

"Sure is," said George. "The company built this place when the oil industry here was booming and in full production, but as I understand it, the entire industry here is not what it was but this company is still doing well and remaining competitive."

"Hopefully for the next three years anyway," interjected Dutch.

"Ha! Yeah, well, seems they built this place here as they thought it was the safest site between the two refineries, but they didn't appear to take into account the amount of travelling involved so there's a *lot* of driving duties using two vehicles, y'know in case of any mechanical breakdowns or problems with the banditos. Always be mindful it's not the boss they wish to harm, it's us they need to dispose of to get to him"

Dutch was taking mental notes of all this new information, and as they drew closer, he noticed an orange coloured windsock, next to a flattened strip of land with a light aircraft parked close to the rear of the building.

"Who's the pilot?" asked Dutch.

"That's the boss. He's got a pilot's licence, uses it for the island refinery or takes his family on holidays or back to the States now and again. Some of the company's big players also arrive by air," replied George.

"Very nice too. I didn't realise that there was an island site."

"Right, yeah, all four of us travel in a two-vehicle convoy to the mainland site most days, but when the boss goes to the island, if he feels like it and the weather conditions are favourable, he will fly there and two of us will accompany him while the one remaining will carry out general maintenance of the vehicles and armoury, fuel up and get any required provisions from the town. We're expected to do simple DIY, but for anything we can't do, we have vetted companies, and when they are on the premises, at least one of us accompanies them the entire time they are here."

"Fair enough, so if we go by road to the island plant, I presume, at some stage, there is a boat involved?"

"If we drive, there's no other way of getting across that stretch of water, buddy; although it's not far, we are extremely vulnerable at that point as they still have pirates in these parts. Not worried about the water, are you, Dutch?"

"No, I can swim okay but don't know a great deal about boats."

George cast a glance at Bo.

"Don't worry about the boat, that's Bo's job to look after it and its moorings, the pea brain can just about manage that."

Bo briefly glanced back in the direction of George and muttered the words, "Chupar mi pene."

The two passengers laughed loudly as they both imagined somewhat correctly the content of his disparaging remark.

As they pulled up at the front of the gates, Dutch was captivated by the palatial, elegant and modern three-storey building with pillars flanking the entrance and balconies adorned with palms and exotic hanging plants on each floor, but at the same time, he felt a sense of guilt about the contrasting conditions of where he would be living in relation to the living conditions witnessed on his journey; it was like two totally different worlds. It certainly seemed to go some way to explaining why there was so much crime in this country, but this, he reasoned, was the way of life here and he had a job to do.

George turned to Dutch and said,

"What do you think about that?"

He gestured towards a large nameplate next to one of the doors with the words 'The White House' in large, black script. "The boss took my suggestion for the name and allowed me to design the nameplate." Dutch just smiled.

"Do you know that shit-for-brains Bo doesn't see the irony in it?"

"Well, it's nearly as big," said Dutch.

"Yeah," interjected Bo, "plenty big, like George's ass."

Dutch saw Bo fumble for something in the centre of the front console and eventually retrieve a remote control which he aimed at a sensor next to the intercom system affixed to the wall by the white metal mesh security gates; the gates then opened slowly and the interior of the vehicle darkened as they drove into the subterranean beneath the complex.

Bo pulled up next to a Ford pickup truck, an American Cadillac and yet another large battered taxi, at the same time, cutting the engine and tossing the keys to George.

"Adios, see you Monday? Nice to meet you, Dutch."

Before he could answer, Bo jumped out of the car and made his way straight to the taxi, immediately started the engine and with a brief salute to the remaining two men, drove hastily out of the compound.

Puzzled, Dutch asked George incredulously,

"He has another job as a taxi driver?"

"No, no, it's his cover."

The big man laughed but seeing Dutch's confusion, he added,

"He lives in a small village not far from here and as far as everyone there knows, he is a taxi driver cos if they knew what he did, a gang might try to use him to get to the boss."

"It's that bad, is it?"

"It sure is, no one can be trusted. C'mon, let me show you to your accommodation."

He turned and started walking along a shady, polished walkway, calling over his shoulder,

"I understand your wife is coming as well?"

"Yes, that's right. As soon as I am settled, I will send her word."

As they left the car park and emerged into the daylight into the centre of the complex, Dutch couldn't believe his eyes. In the centre of the grounds, he first noticed what he could only describe as an oasis with palm trees in massive pots surrounding a large oval swimming pool and a vast expanse of patio on which were scattered stylishly understated chairs, tables and loungers. Next to the pool, under a large terracotta tiled roof supported by heavy posts, were racks of free standing weights, two lifting benches, a treadmill and a rowing machine. Although it was overcast, everything there seemed so clean and bright. Big George turned around and said,

"What are you thinking, Dutch?"

"I'm thinking I've just arrived in heaven and I could handle this for a while."

"Yeah, it's certainly a bonus that comes with the job. I built the gym with a bit of help from that lazy punk Bo. We can use it any time but we can't use the pool when the boss and his family or guests are using it."

"I can live with that. What's the boss like?"

"On the whole, he's fine, an easy-going guy but like us all, he has his moments. He can't be too bad. I've been here nearly two years, and anyway, you'll recognise him when you see him."

"Will I? I doubt it," said Dutch with a somewhat bemused look on his face.

"You will, wait and see."

Once Dutch had stored his bags in the small, clean, comfortable one-bed annex which was to be his new home, George accompanied him to see his new employer who was in the main lounge of his palatial apartment. Having knocked and entered, George announced,

"Mr Chamberlain, this is Mr Dennis French, the new member of our team; he tells me people call him Dutch."

As he walked across the glazed, tiled floor to join George in the room, Dutch noted that the room was styled in what he imagined was typical Spanish décor and felt deliciously cool. As his new employer raised himself from his seat, Dutch was immediately reminded of what George had said to him shortly before; the man's white hair, spectacles and white goatee beard bore a younger, almost identical resemblance to pictures of a certain colonel that appear outside of a chain of worldwide fast food chicken restaurants. He found it difficult not to turn to George and smile and say, "Oh, I see!"

The men approached each other and shook hands. His new employer said in an American accent,

"Welcome, Dutch, you can call me Boss when the four of us are together, but Mr Chamberlain when we are in the company of others, outside of here. You've been in the forces, you understand the formalities."

Dutch nodded in acknowledgement of his statement saying, "Okay, Boss," thinking to himself at the same time that he must try hard to refrain from calling him Colonel.

As Chamberlain stooped to pick up a bundle of papers from a nearby coffee table and stood for a moment, apparently perusing them, Dutch noted his immaculate linen suit and expensive watch.

"I have read your employment record with interest and was very impressed; that is why I made my decision of employing you so quickly. I see you even gained a military honour."

"Thanks, yes, that's right. I guess you could say I was lucky, I was a good runner or else it would have been awarded posthumously."

The boss gave a slight smile, glanced back down at the papers and enquired,

"And we are expecting your wife, when?"

"Melanie has a few loose ends to tie up regarding our property, but now she knows I am here, she should be here within a week or so."

By a barely perceptible gesture, their boss then indicated that George should leave the room.

"We pay top dollar for the security of my family, myself and the company properties; for that, I expect total honesty and loyalty. You may be required at some time to put your life on the line to prevent robbery or kidnapping but with your background, you are aware of that so I need not say anymore. We have tried and tested procedures in place to prevent these things happening, but if you become aware of any improvements we can make, be sure and let me know."

"I fully understand what is expected of me and I won't let you down."

"Apart from the threat of criminal activity, terrorism or sabotage at the plants, fire is a big risk and there have been some devastating ones over the years here, so if you see anyone breaking the fire regulations or spot any potential flashpoints, bring it to my or the site manager's attention straight away."

"I certainly will. I've seen what fire can do," he said knowingly.

"Your days off will be the same as mine, and unfortunately, I don't always know when they will be as it depends on if there are any problems at the refineries but don't worry, I too like to have time off with my wife and kids, so I do try to get as much time off as possible. I doubt if you will find that much of a problem anyway as there isn't much to do in these parts, but if you do, go out, you can use one of the cars if they're available, and I suggest that you travel out a way where no one will guess you are from here."

"Sounds good to me, Boss."

"So, what are your first impressions of a place where you may be living for years?"

"Looks very nice. As you probably read, I am very sporty so the pool and gym are right up my street."

"Yes, it's important that you keep occupied as it can get boring and repetitious in such a small environment, because under our particular circumstances, it is not safe to go out often and certainly not alone. Are you aware that Venezuela has extensive problems with crime and kidnapping?"

"Yes, I did read about that when I did my research on the country."

"Good, good, I wouldn't want anyone to take on this role with a naïve or unrealistic outlook about the difficulties and dangers we face here," he said tossing the papers back onto the table and seating himself on one of the large tan leather settees. He motioned to Dutch that he should also sit and continued, "Your job, together with George and Cesar, will be to look after me, my family and also the security staff at both refineries and any other oil officials you are assigned to; we will get you kitted out with firearms and any other requirements

26

you have and our first briefing together will be on Monday morning. You will have overall responsibility for George and Cesar as you are replacing their former supervisor."

He leaned forward and looked enquiringly at Dutch,

"Are you aware of what happened to him and why the job became vacant?"

"No, the lads hesitated to tell me, they said that you would, but I had a feeling that the immigration officer who spoke to me at the airport knew something."

"He would have, even with all the crime that happens here, it still made the news. Your predecessor, Rock, was an ex-US marine; he was a good reliable guy who prevented one or two incidents while he was here. The problem was that he was divorced and let's say he liked the ladies and as you can guess, there are not many single females in this place; so, against my advice, he, from time to time, would slip out alone saying that he was going to a store or something, but what we soon discovered was that this store was in fact the nearest brothel. Anyway, to cut a long story short, one of the working girls mistook him for me and tipped off one of the local gangs, who kidnapped him at gun point, and we are assuming that he either resisted or they realised he wasn't the man they wanted and so would not generate a ransom, so they shot him. His body was found in the river a few days later and no arrests were ever made, so they are one of many gangs still lurking out there, waiting for an opportunity to strike. This is one of the reasons that we asked for a couple, so you have some female company and it fitted in just dandy that we also needed a teacher about now."

"That explains a lot and it doesn't seem that I'll be doing much of my running outside of here, so I guess I will just have to hammer the treadmill."

"That's certainly the healthier option around here. Hopefully that sort of incident won't happen again as Cesar has his family and big George, well, let's say he entertains the housekeeper and cook on a regular basis."

Dutch laughed, "Good for big George. By the way, is he likely to be resentful in any way for me coming in and supervising him and Bo when he also appears to have all the credentials for the job?"

"There will be no problem there. George made it clear when Rock was found that he did not want any more responsibility; he's more than happy with his present lifestyle. Okay, Dutch? Why Dutch, by the way?"

"Services thing. Surname French so it was always going to be some other nationality."

"Same as Rock then, his surname was Stone. Right, see you in what we call the Ops room at 8 am on Monday for a full 9 am briefing, and we will talk everything through together. If you now go, find George; he will familiarise you with everything before then so you can make yourself at home. If you need any food, George will acquaint you with the cook, that is if he is not acquainting himself with her at the moment, if you know what I mean?"

Dutch laughed again and stood up, aware that he was being dismissed. He stepped forward and shook hands with his new boss before he left the room and was reluctant to knock on George's door in case he was 'busy', so in the meantime, he telephoned his wife, Melanie. On looking at his watch, he deduced that it was early afternoon in the UK, but Melanie had insisted that he call her as soon as he was able to following his arrival there, regardless of the time. He gave her all the positive news regarding their new home, new employer and work colleagues, only omitting any mention of the circumstances surrounding the demise of Rock. Melanie said it sounded more like a holiday camp than a working base and asked if he had seen the children that she would be teaching. Dutch informed her that he had only caught a glimpse of them from his window and their mother looked a great deal younger than her husband and was expecting to meet them all the following day. Following what he calculated would be an expensive conversation, he located George and immediately said, "I see what you meant when you said I would recognise the boss. I will have to be careful not to slip up and call him Colonel."

"Exactly, I once forgot myself in his presence and referred to some food I had eaten as 'finger lickin' good' and I am sure he thought I was taking the piss."

Although tired, Dutch was determined to make immediate use of the facilities and both men completed a short gym session followed by a much longer relaxing period in the pool where they discussed their former lives in the military, realising that on several occasions, they had been in the same war zones at the same time. During their long conversation, they struck up an immediate mutual friendship, but both failing to reveal to each other the true circumstances that had taken them both to this destination.

Following their swim, George suggested that they eat, and a hungry Dutch, whose inadequate airline meal seemed ages ago, followed him to a room in the building that doubled as the staff dining room and occasional bar. Having been shown around, George guided him into a large kitchen explaining,

"Claudia, the excellent resident cook, is off today so we have to fend for ourselves, but there is always something to rustle up. She provides our breakfast and evening meals and you can eat here or in your apartment, it's up to you. I will warn you though that if you decide to cook your own food in your own place, that's not a problem; just give her plenty of notice as she tends to get real mad if she wastes her time as she often has nine mouths to feed."

"Good advice, it's so vital to keep on the right side of the cook wherever you are in the world."

George then opened the door to a huge kitchen cupboard, the contents of which surprised the visitor as all of its long shelves were crammed with various tins and packets of most of the non-perishable foods one could imagine; it was if someone was expecting a siege situation or a nuclear fallout. They then examined the ample contents of the nearby large American fridges and freezers but despite such abundant choice, both men decided that for a quick, easy, no-fuss meal, tinned soup with large slices of crusty bread followed by fruit and locally produced coffee would suffice.

As the two men sat across a table enjoying the simple meal, Dutch found himself wondering if George was in the same boat as himself. He was aware that the USA did have an extradition treaty with Venezuela, who had been known to have refused requests in the past despite the treaty, and as he pondered what had led George to be living in this high-risk-high-reward environment, it occurred to Dutch that George was, no doubt, wondering the same thing about himself. After briefly familiarising himself with the layout of his new surroundings, he felt utterly exhausted and headed to bed, but his brain was buzzing and sleep on his first night in his new Venezuelan environment proved elusive. Sleep seemed impossible despite the fatigue of long-haul travel, and his mind raced in anticipation of Melanie's arrival and the uncertainty of what lay ahead for them both, as he knew such luxuries that he had experienced so far would always come at a cost, especially as he now knew what happened to his predecessor and the real risk factor outside of the fortified compound. Nevertheless, he thought, nothing had ever come easy to him before and he didn't anticipate that changing now. Gradually, his thoughts turned to the life that had somehow brought him to this place, and he knew then that he was in for a long and sleepless night.

Chapter 2
Going Back to My Roots (1977)
Artists: Odyssey   Writer: Lamont Dozier

Dutch watched the fat beads of rain roll down the generous expanse of glass, interrupting the view of the collage of fields which skirted the foot of the South Downs; the large bay window framed the view like a television set and would have been unblemished, save for the recently constructed, dual carriageway, lacing its way noisily across the landscape.

It was the realisation of a long-held dream for both Dutch and Melanie to settle back in their home county of East Sussex, close to family; they were now entering a new phase of their lives together—a more peaceful and settled lifestyle in their modest, newly purchased two-bedroom flat on the extreme northern city limits of Brighton and Hove, which had now gained city status since last living here.

They chose the neat and presentable property primarily for its location with its panoramic views from the lounge and master bedroom and its affordability within this affluent area. The interior was a bit outdated with its mock, white marble-effect fireplace and its dark stained kitchen cabinets, the colour of which suited neither of their tastes, but the units were so clean and in such good condition that they could not bring themselves to replace them immediately. Dutch was pleased that he and Melanie agreed that they did not need to make any significant changes as DIY and decorating did not feature highly on his list of priorities. Fortunately, the flat did not have any allocated land save for a garage, which Dutch had earmarked for a home gym and store, as whilst they both enjoyed the great outdoors, neither of them had any real interest in maintaining a garden.

Windsor Court may not have been everyone's idea of a dream home, but to Dutch and Melanie, it had everything they needed and desired, and it was theirs and not rented unlike their previous home. After 25 years in the Parachute Regiment, travelling the world and serving in combat zones, Dennis 'Dutch' French was relishing the prospect of a more sedate life in a familiar area, which encompassed a vibrant town, coast and stunning countryside, all within a five-mile radius; peace and security were now his utmost concern for them both.

The positioning of the first-floor window had clinched the buying of the flat; Dutch had hoped that he might find somewhere which would give him easy access to good running routes on the edge of the town but had never imagined that he would also find somewhere so ideally situated that it would overlook an area of trees and uncultivated fields to provide the elements for a secure cache and easily monitored surveillance.

As he looked out, he could see half a dozen youths noisily speeding across the rough ground of the field situated on the other side of the road opposite his home.

"Are those motor cyclists concerning you?" said Melanie, his wife, who had just entered the room having returned from a shopping trip.

"Only for the fact that occasionally, they will ride up the slope in between the bushes close to my hide. If they do really give me cause for concern, I will call the police, because not only shouldn't they be there and creating a din, but I'd bet, as none of those bikes are for off-road use and have no number plates, some are stolen."

"Nothing to do with protecting your illegal stash then?"

"Of course, that's the main reason, but they could be a bloody nuisance if they keep coming back. Anyway, I quite like the idea of the local constabulary unwittingly protecting my naughty secret."

"You do worry me, Dennis, by keeping it there. I know you like to keep it as a link to your past but that's what that soldier, Danny, what's his name, did and look what trouble he got into."

As the rainfall intensified, the drenched and mud-spattered youths left the area and disappeared into the distance, prompting him to say,

"My old pal Chris Compton was right when he said that bad weather was a policeman's best friend as it keeps everyone, including the villains, off the streets."

"If that's the case, then we should have a very low crime rate in the UK," quipped Melanie.

Other than Dutch, only Melanie was aware that he was in possession of a gun, and whilst she accepted his apparent desire for retaining it, it was a cause of anxiety to her, particularly when in 2012, ex-SAS sniper, Danny Nightingale, hit the headlines for almost exactly the same circumstances and was prosecuted and convicted for the possession of his memento.

He had hidden it in its present position upon moving into the flat; when the opportunity arose, he retrieved a Walther PPK 9mm semi-automatic handgun with 42 rounds of ammunition, which had been hidden near his previous Essex address that he had acquired when involved in a humanitarian mission of the once war-torn country of Kosovo. When pursuing conflicting fighters fleeing a building, finding himself alone whilst searching a room, he discovered the weapon and ammunition and secretly seized them as a trophy. He had broken down the weapon and smuggled it, together with the bullets, into the UK in amongst vast amounts of stores and tools, as he correctly suspected that due to the volume involved, they would not be vigorously inspected. Reuniting himself with the weapon, he carefully buried the gun in a tin box in nearby scrubland in view of the flat and protected it by way of four battery-operated tremble sticks, large camouflaged pencil type objects that each contained a small radio transmitter, which could be tuned to a standard VHF radio, which he could monitor from his lounge if he saw anyone close to the hide. He became familiar when using such sticks to detect enemy movement by vibration within the ground, and he'd seen their potential as a guarding device and had fortunately retained the obsolete sticks when they were superseded by a new design.

In the event that the gun, container or sticks were ever located by a third party, he would ensure, after each handling, that all surfaces were wiped of his finger prints. If the authorities became aware of these warning devices, they would immediately determine that the small transmitters within the sticks only had a short-range signal and his block of flats would be the most obvious receiving post; therefore, Dutch was acutely aware that in the event of any such discovery, he must always be prepared to immediately change the tuning position of the monitoring transistor radio to eliminate the possibility of his involvement. Since obtaining the Walther, he had carried out some research about the gun and, despite being James Bond's weapon of choice, was disappointed to find that it had some reliability issues, including playing a key part in a famous incident in 1974 when Princess Anne and her then husband, Mark Phillips, were returning by car to Buckingham Palace on the Mall, and the vehicle in which they were travelling was forced to stop by an armed man who began to fire at the entourage; her personal police officer attempted to exchange fire but his pistol, a Walther PPK, jammed and he was shot by the assailant. With its tarnished reputation, the Walther wouldn't have been his weapon of choice, but the chance to bring it home had been too good an opportunity to miss, and its reliability was of no real significance given that he had no plans to use it in anger.

He felt that he needed some kind of firearm, having been in possession of a gun for 20 years, he felt naked without one; he was a firm believer that if you looked after a gun, it would look after you. From time to time, he would retrieve it from its burial place and then enjoy practicing misfiring and jamming drills, breaking it down and cleaning it thoroughly, and finally wrapping it up in waterproof materials before returning it to its hiding place. He kept all of the ammunition hidden in a metal box that he had adapted to fit in the void in the base of a large toolbox, exactly the same way as he had smuggled them in, which he now kept in his locked garage as he would never keep the gun and ammunition together, should they fall into the wrong hands.

Occasionally, when he had prior knowledge that he would be working in the area of the vast expanse of Ashdown Forest in the north of the county, he would retrieve the gun and ammunition, transport them in his personally adapted toolbox, walk out into a remote and uninhabited part of the forest and fire off a couple of rounds just to keep his eye in. Dutch would only use the bullets sparingly knowing that once he had used the remainder, he would not be able to purchase any more without a firearms certificate that every holder of a lethal barrelled weapon in the UK was required to have by law, so he was extremely vigilant when retrieving or using it.

He was only too aware that the penalty for holding unlawful firearms and ammunition was severe, and he would never be able to apply for such a certificate because he would be unable to reveal the true origin of the weapon. He considered that this was the only way he could possess such a firearm because to join a gun club would be too sterile and controlled and, truth be told, the gun and hide gave him a sense of excitement and trepidation to his new-found calmer lifestyle. He had once considered surrendering the weapon and ammunition during a police amnesty, but he couldn't bring himself to part with this link to his past life.

When Melanie had first seen their flat, she too had fallen in love with the view but also prized the place's feeling of security and homeliness; it had been such a relief to find somewhere they both felt able to settle. Melanie: his wife, confidant and closest friend for so many years—outwardly, so sorted, so together, but to the few who knew her well, latterly so fragile and vulnerable.

Dutch found it difficult to adjust to this new, uncertain, delicate Melanie; when they had first met, she had been a confident, gregarious young woman, employed by the army and thriving in the routines and structure of military life.

Out in Civvy Street, however, despite retraining to become a nursery school teacher and a concerted effort to keep up with old friends, her confidence had diminished and the ties had withered, exacerbated by a series of highly distressing miscarriages during their early married life, which had adversely affected her physical and mental health and, coupled with their mutual reluctance to enter into the adoption process, had made her feel the odd one out amongst friends who predominantly had children.

She had become increasingly withdrawn, going out only to go to work or to visit her parents, Molly and Ken, who lived in a smart bungalow in a quiet suburb on the eastern edge of the city. Melanie visited often, fuelled by an unspoken guilt that she felt of having deprived them, as their only child, of the opportunity to become grandparents.

Dutch couldn't help shoulder some of the blame for her isolated life, having taken her away from the army network that she so valued. They had always been close as a couple, relying on each other and sharing the same hopes and values.

Shortly after moving into the flat, in an attempt to refocus their lives outside of army life, they had hiked along the entire South Downs Way, sponsored by family and friends in aid of a Rehabilitation Centre for injured service personnel. Starting in the sedate seaside town of Eastbourne, and following the high peaked chalk hills and low valleys some 100 miles, they had finished in the ancient Hampshire city of Winchester.

It had been a long-held ambition, since being introduced to the route during army training, for Dutch to again complete the walk, and he had felt that the experience would be beneficial for his wife, both physically and mentally, and she had really enjoyed it apart from the initial starting point of Beachy Head, a notorious suicide blackspot, famous for the 162 metre cliff drop onto treacherous rocks below; the sinister reputation of the spot had spooked Melanie and somewhat marred an otherwise idyllic route. Dutch, sensing her discomfort and with thoughts of his own mother's demise, diverted the now solemn atmosphere by light-heartedly hurrying them both from the scene saying that due to recent erosion, they had better move off the cliff quickly. Despite their heavy packs, they ran a short distance, giggling like a couple of kids as they fled.

The Downs hike was the first opportunity that Dutch and Melanie had really had to spend so much time together without the outside pressures of work and other activities and distractions for a long time. They both enjoyed the release from the usual routine and made the most of some exceptionally fine walking weather, dry and warm with a cool breeze and the mile upon mile of beautiful countryside, providing the perfect backdrop to venture. They constantly encountered other hikers, cyclists and a great many dog walkers together with artists, mostly women in isolated vantage points. The couple, from time to time, took the opportunity to stop and not only admire their work but also their determination to reach their chosen site by carrying all of their equipment for some considerable distance. During the second day of their hike, they came across an artist, named Stella, who had become so engrossed in her project and had been painting for such a long period that she had become completely disorientated and had no idea where she had parked her car that morning; she was wandering fully laden with a stool, easel and a large box of paints. As the light was fading, Dutch and Melanie assisted her by consulting their route map and searched for possible places that she may have parked her car, eventually locating it just as darkness fell on a narrow farm track halfway up a steep hill. Neither Stella nor the couple could figure out how she had managed to access and drive to such an isolated spot. Due to the time spent in their search, darkness had fallen, and Dutch and Melanie were forced to pitch their tent nearby instead of their intended destination, and Stella was so grateful to them; she insisted that she took their names and address as she wished to send them a token of her gratitude. Despite them declining, Stella was insistent and once obtained, she wrote their details on her sketch pad.

Shortly after returning home from their expedition, a package arrived by way of courier, and on opening it, Melanie found it to contain the now framed painting that Stella had completed the day that they came across her with a note extending her gratitude. Later, when Dutch arrived back home from work, she showed him the gift saying,

"I am so pleased with this, not only with the picture itself but for the lasting memory of what a wonderful time we had on that trek."

"You're right on all counts. Do you know what the best thing is about it though?"

"The fact that it's so unique and on canvas?"

"No, we can hang it up over that black finger-mark I got on the wall, and that will stop you keep going on about me repainting it."

"That's typical of you, Den, no finesse and always trying to avoid household chores."

"No point in keeping a dog and barking yourself."

"Don't you dare go down that road. Anyway, you are going to like Stella's painting even more when I tell you what I have found after some research on her signature."

"Don't tell me she's signed it Rembrandt."

"Don't be stupid. On googling her full name, I was pleasantly surprised that she is a very accomplished artist whose works sell for hundreds, sometimes thousands of pounds."

"You're right, I suddenly like it a lot more."

Stella's painting did get to hang over the black mark on the wall but not for that reason alone, they both loved it and, despite its possible value, would never sell it as to the memories it held.

Melanie talked more openly about her feelings during the days of the hike than she had for many years. Dutch wondered if it was the feeling of liberty of being out in the countryside that made her so free with her thoughts, or whether it was just that he never made himself so available to listen to her ordinarily; he felt a slight pang of guilt, especially as many of the feelings she confided pertained to her sense of loneliness and disappointment over not being able to have a family of their own. Dutch knew that she had found the repeated, unsuccessful pregnancy attempts traumatic and distressing, but he had tried not to dwell too much on it as he felt there was very little he could actually do about it and Dutch, like most men, was very practical-minded as well; he did not want Melanie to feel that he held her responsible for depriving him of something in his life. He knew she was aware that he had hoped they would create the family, the life, together that he had not really known—God knows they had talked about it enough when they were first engaged, rehearsing their entire life stories and it felt as though they could control everything that life might throw at them to create the perfect plan.

In hindsight, that seemed so naïve and foolish but Dutch was a realist and a great believer in making the most of any given situation and, whilst undoubtedly disappointed, he was determined that their childlessness wouldn't destroy everything good they had in their lives, but he had clearly underestimated how much it had affected Melanie's outlook. Hearing her talk honestly about grief, loss and, at times, outright despair, he realised that he simply hadn't, and probably couldn't, comprehend the depth of her feelings, but he felt heartened by the renewed feeling of intimacy between them.

Dutch was fiercely protective of his wife and feeling keenly a fresh awareness of her unhappiness, and as she seemed very taken with the idea of having a dog, he vowed to himself to do everything within his power to acquire a dog for her as an antidote to her increasing isolation. Their relationship had formed the backbone of his adult life and although it would appear from the outside that it was military career that was the making of Dutch, it was the emotional security and stability of his life with Melanie that he prized above all else; army life had provided fitness, skills and knowledge, but his marriage had held him mentally strong and secure.

As luck would have it, the conditions of the lease allowed for a dog and not long after their return, he acquired Jodie—a bouncy, affectionate, young springer spaniel cross—from a local dog rescue. Melanie immediately took to the dog and in time, they both did. When Dutch was not at home, she would regularly walk her on the Downs, often alone at nearby beauty spots including Devils Dyke—a mile-long dyke valley, the largest, deepest and widest dry valley in the UK. Dutch would tease Melanie about her enthusiasm for walking up there, claiming either that it was the superstitious lure of the legend that the devil dug the chasm to drown the parishioners of the Sussex Weald or, more likely, the fact that there was a pub and often an ice-cream van to be found on the peak.

Gradually, Melanie became more confident and enthusiastic about going out on her own with Jodie and would put the dog in the back of her little Fiat and drive out onto the Downs including Ditchling Beacon—another nearby beauty spot that was popular with dog walkers and hikers. Even though she originally came from the area where she never failed to marvel at the fact that on these peaks, she could look southwards and see ships in the English Channel and then north to the magnificent Sussex countryside, where it was said that on a clear day, you could see the outskirts of the counties of Hampshire, Surrey and Kent.

She felt comfortable and safe walking in these areas alone as it was common practice to see other women walking alone with their canine companions, although she did occasionally wonder whether Jodie would be of any help if she should need it. The greatest threat that she had encountered so far came from the weather; despite their beauty, the Downs could be dangerous in extreme weather, hot or cold; without a map, it was easy to become disorientated and lose your bearings as she had witnessed first-hand on her encounter with Stella, and as a result, Melanie had learned to wear appropriate clothing and footwear and to stick to well-established, well-sign posted routes.

She had never forgotten the eerie and unsettling experience of being caught on one of the peaks when a sea mist had come rolling in, completely enveloping the hill top in a dense, damp fog. She had only been able to see a few feet ahead of her, everything else was swallowed up in the mist, and she had needed to find her way back to her car by following the most clearly used of the white chalk paths.

Dutch was eager to support Melanie as much as possible in establishing their new civilian life together; he knew that she was struggling to find her feet and he felt for her, but he no longer missed military life, only the comradery; he was a glass-half-full, not half-empty person as he appreciated very much all that he had; he was comfortably off with no debts, had a nice home, a loving wife and they were both fit and healthy. He could be best described as a realist, a simplistic man who had no interest in flash clothes, expensive jewellery, big houses or fast cars, and he had certainly experienced enough 'overseas trips' during his previous employment. Luckily, Melanie had a similar outlook on life and never wished for excesses but with their combined income and the availability of her parents to look after Jodie, they were able, when Dutch was not on call, to regularly spend the weekend in London for sightseeing, including taking in a show or travelling to another part of the country to see a particular band that they both appreciated.

Dutch enjoyed driving his work's van as it was so practical; if they'd had a family, it would not be suitable, but for him and his tools, it was perfect and Melanie had her own small car that they used when travelling together. To the man in the street, he would now give the appearance of an everyday, unassuming individual, betraying no indication of his former capabilities and military expertise. Although they had not been able to have the children he'd imagined them with, he was pragmatic in his outlook and considered this gave them more time for each other and for their interests, and he had witnessed that children did not always improve a relationship.

Dutch was not a man to be idle and had always been a fanatical runner. He continued to regularly run 5K to 10K most days on the nearby Downs and created a mini-gym for himself for weight training in his garage in a block, opposite the rear of the flat. Although a very private person, Dutch generally found it easy to make friends and soon got to know a couple of local runners, Terry and Alistair, and whenever he got the opportunity, he would join them in their training sessions or for long runs on the Downs. The only competitive running he now participated in was low-level events such as Parkrun or fun runs on weekends when not working. If he had a particularly long day at work, he would take his kit with him and during his lunch break, secure the van and go for a run. He was conscious that not being able to shower after may cause unpleasant body odour but usually working alone and wearing full body overalls, a good spray of deodorant masked any problem.

His only regret was that his wife was not truly settled in their new environment, but he was sure that, given time, with her personality, things would change for the better. Now that he had returned to his roots, he was able to look up his brother and sister who had remained in the city and his aunt and uncle in Portsmouth who had done so much to change his life. He now felt happy and secure with a wife he loved dearly, a good well-paid job with plenty of opportunity for overtime and the addition of his army pension. He felt that he deserved this peace and tranquillity after the turmoil of his early years and all the service and sacrifices he had given to his country.

Chapter 3
The Year of the Cat (1976)
Artist: Al Stewart
Writers: Al Stewart/Peter Wood

Sharp needles of rain struck relentlessly upon the rooftops and pavements of the small border village of Crossmaglen, County South Armagh, Northern Ireland, locally referred to as bandit country due to its history of lawlessness. Shouts could be heard from a neighbouring street and there was a faint whiff of smoke in the air, as the foot patrol stood vigilantly outside the house guarding local police and colleagues who were searching what was believed by intelligence reports to be a weapons store. It was a dismal November evening, exacerbating the usual hostile feeling of the area. Unrest in the province had already claimed the lives of many soldiers and police officers that year and as Paratrooper Corporal, Dennis French, patrolled outside in part of an area known as Snipers Alley, the unmistakable sound of a single shot rang out and the meticulously placed bullet fatally struck the soldier, piercing a tiny part of unprotected flesh in his neck, and he became another further casualty of the sinister but deserved name and reputation of the place; he left behind a wife, Sadie, and four children, and one yet to be born to his pregnant wife, who would carry his name.

Born slightly prematurely, young Dennis was scant consolation to his already distraught mother and the tragedy of her husband's death was further compounded when she discovered that she was not able to remain in their military-provided home in the garrison town of Aldershot, Hampshire. Whilst she had grown used to her army husband's absence due to his military postings, she had relied heavily on the support of the barrack's lifestyle, surrounded by other army wives, who understood the pressures and difficulties of managing alone. Sadie had always been close to her parents and decided, with her husband's interim death benefit, to acquire a house in the Kemp Town area of Brighton in order to be close to her parents again.

Dennis was the youngest of her five children; Deborah, Roy, Jeanette and Barry—the eldest two being his half-brother and half-sister from his father's previous marriage.

Despite the move to the coast, his mother, struggling financially and feeling unable to cope with her husband's death and bringing up the children on her own, rapidly descended into depression. She had always been an anxious woman, living on her nerves and prone to pessimism but sometimes, it became more than that and she became withdrawn, experiencing long periods of deep misery and despair. Previously, she had always managed to pull herself out of these episodes but when Dennis was only five, at a time when psychiatric help was not easily available, her condition deteriorated and she took her own life.

The shockwaves resonated throughout the family as the children were orphaned again and Dennis' grandmother, Connie, pleaded with social services not to split the children up and, together with her husband, volunteered to care for the three younger ones whilst the elder two wished to go into the care of their maternal mother. As they were both fit and well and had brought up their own now grown-up children, and, with others of the large family living nearby, they were granted an interim care order and all three children went to live in nearby Chapel Street with their grandmother and her husband, Sinbad—a nickname given to him as he was a long serving fisherman. This was an unusual care order due to their advancing years but it was granted due to the large caring and well-balanced family network in the immediate area and a concerted effort by both social services and the family who were all determined and passionate in preventing the devastated children being split up into the care system.

Brighton, over the years, had acquired the name of 'Little London by the Sea' due to it not only being a popular seaside resort since Victorian times but also having built a reputation of providing first rate night life with its many clubs, bars and restaurants, which had now become popular venues and was much favoured for hen and stag parties. It had become a bustling cosmopolitan town with a large gay and lesbian community but, like all large towns and cities, it had a darker side; the crime rate was high and drug use was prevalent. The city provided many hotels and guest houses for holiday makers, and in the summer months, these numbers were swelled by day trippers from near and far, and with all of these people with time on their hands, business had been good for local residents including Grandma Connie, who had enjoyed a long career as a fortune teller and clairvoyant for many years on the nearby famous Palace pier.

For well over one hundred years, this 524-metre-long structure, stretching out into the English Channel, had given great pleasure to holiday makers when visiting the amusement arcades and refreshment stalls. Connie had used the name of Madam Crystal Gaze and, when asked by punters, would assure the enquirer it was truly her real name. Even after her retirement from her tiny kiosk on the pier, she still carried out private readings from her home or visited local clients, also writing a weekly column in the local newspaper. In the past, if a holiday visitor considered that she had carried out a particular good reading, they would return from miles away to see her for a further session; she had built a fine reputation amongst such followers and once had a lucrative business.

Dennis' grandfather, Sinbad, did not share his wife's mystical beliefs and one look at him would make it immediately apparent that he was a seafaring man and had been so all of his life. His facial skin had the appearance of old, tanned leather with deep weather-beaten wrinkles. He was tall, with greying hair always covered by a cap which had seen better days; he usually wore a series of thick ancient woollen turtle neck pullovers under his waterproofs. He was one of the few remaining men of the small fishing fleet community that still operated from the nearby beaches and because of this, all varieties of fish and seafood were regularly on the family menu; hence why Dennis, in his later years, only ate it occasionally. All the grandchildren had the opportunity to go out to sea with him occasionally, but they rarely took up the offer as the boat reeked of fish, leaving him to work alone with his ever-faithful Jack Russel terrier.

As a quiet hard-working family man, his only tenuous claim to fame was allegedly being the last person in Sussex to have received the ancient traditional punishment of "Rough music". This ordeal was carried out by residents of a community who considered that the recipient had wronged them. This occurred when Sinbad wrote to the Chief Superintendent at Brighton Police station complaining of a 'lock in' at the public house opposite his home, when on many evenings the landlord would allow customers to continue drinking behind locked doors after licensing hours. The noise created by the revellers would keep his entire family awake into the early hours. Due to his complaint, the police cracked down on the pub forcing it to close on time causing annoyance to some of the participating members. Somehow it was discovered that the complaint had been made by Sinbad and, over a period of nights, in shifts they camped outside his home continually banging on metal objects and blowing whistles. This continued for several nights until the police halted the disturbance. Ever since the event there had been tension between the family and the pub, but this never bothered Sinbad as he could never risk going to sea either tired or intoxicated.

Connie's own children had long since left the nest, but even though she remained fit and active, she soon found it difficult to cope with the boisterous youngsters, even with the financial help from the local authority. The children would all wear second-hand clothes obtained from charity shops and were often helped by local shop keepers, who respected the family, having known the grandparents for many years. They would receive dented tins, broken biscuits and food products where the best before date had expired. The nearby fish and chip shop would also contribute by giving them any food left over after business hours. The family were also helped by an armed forces' charity organisation, the Soldiers Sailors Air Force Association, but Dennis and his siblings would regularly be taunted by other children regarding their clothes and poor lifestyle.

The children dreaded going to school being prey to constant bullying and humiliation by others bragging about their latest acquisitions: skateboards, Walkmans and chopper bikes; his sister would be upset and cry but Dennis started to get into fights with those responsible and became generally unruly. Dennis was big enough and strong enough to handle the boys of his own age and older, but he was always in the minority and often found himself outnumbered and took some terrible beatings as he would never submit to them. The Social Services department were aware that there were difficulties with the situation but all efforts were made to keep the family together, and Connie was granted a full care order and the situation was regularly monitored by the department.

Dennis was a physically unremarkable child, an asthma sufferer of average height, build and weight but the stigma of not having either parent had a significant effect on him, rendering him deeply insecure and giving him an air of nervousness. His lack of self-confidence eventually caused him to develop a slight stutter and to stare at the floor to avoid eye contact with others; he became a difficult and disruptive child. The bullying seemed endless for Dennis and his siblings and the only solace and uplifting moments he experienced in those early years were when Connie, who adored music, would, despite her age, turn the radio or cassette player up loud and dance around the room to the popular music of the time. Dennis found the music infectious and an uplifting experience, giving him pleasure that he had never felt before. He then started to listen to music whenever and wherever he could, especially when he was feeling down, which was often, but he had now found a new friend in the world of music and, for a short time, could drift away into a contented world of his own; his taste in music was forever influenced by genres she liked.

Life 1: At a young age, Dennis was involved in an accident with a fast-moving car when running onto the road whilst being chased by bullies and had a remarkable escape when thrown onto the windscreen and onto the road but received only cuts and bruises.

Whilst his grandmother dressed his wounds, she told him,
"What comes around, goes around and believe me, all bullies will get their just rewards in the end."
Dennis replied angrily,
"I hate bullies; they just do it for fun. One day, I will get them back," and he took little comfort in his grandmother's assurances.
Referring to his lucky escape, she explained to him that if he were a cat, who were said to have nine lives, he had just lost one, but he had plenty to last him his lifetime. He was curious about this statement and so she explained that it was only an old saying and not factual, but the myth was that in the event of someone avoiding death or escaping a significant life-changing moment, they lost one of their allocated nine lives. As an impressionable child, he always remembered this and was fascinated by how extremely superstitious his grandmother was. She was constantly saluting magpies, knocking on wood, avoiding black cats crossing her path and other similar customs. He once overheard her telling one of her clients that she had almost been prepared for having the grandchildren living with her as she had foreseen tragic circumstances within the immediate family network. It was from this conversation that Dennis first learnt the truth as to how his mother really died. The family had decided to keep

the true circumstances from them until they were older but their hand was now forced to inform them all.

Not long after learning the devastating truth about his mother, he witnessed an incident involving Connie's cat, Lennie, which almost justified her words when he saw it chase a squirrel up a tall tree; when the squirrel reached the top and having nowhere else to go, it leapt onto a branch of another tree; the cat followed but was too heavy for the adjoining branch and fell to the floor. On its way to the ground, the cat twisted in mid-air, landed on his feet, ran off and continued his pursuit of the squirrel. Dennis began to wonder whether there was any credibility in Connie's belief about this 'nine lives' theory; he was young and cynical but she seemed to be proved right time and time again, and he questioned whether he might need to take her more seriously.

At the age of ten, Dennis was caught breaking into market stalls in Carlton Hill and stealing fruit with his brother, Roy; they had done this on four previous occasions by sneaking out of the house at night, but on the fifth time of doing so, they were caught by a security officer and his dog. They had not only been eating the fruit but also selling it to support their sister without their grandmother's knowledge. On initially being dealt with by the police, Dennis gave false particulars but this was soon discovered and he was dealt with by means of an official police caution.

Consequently, it was decided by the authorities that his grandparents were finding it increasingly difficult looking after all of the children as prior to this, the school and social services had noticed that the behaviour of both boys was deteriorating, and it was reluctantly decided that Dennis and Roy would have to go into the care of others.

His aunt, Susan, his mother's sister, and her husband, Jim—both natives of Brighton—had, during their return visits to their home town, grown fond of Dennis despite the problems he was presenting, but both appreciated as to why he was reacting in this way. The couple, who had now moved to the Hampshire village of Denmead in order to be nearer Portsmouth Naval Headquarters, where Jim was a petty officer in the Royal Navy, volunteered to take Dennis in with their two sons, James and Richard, who were both of a similar age, whilst Roy was placed into the care of another responsible local family member.

Before his emotional parting from his grandparents, Connie took Dennis aside and told him,

"Good luck and goodbye. I have seen you will do well but be sure to look after your lives."

Immediately following their farewells, on the car journey to his new home in company with his newly adopted family, there was a jovial discussion about his grandmother's reference to the word 'lives' and not life and her spiritual ways. Susan jokingly said,

"We always said, what with her fortune telling and superstitious behaviour, if she had been around in the Middle Ages, she would have been burned as a witch."

Dennis got on well with James and Richard and attended the local schools in the area. At first, it was difficult for him to adjust from moving from the big city to a rural village and due to past bullying and humiliating experiences, his now deep-rooted mistrust of his peers, and being a newcomer to the area, he remained a target for similar aggressors; his readiness and ability to defend himself initially landed him in trouble, but he learned to fit in and under these new circumstances, the bullying eventually ceased. He lost the need to constantly defend himself, both physically and verbally, and became a calmer, more confident boy, no longer requiring to adapt an unnatural aggressive persona. He still, however, remained a very guarded person but now had the ability and presence to have friends; his former experiences had left mental and physical scars and he would fully trust but a few, not allowing many people too close until he knew them well enough to do so. Dennis was happy with his new-found family; he settled down and started to take more of an interest in his education but always yearned to be outside in the open air, wishing he was on the school playing fields or in the distance where he could see the route of the cross-country course rather than sitting behind a school desk. He was determined to escape from the feelings of humiliation and inadequacy, and after a time, despite his teenage facial spots that haunted him, he became much more self-assured, losing his inferiority complex and social awkwardness, though the scars would remain forever.

As soon as he was old enough, he obtained a job as a paperboy at the local village newsagents. He got on extremely well with the proprietor of the shop, Frank Kingswood, and his son, Paul, who was older than him; they identified him as a good, honest worker and in time, employed him in the shop at weekends and holidays. This included him accompanying Paul in a small van which was, in effect, a mobile shop that serviced outlaying districts with newspapers, cigarettes, tobacco, confectionery and various food and drink items. Paul was very generous, and they would both eat and drink as much as they wished from the goods they carried. It was on such a journey that Dennis smoked his first cigarette, but was not impressed and was glad that he hadn't had to pay for the privilege. Paul would also let him drive the van on some of the long private roads on their round; he couldn't wait for the day he could do it legally and would always remain indebted to the father and son. When not working for the Kingswoods, he would go to the local wood yard owned by the Jones family, where local boys were paid for chopping and bundling up small logs. He was forever grateful to both employers, not only for being given the opportunity and for the wages that he received but also for giving him a good work ethic and a renewed confidence. Although his life had completely changed, he still retained his interest in music, never forgetting how the song and tunes helped him through his darkest moments, and now with money in his pocket, he could now start his own music collection.

Although he was a naturally keen and energetic person, he attributed his enthusiasm for work to Sinbad, the man who had kept the house going by being out at sea, oftentimes seven days a week, at first light, in all weathers. Then, on returning to shore, had to sort and clean his catch and then spend the remainder of the day selling it to local restaurants or from his small pitch on the beach. All this and he would still find the time to clean and service the boat and mend any damaged nets.

For the first time, Dennis now had extra money in his pocket and felt proud about the fact. Life was now good, but he couldn't help wondering about the fate of his brothers and sisters and wished that they too could be experiencing it with him.

Dennis treasured the photographs he had of his father in uniform, and he had always harboured a secret wish to join the army and become part of the parachute regiment.

And at the age of 14, he became aware of the Military Skills Academy located at Portsmouth that accepted students between the ages of 14 and 16, which was predominantly founded to prepare young people for a career in the British armed forces, and he asked Susan and Jim if they could help him enrol. The comprehensive school that he was attending agreed because they were aware that this was the only career he wanted to follow and both college and school allowed him to transfer as a full time, five days a week student, which he was able to do as a day student, as he only lived 11 miles away, a 30 minute bus ride from the college. Jim especially supported Dennis' ambitions as they were similar to his own when he was a teenager, and he was often able to give Dennis a lift into Portsmouth on his way to work at the city naval base. Dennis' only intention was that as soon as he became 16, he would join the army. His weekends and holidays were occupied by maintaining his part-time jobs in the village.

Whilst at the college, now free from spots and asthma, he excelled at boxing, rugby, running and swimming; he joined local clubs, becoming extremely fit, resulting in him winning the Hampshire schools' cross-country title—an achievement he knew would serve him well in his proposed future career. Following this victory, he was approached by Phil and Tim, two likeable characters who requested him to join their newly formed athletics club, which he did and felt honoured to have been asked. He credited his sporting prowess to the enthusiasm and coaching given to him by the arts and sports master, Mr Griffiths, who he knew to have once been a Welsh ABA boxing champion. These new experiences assisted in his ever-increasing popularity amongst the other students, giving him newly found confidence and self-esteem, especially with the opposite sex and took an interest in girls and from time to time, dating the occasional girlfriend but nothing serious as he was determined not to have any distractions from his training as the army was to be his security blanket, giving him the family of which he felt he had initially been deprived.

Due to the amount of daily physical activity, his 5'10" frame was now more muscular; he was a polite, confident young man with a kind face, crew cut, dark hair and no striking features—only it could be said that he had a larger than average nose. His southern English accent now had a calm air, giving the impression of being in total control of the environment and situation he was presented with, but when perplexed, showed that he was not a person to be messed with, with a face now showing some marks and scars from past scraps and numerous rounds of boxing.

The college motto, "By failing to prepare, you are preparing to fail", a quote by Benjamin Franklin, had a lifelong influence on Dennis, as he could see the importance of such a statement, especially within the armed forces. His thoughts were that if he remained prepared for every eventuality in his proposed career, and life in general, he might just come out the other side alright. The fact that he attended the college fascinated his cousins and other acquaintances; in some ways, they were jealous of his diverse form of education but most were deterred from ever following his path when discovering the amount of daily drill, discipline and physical activity involved.

For the first time in his life, he felt equal to his peers; despite their intelligence or background, he now suddenly had a place in society. As a result of his early turbulent years, he had fallen behind with his education and when it came to exams, he was usually in the lower half of results, but he was always able to make up for it when it came to practical or physical demands, where he would excel. He soon realised that if he was going to succeed in life, he must look after his health and fitness and never go down the excessive drinking or drugs route that he was witnessing with some and could understand, perhaps more than most, why some would look for a form of escapism and not take heed of the pitfalls. But this kind of escapism wasn't for him; his only drug was adrenalin. He didn't see himself as completely innocent, as after all, he had stolen and knew he was capable of responding extremely violently when pushed to his limits.

Chapter 4

In the Army Now (1986)

Artist: Status Quo   Writers: Bolland & Bolland

On a typically shower-filled April morning, having reached the age of 16, Dennis attended the local Army recruiting office to sign up to his dream occupation, accompanied by his uncle, Jim. He successfully passed the entrance exams and was given a date for joining. To honour his success, Susan and Jim held a farewell party for him, and it was a truly emotional moment for Dennis as he realised the kindness that the family had shown him, giving him the opportunity to make a success of his life, when he knew that it could have all been very different and his life might have followed a far less-fortunate path.

Joining as a junior soldier, he successfully passed the parachute regiment aptitude course and a series of physical fitness assessments. This was followed by completing mainstream training during which he attended a pre-parachute (P company) selection course at Catterick Garrison, Yorkshire and put through additional physical assessments designed to test fitness, stamina and teamwork skills, described by some as the most arduous training carried out by any army in the world. He went on to pass the pre-parachute selection tests, and his acceptance into the parachute regiment was complete when he made the mandatory five successful jumps at the basic parachute course at RAF Brize Norton to acquire the status, for which he had long wished.

How proud he was when he received the famous maroon beret with its winged cap badge—a moment that he had been waiting for since becoming a teenager. As soon as his training was complete, he was posted to Third Battalion parachute regiment headquarters, Aldershot, and shortly after joining them, his company were deployed to the conflict in Northern Ireland. At 17, he was the youngest and it was official policy that no personnel under 18 were sent to combat

51

zones, so it was decided that he, together with others, would be required to stay and secure the day to day running of the barracks, whilst part of the battalion were on the tour of duty.

Dutch, as he had now been nicknamed by his colleagues, was thoroughly disappointed as he was only a few months younger than eighteen-year-old Private Derek Bowman, who was selected for the tour, but Dutch, at his age, with so little experience, didn't feel that he could argue his case, although he did make his feelings known to some. It was with great disappointment that he accepted the fact that he was missing out on his first real action, especially as his father had given his life in the same peacekeeping role. It did cross his mind that, apart from his age, this may have been the reason he had been overlooked, but he wasn't sure if any of the persons making such decisions knew about the circumstances surrounding his father's death. Once his unit had departed, he was engaged with others in rear-guard duties, involving the general running and security of the barracks. The fact that he now had all the facilities and plenty of time to attend extra courses and carry out his fitness programme was of little consolation but kept him focused from the daily boredom. So, when he was approached and informed that he was considered a model recruit and had been selected to go on attachment, to what is known in army terms as the 'satisfied soldier scheme' to Brighton Army recruiting office for a short period, in order to talk to other prospective recruits about the Army career, he jumped at the chance, especially given the location. Dutch was disappointed at not being involved with his battalion but was excited about going back to his home town, and the transition was made easier by being able to stay in accommodation at the recruiting office whilst he was there.

As he had been away from Brighton since he was a child, he now had very rusty knowledge of the area, only having once returned when he had learnt of the sudden and unexpected death of his grandmother. Her funeral had been a grand affair and, as she had wished, was a spiritually themed non-religious event, attended by many of her family, friends and ex-clientele. All of his brothers and sisters were present, and it transpired that none of them, apart from Jeanette, who was now living permanently with her partner, Martin, and the ailing Sinbad, had kept in regular contact with her; a fact that they all now regretted as she was the anchor that had given them a home and had attempted to keep the family together.

Dutch was disappointed to find that Roy, still living in Brighton, had had further brushes with the law and was now living in a hostel, mixing with a bad crowd, and Dutch feared for his future. They still got on well but the disparity in their lifestyles and interests put an inevitable distance between them, and the only thing they now had in common was their shared past. Dutch couldn't help but be concerned for his brother, especially as he was certain that he could smell an odour of cannabis about him after he returned from a smoke—a luxury indeed for someone in and out of work—but he made no mention of this to his older brother as for fear of falling out on such a rare meeting with him and on such a solemn occasion. He did, however, wonder whether his own life might have followed a similar path, had he remained in the town, and had he not pursued his only ambition?

Dutch spoke with his half-brother, Barry, and sister, Deborah, for the first time for many years and learnt that they were both happy and now living in Swindon; Dutch had great affection for Deborah as she had, despite her young age, once been a mother figure to them all, and he was pleased to reunite with her.

Dutch found that he had a lot of spare time on his hands in the evenings, and now being unfamiliar with the town, he was only too pleased when he caught the attention of Melanie Warwick, a petite but confident, dark-haired girl, who worked within the recruiting office, having moved to the city in her early teenage years from a small Cambridgeshire village due to her father Ken's employment for a multinational financial services company relocating there. As an only child, she had been reluctant to move from her friends and other family members, but the lure of the sea and the bright city lights compared to her sedate rural location swayed her to leave without serious protest. The enforced move proved to be successful in many ways as she was to enjoy her comprehensive and college education and all the entertainment and interest the city held for her newly found friends and herself. Melanie was never to be a serious student, and at the completion of her college education, she was still unsure as to what career path she should take until by chance, her father learnt from an acquaintance, who was a member of the Territorial Army Reserve, that there was a position vacant at the local Army Recruiting Office. On hearing this, Melanie made enquiries regarding the work, and it appealed to her, coupled with the facts that she had the qualifications requested and the location could be reached by public transport; she applied and was accepted as a civilian recruiting coordinator within the office. Dutch and Melanie, who was a few years older than him, hit it off right away and were soon spending all their free time together, making the most of the city's many amenities and vibrant nightlife. Whilst they shared many interests including music, Melanie's background differed hugely from Dutch's, as she was an only child with doting parents, but her secure sense of family and belonging anchored them both, and Dutch felt able to trust and rely on her, and they quickly became inseparable, much to the interest and amusement of their co-workers at the recruitment office.

Dutch found himself involving Melanie in more and more aspects of his life, and their mutual interest in music drew them even closer together as they travelled up and down the country together to many gigs and festivals; she inspired trust and confidence, as well as being a fun and attractive girlfriend. Before long, he decided to take her to see Jeanette and the ailing Sinbad, which Melanie teased him good naturedly about, saying that she hoped she was going to impress him enough so as not to be forced to walk the plank. . Dutch took great pleasure in regaling her with an infamous story from Sinbad's past, when his own teenage daughter had arranged for a young man to call for her at the family home, and her father had answered the door first. Due to his age and lifestyle, he was very tactless and blunt, and he took one look at the youth, decided that he didn't like the look of him, especially as he had a large earring in each ear. Apparently, according to the youth, Sinbad said to him, "The only men who wear earrings are poofs and pirates, and neither are welcome in my house," then immediately closed the door, leaving him on the step outside. Although Dutch would never have considered wearing an earring himself, he didn't agree with his grandfather's sentiments but found the story amusing as it summed up Sinbad's archaic views and felt sure that Melanie would have little to worry about from him.

But then, Melanie was almost universally well liked; she was slow to anger and quick to laugh, and her ready smile conjured deep dimples in her cheeks, giving her an appealing girlish look. As Dutch said his farewells to all, the old sea dog hugged him and whispered, "You look after yourself, Son. The next time you see me, I will be laying horizontal."

Dutch returned the hug, kissed him on the cheek and on looking at the deteriorating figure of his once big, strong grandfather, suspected that what he was indicating was probably correct. It was to be the last time Dutch saw him alive.

Life 2: During his stint at the recruiting office, he was informed by the staff sergeant that Derek Bowman had been shot and killed by a terrorist bullet whilst manning a vehicle checkpoint in Belfast. Dutch was duly shocked at this news as he realised that if he had been just weeks older, it would have been highly probable that it would have been himself at that checkpoint instead of Derek. He recollected, not for the first time, his grandmother's words about having nine lives, and he wondered whether this would count as one of his own 'lives' having been lost.

Melanie was taken aback by how shaken Dutch was by this news and even more surprised by his preoccupation with superstitious belief.

"What is it with you and this 'nine lives' business? I really think you believe you've got some sort of a charmed existence." Melanie looked at him slyly, through her long, dark lashes, raising an eyebrow quizzically, clearly inviting him to challenge her statement.

"I've told you about this before, Mel, it's just something I can't shake off. I know it's probably just coincidence, but I can't help believing that there's more to it, and I don't want to tempt fate by saying it's all a load of cobbler's and going against Connie's beliefs It's not that bad, it's just a feeling I have ingrained within me, especially as I consider I have now twice cheated death."

"There you go again, 'tempting fate', it's all superstitious stuff and nonsense; you've got one life and you need to live it."

Dutch didn't want to argue with Melanie and he knew that she was mostly just teasing him for the sheer fun of it, but he had grown up with these beliefs, and they were something he had held onto as part of his sense of identity and belonging to the family, and besides, he really couldn't quite dismiss it all as groundless, however improbable it seemed.

"If you'd met Connie, you might have felt differently," he said, "it's a real shame you never got to meet her."

"Yeah, that's true, it would've been nice to meet the famous Crystal Gaze, well, *your nan*, of course," she added hurriedly, softening her stance considerably, as she could see that she had clearly touched a nerve.

"Look," she said, "if you think you've got nine lives, then that's okay by me; just make sure you spend plenty of them with me."

"As sad as I am for Derek and his family, I can't help thinking that if I had been there instead, not only is it possible that I could be dead, but there is also the fact that if I had gone, we would never have met."

Dutch smiled and thinking of the words of a 'Different Corner' by George Michael, slipped his arm round her waist, pulling her close to him, and held her face in his hand gently.

"I know how lucky I am, finding you," he said. "You need to understand that these things really matter to me. It's my past, it's sort of who I am and I need to hold onto that."

"Yeah, I know, I get that. It just seems funny when you're a soldier and all...you know you'll jump out an aircraft but don't want to step on a crack in the pavements or walk under a ladder."

"Well, when you put it like that," Dutch laughed, "but I'm not that bad, it's just the nine lives thing that really gets me. It's kind of like a code that I feel I need to live by, something to believe in, I suppose."

Melanie smiled mischievously,

"Whatever it takes to keep the Satisfied Soldier happy," she quipped, depositing a rapid kiss on his lips so that he could not take offence at what she had said.

"You'll do for me, Melanie Warwick," he said, feeling as though things couldn't get any better in his world. His assignment at the recruiting centre was relaxed and enjoyable in which time he was confident that he had been instrumental in encouraging a number of enlistments.

Their bubble looked set to burst though when Dennis was called to re-join his unit, which at the time was based at Aldershot, Hampshire; but they managed to navigate the difficulties of a long-distance relationship by both passing their driving tests within weeks of each other, and their perseverance paid off as they eventually became engaged and subsequently married, settling in army accommodation. .

As a couple, they were very close, still choosing to spend most of their free time together. Melanie really took to Army life and took up a post working in the Army pay office and quickly made lots of friends within the barracks. Dutch was so much happier as a part of a couple, he enjoyed the security of being married and living within the structure of the army 'family'; it was such a contrast to his early life of uncertainty and a constant nagging sense of inadequacy. Dutch considered himself to be really lucky to have someone like Melanie and he was very protective of her; he tried hard not to be possessive or jealous but she was so very precious to him, and he vowed to himself to always protect her from any harm.

His newly found happiness had a somewhat minor detrimental effect on Melanie as he had now developed a habit of, when getting up in the morning would, sing or whistle an appropriate tune as to the mood that he was experiencing at that time. For instance, if it was raining or in the shower, *'Raindrops Keep Falling on My Head'*; if he heard birdsong, *'Rockin' Robin'*; if sunny it was, *'Lazing on a Sunny Afternoon'* or similar, all bellowed out from behind the bathroom door. As he was an early 'go get 'em' riser, she was not and would get infuriated by his interruption to her early morning sleep, but underneath, she was pleased that he was so obviously happy with their life together. Dutch was not intentionally being selfish; by the time he was conscious of his crooning, it was generally too late and he had awoken her. Evening bath times took on a similar role as he would 'belt out' tribute sessions; one of the worst she could remember was one dedicated to the Kinks, when *'You Really Got Me'* caused her to shut the lounge door and turn up the television to drown out the commotion. The icing on the cake was the night he tried to impersonate the falsetto sound of Frankie Valli, and Melanie rushed up the stairs to the bathroom genuinely believing that he was in some form of distress. Alarm bells rang with Melanie when Dutch considered learning to play the guitar but later decided that his full lifestyle would not allow him the time to reach the standard he would wish for. Melanie readily agreed with him as she considered that the world was not yet ready for another 'Dennis Dutch Denver', churning out similar songs to the late John Denver of his love for the natural world.

They each made sure that they had their own separate interests though, and he kept up his fitness training and hobbies. He was a good boxer and reached the army boxing semi-finals for his weight on two occasions, and knew he could do even better, but he was not prepared to give his all to it, as he favoured the freedom of cross-country running. He appreciated that boxing had acted not only as a sport and a method of defending himself but, above all, had given him confidence and had taught him controlled aggression. On the other hand, running calmed him, taking him to a place where he could enjoy peace and solitude and the feeling of being back to nature, escaping for a short time at not seeing either people or vehicles; he felt most relaxed in life when running. Although he loved music more than most but found it difficult to comprehend as to why many runners listened to earphones as personally, he thought that not only should technology be left behind for that short period but also, it was distracting and dangerous, because the listener had a limited idea what was happening around them and in the past had witnessed several near misses involving such users.

Life 3: His sense of self-survival was tested early in his new career, not in combat, but in a busy city centre night club on a lad's night out with two fellow soldiers. During the evening, a group of local drunken men identified them as being army personnel and started goading them. This eventually resulted in a vicious fight; with the soldiers being heavily outnumbered, his two colleagues were forced outside where the fighting continued. Dutch became trapped inside and received a stab wound to the neck which partially cut into his carotid artery; he was bleeding heavily and realised that he could bleed to death very quickly and needed immediate medical attention. Despite his wound, the doormen were trying to eject him from the club because blood was spurting everywhere and was causing distress to the remaining clientele. Dutch thought that if he went out into the street and collapsed, he could not rely for certain on anyone calling for an ambulance immediately. So, he grabbed a candle from a table, using the tablecloth as a pressure pad on his neck wound and held the candle close to the huge net curtains and drapes in the reception hall and threatened the staff that if they did not call 999 in his presence, he would set fire to the curtains. As a result of this threat, the receptionist called the ambulance, which arrived quickly. Due to his heavy blood loss, he was required to spend several days in hospital, requiring surgery and monitoring. Melanie, frantic with worry, barely left his bedside and, as soon as he was coherent enough, he was desperate to set the record straight with her.

"Sorry about this…it really wasn't our fault…they realised we were army…they were hell-bent on a fight," he spoke in short, staccato bursts.

"Yes, I know, it's okay. I've heard the story, the police told me; that's exactly what witnesses have said. They've arrested the ringleaders, by the way, so you can lie back and relax and recover."

"Good. Can't afford to get into trouble so early in my service."

"You have nothing to worry about, honestly. You just need to concentrate on getting better."

She leaned over and smoothed his hair, kissing him lightly on the forehead in a slightly motherly way, which made Dutch smile.

"Yeah, I'm lucky to be here, considering the amount of blood I lost. I knew straight away it was an artery. Perhaps what I told you is true and Connie was right…I am blessed with extra lives. This will be my third lucky escape."

He exhaled deeply, the effort of speaking tiring him.

"I don't know about that. I'm just glad that you are okay."

"Did they get the one that did me?"

"Yes," Melanie replied, laughing, "he's here, somewhere under police guard; unlucky for him, he ran straight outside into Ron Page and according to Ron he bumped into him and fell over, knocking himself unconscious but apparently, his injuries are worse than a simple fall would cause."

Dutch smiled, "Bumping into his massive fists more like. Sounds like I owe Ron a big drink, but I won't be joining him. As you know I've never been a big drinker and since being in here, I've done nothing but think about what happened, and if I had been sober and had all my wits about me, I would have seen that blade coming and could have dealt with him." He paused, looking fatigued but determined to finish what he was saying. "But due to the drink, my reactions were slow, so from this day on, I'm planning on keeping off alcohol."

"That's good news, I supposed, but you only usually drink on special occasions anyway. Anyway, is there anything I can bring you in as I know you'll soon be getting bored stiff as you hate being still?"

"Actually, yes, there is. As I'm going to be out of action for a bit, do you think you could pick up a book I'm after? It's just you won't like it, when I tell you what it is."

Melanie raised an eyebrow and paused before she replied,

"Something dodgy, is it?"

"No, nothing like that," he laughed. "I think it's called *'Myths and Superstitions'* and it's got a picture of a dragon type thing on the cover."

"Hmm, I see, going to test out a bit of hocus pocus from your sick bed. I think you'll find stitches and antibiotics will work just fine."

"Just wanting to check something out, whilst I've got time on my hands."

Melanie could see how tired and drained he looked, and she knew that he would soon become restless, once he started to improve.

"Okay, leave it with me and I will see what I can find. In the meantime, I think you need to take it easy, you look shattered."

"Thanks, and yeah, this lying around, recovering really takes it out of you. At least it's given me the chance to listen to some of my music without disturbance."

"Is that comment aimed at me?"

"No, but you know what I'm like. I don't usually sit still long enough. The only time I get chance for a sing along is in the bath, shower or in the car."

She bent to kiss him, dodging the obstacles of IV tube and dressings.

"I'll be back tomorrow then, hopefully, with your special request. I can't believe that you are going to read something else rather than military or fitness related."

Melanie was as good as her word and returned the next day with a book closely resembling the one he had detailed, but it was a while before he felt up to being able to look at it properly. Once he was ensconced in the medical centre situated at his barracks, to continue his convalescence, he made a beeline for information regarding the myth surrounding cats having nine lives. Consulting the index of the book, he turned to the appropriate page and read the chapter whilst his wife browsed through the local newspaper. After a while, Dutch interrupted her reading.

"Listen to this, Mel, it appears that the myth of a cat having nine lives derives from ancient Egypt, where they worship cats as divine creatures with psychic or supernatural powers. Many other ancient civilisations also regarded the cat as some kind of mystic spirit too."

"More of a dog person myself," retorted Melanie, "and anyway, what's that got to do with them having nine lives, anyway?"

"Like most superstitions, it's all very vague with no real facts to back it up, but the belief that cats have multiple lives seems to exist in many cultures around the world. One theory is that the number nine appears to come from either the ancient Egyptian sun god, Atum-Ra, who took on the form of a cat for visits to the underworld, giving birth to eight other gods, thus representing nine lives in one, or just the fact that the ancient Chinese and Greeks, who also held the cat in high esteem, regarded nine as a lucky number and called the belief the 'trinity of trinities'."

"So, what you're saying then, Dennis, is that you think you may have taken on some god-like power? Mind you, like a cat, you are very resilient and always seem to eventually land on your feet," Melanie smirked.

"No, c'mon now, don't be silly, gimme a break. I'm just interested, that's all, cos of my Nan's superstitious behaviour and beliefs, and I find it genuinely interesting. She was a legend in mystic circles, so who are we to say that there's no merit in her theories. Who is to say that there's not some kind of unseen force out there that governs our lives, monitors every move we make, dictates our fate, chooses who is lucky or unlucky, who lives and dies, depending on their next decision or direction in which they turn. It's just as easy to believe in that theory as it is to believe in any of the popular religions. Anyway, reading this book will give me something to do while having to take it easy, I'm bored with this laying around already."

"That's true, you rarely read a book, you're always too busy for that, and you're not exactly malingerer material. Just don't go getting like Connie after you've read it. I don't think I could put up with that."

"As if! I can still remember how her superstitious ways used to drive everyone nuts. Bless her."

The couple were forced to move their base when after 63 years since its formation the parachute headquarters was relocated to the Colchester Garrison, Essex

From the day Dutch joined the army until the day he left, Britain was involved in six major conflicts, and he had some involvement in most of them with many tours in war-torn countries including the stabilisation of some in the aftermath. Without exception, each one he was engaged in was eventful and played a major part in his life.

In the majority of these hostilities, he had no firm beliefs of how they would ever be resolved due to either corrupt or inept politicians, or different tribes, religions or customs, which all seemed to cause friction. Although, at times, he gave out sweets and other goods in order to win over the civilian populations; he realised that none of them could be trusted, not even the children, due to the threats that hung over them from the terrorist organisations. At times, whilst in the Middle East when troubled by the heat, flies and sand, he flippantly considered that there was little wonder that the inhabitants were so ill tempered and in regular conflict with each other.

Life 4: It was in such heat and sand that Dutch considered that he had lost another of his 'lives' when in a unit at the side of the road, awaiting confirmation from a forward party that their path was clear of IEDs (Improvised explosive devices) when they heard the approach of a small motor cycle. One of the soldiers stepped forward and indicated for the moped to stop but as the rider and machine drew closer to the convoy with no sign of slowing, it became obvious that it was not going to comply and headed straight for the group of gathered soldiers. The soldiers scattered and some fired their weapons, but the rider, although hit several times, continued forwards and crashed into a parked, armoured troop-carrier, instantly killing the rider. As the soldiers tentatively approached the dead, bearded, traditionally-robed male, they noticed an electronic triggering device strapped to his wrist and immediately evacuated the area. On the examination of the corpse, the bomb disposal team found that he was wearing an explosive suicide vest together with a rucksack on his back containing hundreds of large nails; but for a fault in the trigger switch, had the explosion occurred, it would have killed and maimed many of the group including a certain newly promoted Corporal French, who was standing close to the armoured vehicle when struck and was more than grateful to a shaky moped travelling on bumpy terrain that had probably caused a wire in the detonating device to come adrift of its terminal.

From time to time, he would work with special services in clandestine operations, entering and leaving countries without trace or clues as to what nation had carried out a particular attack or hostage rescue. The details of these operations never entered the public domain, with all personnel involved strongly advised that having signed the official secrets act, there would be no hesitation in dismissal from the service and prosecution should they communicate any of the facts.

Life 5: It was for such a mission that he was awarded the Military Cross medal when his bravery and tenacity were demonstrated whilst engaged in an operation in Afghanistan; when, in order to release hostages from Taliban fighters, he was required, under cover of darkness, to blow open a large, metal door and grill in order for troops to enter the compound. Whilst setting the explosive, a fuse proved to be defective and failed; with no spare at hand, Dutch was forced to substitute it with an improvised firing method, knowing that he would have very little time to get clear to escape the blast. Having primed the explosive, he ran for cover as fast as he possibly could, but before he reached the shelter of a low wall, the device exploded, and he was struck in the back by flying shrapnel, leaving him with serious but not life-threatening injuries. Despite this, the operation was a complete success, and Dutch was awarded the honour for his bravery, and whenever he got the opportunity, he would willingly show the scars and tell how, although not being a natural sprinter, during his run for cover, he would have given Usain Bolt a run for his money.

Chapter 5

The Cowboy and the Lady (1981)

Artist: John Denver   Writer: Bobby Goldsboro

The early years of marriage were happy and gratifying for them both, just as they had both wished. Although Dutch was regularly away on tour with his unit, Melanie became familiar with his absences that came as no surprise to her as her own employment had well-prepared her for such sudden interruptions. She would always be concerned for his welfare whilst engaged in conflicts but was always inwardly confident that her man would come home unscathed.

Although his love for Melanie was never in question, like many married men, he was still occasionally attracted to the opposite sex but had no intentions of pursuing any other relationship. The one and only blot on his copy book occurred whilst on a colleague's stag night, many miles from home in the future bridegroom's home town of Warrington, Lancashire.

Dutch, who was almost teetotal, only drinking alcohol in small quantities on social occasions since his stabbing incident, was not relishing the thought of a booze-filled weekend with lads fully tanked up whilst he was stone-cold sober, witnessing the loud raucous behaviour that accompany such occasions, but as he knew the host well and he was to go with Melanie's blessing and encouragement, as, although she appreciated his predicament, she thought it impolitic to turn down the invitation.

As it wasn't entirely a 48 hour pub crawl, as the groom had family connections at Old Trafford, and consequently, a hospitality box was reserved on the Saturday, followed by a trip into Liverpool the following day where Dutch could fulfil one of his lifetime ambitions and catch a ferry across the Mersey, just as depicted in one of his favourite songs, so he agreed to go with the proviso that he was allocated a single room, knowing that apart from him, the rest of the group would be absolutely paralytic. Thinking in this way made him feel like an old fart but drunkenness nearly killed him and that was not happening again.

Having arrived at the small, mid-standard hotel on the Friday evening, failing to divulge that they were a stag party in case of rejection, the lads took little time in getting the extended party started, a few drinks in the small resident's bar and then out on the town. Before leaving, they had discussed that the town had been subjected to two separate bombings in 1993, the first of which resulted in a policeman being shot, the second causing two children to lose their lives. They decided that due to some past high-profile attacks by terrorist sympathisers on off-duty servicemen, they could be credible targets, so if speaking to anyone outside of their group, they were to say that they were all construction workers.

By the time they reached their first venue for the evening, the whole group were pissed apart from Dutch who, after a couple of small beers, was now drinking tonic water so as to at least give the impression that there was alcohol in his glass and not make him a constant target as a lightweight. The inevitable happened: as the group moved from pub to pub, they got more noisy and boisterous as they played out their drinking games. At their final destination before the obligatory curry, which would be followed by those still standing finding a late-night club, Dutch was viewing the nonsense antics and piss taking with an interjection whenever he could be heard, but feeling somewhat detached from the rest with their loud and juvenile behaviour, which almost made him feel like drinking himself in order to fully interact but he resisted.

Feeling bored, he started to look around the packed bar, as he was aware that the group were drawing attention to themselves, when he noticed a group of young women a couple of tables away. Occasionally, some of them sitting nearby would look towards the rowdy soldiers when the volume of their rowdiness increased. As he sat there, hoping that one of his motley crew would soon feel hungry and suggest moving on, he noticed a very slim, attractive lady, several years older than the rest of her group, looking directly at him and smiling. He ignored her glances at first as he thought that he was imagining it, or she was smiling at someone else nearby, but each time he glanced back, he got the same reaction and realised that she was regularly looking directly at him. Dutch felt himself blush and looked around at his mates hoping they had not noticed, as if so he would be in for some stick. He now couldn't help looking in her direction occasionally because he had become completely bored with the drink-fuelled banter between them all, and each time their eyes met, she smiled, and he now found himself discreetly smiling back without any other members of the two groups appearing to notice the silent communication between the two.

All of a sudden, Dutch felt a heavy poke in the ribs, it was 'Chopper' loudly announcing, so much so that the whole pub must have heard, that it was Dutch's round, which they had decided were even more tequila shots. Dutch was more than happy at such a simple order because there was no way he could now understand the ramblings of most of his crew. On reaching the bar and making the mammoth order, realising more than ever that it was a bad decision for a virtual non-drinker to attend a stag night, he suddenly became aware that 'lady eye contact' was standing at his side, looking up at him, saying in a soft, educated northern accent,

"Your lot seem to be enjoying yourselves; special occasion, is it?"

Feeling flustered, not being a natural small talker with strangers, especially with such an attractive woman who was wearing what appeared to be elegant designer clothing, making him feel much underdressed in his t-shirt and jeans.

"Yeah, my mate's stag weekend—can you tell?" he smiled. "He's originally from here."

"You all sound as if you are from down south." She fleetingly looked him up and down. "What do you all do? I take it you work together?"

Dutch didn't like to lie unless absolutely necessary but remembering what the group had decided and knowing how word would soon get around the pub, he said,

"Most of us work for the same construction company; noisy bunch, aren't they?"

"Only to be expected, but you seem to be on the edge of it a bit, not as noisy as the rest of them."

"I don't drink much, so yeah, I am a bit out of it, I suppose."

Dutch could feel the back of his neck flushing and hoped that it didn't show in the dimly-lit pub.

"I'm in exactly the same position, I'm out with my staff. I'm treating them as we have had a particularly good week at the boutique and because I'm paying, they've all had a lot to drink."

"A boutique owner, well that makes sense. I thought you looked very glamourous."

"Thank you and if I want to stay that way, I better not have any more wine; two glasses and I am anybody's."

Dutch wondered if he should ask this but felt mischievous and said,

"How many glasses have you had then?"

"Two."

Dutch swallowed and wasn't sure where to go from here; was her reply a come-on? Was he being propositioned? It certainly seemed like it, but he was in unknown territory, not looking for female company and had little experience as to what appeared to be happening in his largely male-dominated world, but as he looked across at his buddies, he saw 'out of his skull' Jock fall off his chair and immediately knew what his best option was to be.

"Er, can I buy you a drink, something non-alcoholic, perhaps?"

"No, I'm just buying the final round for the girls, then I'm off, working tomorrow."

"Early night then?"

"Not really, just want to get away from the gossip and the small talk. It's not so entertaining when you haven't had much to drink."

"I know exactly what you mean, same problem. How about..." he stopped mid speech. "No, perhaps not."

She smiled and said, "What were you about to say?"

Dutch said bashfully and knew, from the moment the words passed his lips, he shouldn't have done.

"How about us going for a meal or something? My lot are all going for a curry, and I really don't fancy going due to the state they are in, and if you are thinking of leaving early?"

"Why not? You seem alright and it looks as if we both could do with each other's company. I'm sure that we are the only sober ones in here."

"What some would call two boring farts?"

"Hey! Speak for yourself. I can have fun without booze."

"Sorry, yeah, well, I'll just go and make my excuses but the state they're all in, they won't even know that I've gone. I'll meet you outside shortly. What's your name, by the way?"

"Kerry, what's yours?"

"Dennis. Is that Carrie as in Carrie doesn't live here anymore?"

"Who? What?"

"Never mind, it's an old song, one of my Nan's favourites. I'm having trouble with your accent. Does your name start with a C or K?"

"K as in County Kerry, Ireland. You're not that easy to understand yourself, perhaps we will need an interpreter?" she said smiling.

"In that case, I'm presuming that your family originated from Southern Ireland."

"Wrong, Sherlock. They are all Welsh, but they didn't think the names Caerphilly or Aberystwyth suited me."

Dutch laughed out loud, realising that her immediate humorous response was a result of his incorrect assumption that had also been made by others in the past.

By the time he reached the table with the drinks, the pub's two doormen were at the table giving out some strong advice to his revelling friends, who were belting out 'Jerusalem' as it had never been sung so badly before.

This was a good time to depart, he thought, as it could only get worse. He had no sooner put the drinks down on the table, and they were snaffled up immediately, reminding him of pigs around a trough, and he was correct in his assumption that his presence wouldn't be missed, as when he made an excuse regarding his departure, apart from a few feeble pleas and piss-takes, they soon resumed their party routine. He looked over to the girls table and saw that Kerry was missing from the group. As he made his way outside, he became concerned by thinking that this was obviously a lady of expensive tastes, and if she chose to dine at a really expensive establishment, how would he explain the amount paid on the credit card as he and Melanie had never kept any financial secrets. He couldn't see her at first and felt a sense of both relief coupled with disappointment, then she appeared from a doorway, having been sheltering from the rain.

"Where shall we eat? I don't know this town at all," he said.

"I do, so what do you fancy?"

Dutch, feeling mischievous, thought about making a suggestive remark but resisted.

"I really don't mind, just avoid all curry houses as we could get some drunken company."

That's something Dutch could do without as the guys knew he was married, some had even met Melanie. Although the maxim

'What happens on tour, stays on tour' was always adhered to, but how much personal flack he would have to endure from them wasn't worth thinking about.

They both then strolled on the rain-soaked pavements until they reached her recommended standard Thai restaurant where they chatted about life in general and laughed a lot over her one glass of fine wine and his small beer that they had each permitted themselves.

"That's three now," Dennis said, remembering what she had said earlier.

"You had better watch out then, hadn't you?"

During the conversation, Kerry mentioned that she had just recently ended a long-term relationship and was coming to terms with being a single girl again.

"Are you married or seeing anyone, Dennis?" she said.

"Yes. I'm married but it's not a problem, is it? We are only here to keep each other company, away from our rowdy mates?"

"No problem to me, let's just have some fun."

As they sat at their table, to any observers, they would have appeared as an unlikely couple. She was apparently a successful, wealthy businesswoman, petite and elegant, looking as if she was about to attend a glamorous function; in comparison, Dutch felt he looked like the rough and ready combat soldier that he was, but despite the appearances and her being about ten years older than him, they seemed to hit it off, laughing and joking with no awkward silences during the two hours they spent dining. At one stage, he did let slip a reference to the army and not wishing to admit his initial deceit, covered any further discussion about it by saying that he had once been a short-term soldier. He so disliked his dishonesty as the old adage of 'One lie leads to another' immediately came into his mind, but the roller coaster had started and he couldn't get off.

When they were asked by the waiter if they required coffee, Kerry interjected saying,

"Shall we go back to yours for coffee?"

Dennis, trying not to look surprised or anxious, again knew what he should say, but instead, not relishing an early night, said, "Yeah, good idea."

When the bill arrived, Kerry said, "Let's split the bill. What do you call it when you do that?"

Dutch burst out laughing.

"What's so funny about that?"

Still laughing, he replied, "It's called going Dutch."

"So, what's so amusing?"

"Dutch is my nickname, everyone calls me that."

"Why?"

"My surname is French."

Kerry said smiling, "I see now, my little Dutch tulip, or should it be my little French frog prince?" and lent forward and kissed him on the cheek.

"That was very nice, my little, northern balm cake".

"Balm cake, why balm cake?"

"The word balm fascinates me, it's a word I hear regularly used up here but very seldom heard down south."

"That's because you're not only a load of southern softies, you know nothing about good food either."

Dutch responded, "That Hadrian fella should have built his wall south of Birmingham."

"Who's Adrian?" she knowingly and inquisitively gestured.

"Ah, just some Italian brickie I once read about in a school history book."

They both burst out laughing.

Although he protested regarding the sharing of the bill, he was inwardly pleased that the resulting cash card statement would show the purchase of just one meal.

As they left the restaurant, the heavens opened, and as his hotel was only a short distance away, they decided it wasn't worth waiting for a cab so started to walk, but due to her expensive high heels, she was unable to hurry so in frustration, removed them and paddled the rest of the way in her stockinged feet, both laughing as she did so.

On entering the hotel, both dripping wet, Dutch was relieved that the reception desk and bar were now closed, so there were no embarrassing moments with staff seeing him going to his single room accompanied by a female.

Once inside of the room, Kerry entered the en-suite bathroom whilst Dutch selected some clothes from his case. After removing and secreting his tell-tale dog tag, he put on a pair of shorts and a running singlet, then placed a t-shirt and a pair of jogging bottoms outside of the bathroom door, at the same time informing Kerry that they were there and suggesting that she hung her wet clothes in the warm bathroom in an effort to dry them. Following drying his hair, he commenced to make coffee for both of them and was doing so, when he became aware that Kerry had silently walked up close behind him.

"How do I look? You could have got a smaller pair of trousers?"

Dutch turned towards her and saw the stunning sight of the pretty, well-educated lady, whom he barely knew, standing before him in his t-shirt with the nipples of her small breasts clearly visible, pressing against the thin material. There was something very erotic about her naked body inside of his clothing, and he became immediately aroused and turned his back to her, continuing to prepare the drinks in an effort to hide the increasing prominent bulge at the front of his flimsy shorts.

He swallowed heavily and diverted his attention to the boiling kettle in an effort to avoid her sensing his nervousness of the occasion.

"Very nice, it looks as if we are both ready to go for a run."

"I don't think that we would get very far after that meal and in this weather".

As he replied, "A few yards perhaps. How do you like your coffee?"

It was as if she had felt both his desire and tension, as she gently took his hand in hers and lead him the short distance towards the side of the bed.

"As my clothes are soaking wet, I will have to stay the night so let's make the most of it."

Before Dutch could reply, she was kissing him gently and seductively on his lips and he automatically responded.

Without the usual petting, which may have resulted in Dutch getting cold feet, she lay on the bed gently, pulling Dutch towards her and the little clothing that they were wearing was soon hastily removed and tossed to the side. As they both lay naked, kissing and fondling in the small bed, Dutch was finding it difficult to get a full erection as his brain was telling him not to go through with it, but Kerry proved more than capable in orally stimulating his temporary malfunction, and her continued erotic foreplay soon dispelled all of his doubts, and he soon became a very willing partner in the all-furious sex that followed. Dutch was a relative novice in the bedroom; apart from Melanie and a few encounters with a couple of casual girlfriends before they met, all of which he considered was standard sex, here he was being pulled and pushed into every conceivable sexual position by an obviously very experienced practitioner.

Later that morning, the exhausted Dutch was awoken by Kerry, who was fully awake, showered and having got fully dressed without disturbing him.

"I have to leave for work early as I need to change my damp clothes before I open up the shop. I'm lucky I have plenty to choose from."

Barely awake, Dutch reached for her hand and kissed it, saying, "You still look good to me."

She then said, "I've written my phone number on the hotel note pad should you wish to see me again tonight. If not, it was nice meeting you."

With that, she then lent forward, kissing the slumbering man on the forehead and left closing the door quietly, with Dutch hoping that none of the others would see her leave, although that was highly unlikely as he had heard the rumpus that they kicked up on their return in the early hours, at the same time feeling sympathy for other residents.

He lay there for a short time not quite believing what had happened as the night's events were not really him; it had proceeded so naturally, which gave him great pleasure at the time, but now, when thinking of his wife, filled him with guilt and trepidation. He had always felt that he shouldn't have gone on the trip but for entirely different reasons. He didn't know the definition of a nymphomaniac, but he thought he may have just experienced one as three more times that night, she had woken him for sex, and he even surprised himself when able to oblige each time; she had been a very noisy love maker but hopefully, his comatose pals never heard a murmur. He later looked at the number she had left him and immediately knew that he had to dispose of it, because if the evening was to pan out like the last, he would be tempted to call her—not purely for sex, because he wasn't sure he would even be up to it again so soon, but because he liked her, for her attractiveness, humour and good company. He was under no illusions that he had suddenly become a love god or a gigolo overnight. He was just her bit of rough for the weekend, the only sober male on the premises at the time. It had probably been her way of coping with the disappointment of her recent break up; she probably felt that by doing it, she was giving her ex-partner a kick in the bollocks. With a sense of regret, he tore it up into minute pieces so he could never reassemble them and placed them in the bin.

When the lads eventually arose, long past the final hotel breakfast sitting, they congregated in the foyer and made their plans for the journey to the football in Manchester. During the journey, they all chatted about the previous evening's experiences and commented on Dutch not drinking and not feeling able to fully enjoy himself. He would have dearly loved to have told them how non-boring his night had been, but firstly, they wouldn't have believed him as he was considered the 'Steady Eddie' of the bunch, and secondly, it was a guilty secret that he must keep from Melanie forever.

The remainder of the weekend was enjoyable and so much more sedate as the group, as a whole, was too tired and hungover to repeat the antics of the night before, which suited Dutch just fine as he too was really tired but for other reasons.

On his return home, he gave Melanie some gifts that he had purchased whilst in Liverpool but knew that whatever he gave her then, or in the future, would never rid him of his guilt and concerns. He never viewed Kerry as agent provocateur as to his infidelity; she was apparently free and single and able to do as she pleased in such matters, but he wasn't and had been a more than willing partner, who should have been stronger and resisted the temptation. He did consider that many men in the same situation as himself would have also succumbed in such circumstances, but this was of little compensation as to the realisation of the betrayal of his wife. The fault rested firmly on his shoulders, so much so that he feared that Melanie, who knew him so well, would sense that something had happened over that weekend.

The resulting wedding and after-party were a much more sober affair with Dutch firmly in the knowledge that no one present had any idea as to his weekend misdemeanour and therefore, would not accidently alert Melanie to his guilty secret. He would never again be able to play the song track that he likened to his experience with Kerry in the presence of Melanie, as some of the words were too close to the reality. In the future, he did occasionally have fond thoughts of Kerry and wondered if she had found love and a man fit enough to fulfil her needs. In that short while in her company, he felt more relaxed than he had for a long time and considered that this was due to the fact that in those few hours, he was not living and breathing his work—not that he would ever dream of changing his employment— but it did bring home to him how his work regime and his idyllic home life with Melanie made him a more sober and responsible person and, for most part up until now, had kept him on the straight and narrow. As exciting as the experience with Kerry had been, he must, at all costs, avoid any such pitfalls in the future that would jeopardise all that was so dear to him.

He often wished that he had just got pissed with his mates possibly making a fool of himself rather than have the guilt that hung over him regarding his cheating and he didn't even have what he considered was the pathetic excuse of being drunk. He could have halted proceedings at any time, but the temptation had been too great, knowing the old adage of an erect penis had no conscience would haunt him forever.

The episode was to remain undiscovered and their married life continued as before, contentedly. Everything seemed to be as good as it could be when Melanie discovered that she was pregnant, and both were overjoyed at the prospect of starting a family, but the joy was short-lived when after 13 weeks, without warning, Melanie miscarried. They were both devastated but Melanie especially so and Dutch saw a fragility and vulnerability in her that he had never seen before. Melanie had always been such a bubbly, optimistic person that he found it hard to recognise this new version of her, and although he did his best to be sympathetic and supportive, he just wanted her to go back to being the way she was, as soon as possible. She had been the rock in his life for so long that he did not know what he would be without being able to rely on that security and felt the bitter pang of regret again at his earlier indiscretion, realising that it could have cost him the very thing that mattered the most to him. Fortunately for them both, Melanie made a slow but good recovery; their relationship weathered the strain and, being young and hopeful, they decided that in time, they would try again.

Some 18 months later, Melanie fell pregnant once more and due to her past history, the progress of the pregnancy was monitored extremely closely by local antenatal clinic but again, complications occurred and a termination and a hysterectomy became necessary. Although the first incident had caused her considerable distress, the second attempt dealt her a far more serious blow; she rapidly lost all confidence and become psychologically fragile. Crippling anxiety prompted her to cut herself off from the world for quite some time, refusing to go out and only wishing to see her parents and a couple of her closest friends. Echoes from his childhood, with his mother's instability, prompted Dutch to urge Melanie to seek professional help and was relieved when she willingly agreed.

In time, as Melanie improved, they were able to discuss the prospects of adoption or fostering, but both eventually decided that after the trauma and Melanie's continued high anxiety, neither of them were prepared to take any more risks and would try to return to their previous contented lifestyle together and try to forget the prospect of having children.

During the subsequent years, especially when Dutch was deployed overseas, Melanie drew on the friendship and closeness of the army community to help her through some very dark days. She had never experienced again the high anxiety and reclusive behaviour that she had in those earlier episodes, but neither did she ever feel quite so confident or secure in herself again; it was as though a shadow had been cast over her carefree, independent spirit and she couldn't quite shake it off.

Over his years of active duty, with an exemplary military record, Dutch was promoted to the rank of sergeant and, aware of Melanie's vulnerability, in order to remain near to her, he considered it was time to take himself out of the front line. At his request, he was transferred to 3 Para Training HQ as a drill and physical training instructor. He was especially proud when seeing troops under his instruction efficient enough to quick march to the regiments adopted music *'The Ride of the Valkyries'*. Although now in his mid-thirties, he was still as fit or fitter than most of the younger recruits in the regiment, organising training and fitness programs including a cross-country team, which in the winter months competed in a series of league races against other regiments and services at various bases in the Southern Counties.

He felt more relaxed knowing that he would not be required to leave his wife for any significant time now, and in addition to the physical side of his new position, he also could pass some of his twenty-plus years of knowledge and experience onto new recruits. Dutch had a maxim that he told each and every one of his junior soldiers personally, and with sincerity, "Remember this, I'm only going to say it once. Do not try to buck the system and do not take unnecessary shortcuts, because almost certainly, they will turn and bite either you or your colleagues in the arse. Do everything the way you are instructed, and you will be a good soldier and a credit to yourself." He also liked to introduce them to the military college motto in which he so believed.

It seemed like only yesterday that he had been at the college, and he would often reflect on how fortunate he had been to have been blessed with good instructors and, on the whole, good mates; he was only too aware of how easy it would have been as a junior soldier to have become susceptible to bad influences. Dutch had always kept his sights firmly focussed on his military career and his sporting interests, and whilst he was not unsociable, he did not easily become distracted by fads and fashions and had always avoided the soldier's habit of cataloguing their exploits with tattoos. Whilst Dutch did not share Sinbad's intolerance of earrings, he had a real dislike of tattoos; he put this down to the amount of occasions he had seen young men regretting the image left on their skin, which had often been done as a lark or dare or whilst under the influence of alcohol, later regretting that a former girlfriend was well and truly permanently printed on a part of their body or some unsuitable picture or sentiment was now a total embarrassment to them, and he was a firm believer in prevention being better than cure.

It was a further part of his brief to speak to new recruits to the regiment regarding the misuse of recreational drugs and the severe consequences of such practice. He was well aware that there would often be some amongst them using some form of unlawful stimulant, and if he got the hint or proof of such practice, he had no hesitation in informing the military police and searches or blood tests would be carried out on those concerned. He had no regrets for these actions as in their world, on duty personnel under the influence of drugs or alcohol were a danger and liability to all. Part of his working brief was to remind younger soldiers regarding casual sex, either at home or abroad, including the danger of unwanted pregnancies and sexually-transmitted diseases, and when doing so, he always felt a touch of hypocrisy reflecting on his stag do escapade with Kerry, when as a young man, in a moment of passion, he failed to consider either.

Dutch was soon to become a father figure in his new role and gained a reputation of being a man who would get certain problems solved by sometimes not going through long winded, bureaucratic, red-tape procedures. One such occasion, he became concerned when an efficient and well-liked female recruit working on the base appeared to be preoccupied in her thoughts and started to show signs of anxiety. When he questioned her about the recent change in her demeanour, she informed him that it was due to the worry that her elderly grandparents, who she adored, lived in a flat on a rough London housing estate and were the subject of constant threats and abuse from their next-door neighbour, who was the local drunken bully. Although the police and local authorities had been informed; since their intervention, the problem had worsened which, together with his loud late-night music, was causing them to be ill and sick with fear. The soldier had attempted to talk to the man, who had a fearsome reputation, but also received threats of physical abuse. Dutch, with his hard-line view on bullying, took it upon himself that one Saturday, when the soldier and he were off duty, they travelled together to the grandparents' third-floor flat and spent the afternoon and evening with them. Late that night, as expected, there was loud hammering on the grandparents' door followed by loud, verbal threats as to what would happen should they complain again. As this persisted, Dutch opened the door quickly and was confronted by a surprised looking, unkempt, alcohol-fuelled individual in his late twenties, who upon seeing the unexpected and formidable sight of an angry looking Dutch, immediately clenched his fists and took up an aggressive stance. Before the yob could finish his sentence of 'Who the fuck are you?', Dutch had charged at him and pushed him backwards with force, until he crashed into the brick pillar behind him, winding him in the process. Whilst the man struggled to regain his breath, Dutch pinned him against the pillar with one hand tightly around his neck. Dutch was about to try to speak with him when he moved his hand suddenly as if to attempt to punch or go for something in his pocket, spurring Dutch to instinctively aim a heavy punch to his alcohol-filled stomach, causing him to further gasp for air and sink slowly backwards down the pillar onto the floor. After a short time, the drunk attempted to get to his feet but was pinned back to the floor by the soldier's size nine boot forcibly resting on the chest of the now heavily panting and vomiting individual who laid still, indicating that he had had enough. Dutch then said in a firm commanding voice, "Right, you pissed up piece of shit, your conduct towards these people stops from now. If I hear of any more complaints, I will be back and next time, I won't be alone and we may need to take you for a little trip that you will not enjoy. If you fail to comply, I suggest that you invest in some crutches." Dutch then released his foot from the man's chest, and he staggered to his feet. He looked at Dutch in an aggressive manner as if to say or do something but thought better of it. After many futile attempts to locate the key in his pockets, the man unlocked his door and lunged inside, leaving Dutch to slam the door behind him.

Dutch and the other occupants of the flats spent the rest of that night in undisturbed sleep. He last heard that circumstances had improved, but Dutch realised that he had only temporarily plugged a hole as such a character wouldn't change overnight, and in time, he would revert to his old ways; but hopefully, before he did, the couple with the aid of their granddaughter, may have made the transfer to other council accommodation.

A number of times, he used his initiative in assisting colleagues in avoiding or preventing them getting into further trouble. On another occasion, a young male soldier, who he knew and liked, did not return from home leave; several official attempts had been made to locate him, but he was obviously evading return so he was now classed as 'absent without leave' (AWOL). Dutch learnt that the absconder had recently split up from his partner and was concerned about the welfare of his young daughter with the new boyfriend. It further came to his notice that because of a number of similar absenteeism's in recent times, the authorities, in order to deter such indiscretions, were to make an example of this particular soldier if he did not return soon. With this in mind, Dutch took an unofficial trip to the soldier's former address and spoke to the estranged partner who, out of loyalty, denied having seen him but did let slip in conversation that she was shortly going to watch her daughter participate at the school sports day. Later that day, Dutch went to the nearby junior school where he saw a large group of adults cheering the children on their various activities and races. He was dressed in civilian clothes but suspecting that the soldier's partner had informed him of his visit, he observed the throng from a distance and amongst them, he saw the soldier concerned. Dutch was unsure how to tackle the problem as he didn't want to confront him in the presence of the crowd, especially his daughter, in case he resisted, so he patiently sat on the grass, enough distance away so as not to be recognised by the individual and awaited for the proceedings to finish. Following the final race, the head teacher addressed the children and spectators, and the pupils then filed back into the school building. The parents then commenced to disperse in various directions across the large playing field with Dutch following his prey at a discreet distance, but the now alerted soldier turned suddenly and spotted him and made a run for the far corner of the field. Dutch took off after him and he was no match for the fleet-footed PTI who, when they reached a remote corner of the field with no other persons nearby, executed a well-timed rugby tackle that sent him crashing to the ground. The shocked soldier laid motionless and explained to the man he liked and respected that he had remained home, avoiding return as he knew nothing about his partner's new boyfriend and wanted to be confident of ensuring the welfare and safety of his daughter before returning to his unit. Dutch respected his concerns and explained how he could, with his assistance, address such concerns through official channels, but now he was regarded as AWOL and would be looking at a punishment and the longer he was absent, the more serious it became. Dutch suggested that they get his belongings from where he had been staying, and he would drop him off outside of the barracks where he could enter voluntarily and with his explanation should lessen any charges. This was done and the soldier's case, presented by an accompanying testimonial from Dutch, coupled with the fact that it appeared that he had returned on his own accord, was looked at favourably, and he received a minor punishment and was allowed the time and facilities to address his concerns.

In deserving cases, Dutch carried out many such acts as he knew how important it was in life to have a helping hand on the way as he had been so fortunate to have had himself.

Chapter 6

You've got a Friend in Me (1996)
Artist & Writer: Randy Newman

Army life had treated Dutch well but after 25 years of service, he started to consider a move into Civvy Street. After such a long spell of service, he wasn't sure how to pursue a life outside of the certainty and security of the military, but a conversation after a services cross country league race at the Sandhurst Military Academy with one of his closest rivals, Chris Compton, planted the seed of an idea in his head. Chris ran for the Police Team and, although fierce rivals, the two men, who were of a similar age, regularly conversed at the finish of each race at one of the urns that distributed the good old-fashioned army brew of tea that was most welcome at the completion of what was usually a five-mile slog through extremely wet and muddy conditions.

Chris found Dutch to be a tough but warm, interesting character, whom he took an instant liking to—the type of person who would make a good friend but a very bad enemy, because despite all of his pleasant characteristics, there was an edge to the man which he couldn't explain, an edge that indicated he was not to be crossed. The policeman put this down to his present training of recruits where he had to give such an aura, but wondered if that was the only reason.

As both men discussed the race sipping from their steaming plastic cups, Dutch said to Chris,

"I'm considering leaving the Army and thought about applying for the police. Do you think at 40, I would be too old to join now?"

"There is no upper age limit to join but your age could go against you. I reckon the majority of new recruits would be between 20 and 30. Apart from your army experience, what other exams or qualifications have you got?"

"I passed a couple of low grade exams at college and then joined as a boy soldier, so none to speak of."

"That could be a problem then," he said, grimacing slightly, "because even with all your worldly knowledge, fitness and skills, in recent years, there has been an emphasis on enlisting recruits with academic qualifications. I think it's to do with the ever-increasing technology that now affects us all and I, for one, struggle with it. I know for certain that if the same criteria existed when I made my application, I would definitely not have been accepted."

Dutch raised his eyebrows in genuine surprise. Chris had always struck him as the sort of fella who was born to do the job.

"I had very few qualifications", Chris continued, "and I'm certain that they only took me on due to my fitness at a time when Bobbies were still walking beats and chasing criminals on foot. In those days, police forces favoured ex-military personal for all their discipline and practical experience, and in my opinion, to the detriment of the force, this is no longer the case."

Dutch sensed that Chris may have an 'axe to grind', and he might be about to receive a rather long lecture on the subject but he merely said,

"But please, don't let what I have said put you off applying. I just feel very strongly that the authorities have taken their eye off of the ball, forgetting the grass-roots policing where only a certain type of person can gain the respect and cooperation of the public, no matter what their education. Don't get me wrong, some officers with university degrees are essential in the job but those, like yourself, who have had a long stint at the 'University of Life' are equally necessary. Take me as an example, I can fight or talk my way out of most situations but have difficulty finding my way around a computer."

"That's interesting because I had heard the same sort of thing from other sources. It probably won't help me either that I have a conviction as a child for theft from a market stall."

"No, no, you don't need to worry about that. A minor juvenile conviction so long ago is unlikely to be still on record and even if it were, it would still not necessarily exempt you from joining; applicants with similar minor convictions have been recruited in the past."

"From what you've said, I don't hold up too much hope, but I will give it a go as I need to think ahead."

"Honestly, don't let what I've said put you off, as I personally think that you would make a great copper but regrettably, from the public view point, that's the realistic truth of the system today, and

I'm just trying to give you a realistic opinion. C'mon, if you can stomach this tea, you can cope with the police recruitment process."

Dutch smiled ruefully, he wanted to pursue the application but was now even more apprehensive as he had gained very few school qualifications; as he had put most his efforts into sport and his fitness regime, having no real interest in serious study until it came to army-related matters.

Nevertheless, after talking it over with Melanie, he applied to join the police and spent time in studying basic police procedures and began to look into the qualifications and route of study necessary for forensic science as he thought a scene investigator would be a position that he would eventually like to be involved in if successful in his application. He couldn't help but think that it may be out of his league academically, but the more he looked into the development and techniques involved in forensic policing, the more intrigued and fascinated he became, and it quickly began to overtake his preoccupation with superstition as a source of reading and research.

Ultimately, despite his best efforts, he was unsuccessful due, he imagined, to the reasons that Chris has initially speculated. He was disappointed about the rejection as this was his first real experience of failure since leaving school but, nevertheless, had enjoyed gaining the knowledge of his research into forensic matters and remained fascinated by this science and continued to take an interest in new developments in this field. This interest came to the attention of his colleagues as he was regularly reading books and magazines on the subject and as a result, received extensive ribbing as of the reason for his interest. The popular light-hearted assumption was that he was about to commit another Brinks-Mat gold bullion job but unlike others before him, was going to remain undetected.

Chris felt that the force had missed out in some ways, as he has witnessed how the other soldiers in his team looked up to him as a father type figure and was obviously well respected, but he wondered if it was not for the best, as he could not imagine Dutch taking the abuse that that police officers received on a regular basis without dishing out some justice of his own, and he could not imagine Dutch being satisfied with the lenient sentences passed on some dregs of society and thus, would be a very frustrated man. He wondered if the police interview panel had picked up on this, in the same way that he had.

Dutch had a deep-seated and fierce dislike of men who abuse women and to bullies in general, due to the bullying that he had endured in his early years and also witnessed in the army. He made it his business to ensure bullies, and those with racist or homophobic behaviour, regretted their actions and made certain that their practice ceased whenever and wherever he could. He seldom had a problem enforcing this as due to his reputation as an extremely fit, strong fearless soldier and competent boxer, even the toughest did not wish to tangle with him, and in some cases, this was the only way to gain their respect but he was a realist and knew that he couldn't eradicate such practices completely.

Following the disappointment of his police job application and still feeling the need to leave the Army, he contacted his old friend, Jon Shipway, a former soldier, who had now left the service and was working as a successful private contractor for large clients such as Southern Waterways, which was a job for which Dutch had more than enough qualifications and experience.

They had first met when Dutch, acting as a representative for his regiment, attended the Royal Engineer's depot where Jon was stationed to give a talk on the cooperative roles between both units in war and in relief situations. Jon had been so inspired by the presentation that he spoke with Dutch after the meeting and subsequently applied for a transfer to 9 Para Royal Engineers, which following the necessary training, was granted.

Dutch would eventually enjoy the easy-going company of the former Lance Corporal through cross training unit exercises and having been deployed at the same time on humane missions to Africa, including Rwanda, where both regiments combined to help rebuild and stabilise the country's infrastructure in the aftermath of the civil war, which had left thousands dead and millions displaced. Their duties included the re-connection of essential sterilised water supplies, constructing roads and bridges and mine clearance. Dutch, like Jon, had become knowledgeable in many aspects of water management in flood and drought situations, gaining transferrable experience of bridge building, diverting waterways involving explosives and water sanitation.

Ginger-haired, freckled and wiry, Jon Shipway had a reputation of being a courageous and hardworking soldier but was a quiet and unassuming individual, who could be best described as shy and bit of a loner, but like many red-haired people, had a fiery temper when pushed to his limit, and once his touch paper was lit, one learnt to stand well back.

Like Dutch, he was not overly academic and during his school years, normally had his mind on what he considered were more interesting subjects such as fashioning, homemade explosive devices or re-living the excitement of his last free fall from a tall tree and being cushioned by the branches below as he dropped towards the ground. He was a born paratrooper who had no fear of heights and never considered himself to be beaten; 'surrender' and 'give up' did not feature in his vocabulary. He was a practical person, a quick learner and could pick up a new task easily, without any fuss. These features were what made him not only a successful soldier but also a civilian and armed services pole vault champion, and as both men shared a love for athletics, they would often work out together, encouraging and motivating one another.

When regularly asked why he chose the pole vault as his favoured sport, Jon would jovially respond that in his opinion, apart from heading the shot or catching the javelin, it was the most exciting event in track and field athletics.

He and Dutch were of a similar age and nature and soon teamed up as close and trusted friends within the army, particularly as they shared the common factors of both originating from the same county and neither couple having children; this, together with the fact that Melanie and Jon's wife, Sally, got on well, they had, in the past, spent many enjoyable days together as their respective barracks had only been 30 miles apart.

Although disappointed not to be accepted by the police, the application process had caused him to realise that he was ready to seek a future outside the military, and Dutch, having consulted his contact list on his mobile phone, called his old friend, who had also returned to the county of his birth to see if he could help him out.

The call was answered by a familiar friendly voice,

"Good morning, Clearwater Revival, how may I help?"

"Jonny boy, it's Dutch. That's a catchy company name for a business such as yours. Who could have ever thought of that?"

"Dutch French," came a surprised but jovial response, "it's a miracle! Someone told me that you were brown bread. Yeah, OK, you came up with the name, but you didn't tell me that I would get some punters of a certain age, asking if I have a connection with the band, or some anonymous jokers calling just to sing *Proud Mary*, or *Bad*

Moon and think they're hilarious. But I suppose, it gives the company some credence."

Dutch laughingly replied, "No chance of either me singing to you or checking out any time soon, you know I'm not due to go yet."

"You still believing in that crap? Mind, you've always been a lucky fucker. You had some close calls. Some referred to you as dead man walking."

"Lucky, or is my old Nan's belief in the myth still working?"

"How many have you got left now?"

"I reckon if I remain lucky four. Anyway, how are you surviving?"

"Bloody busy, not enough hours in the day at the moment... How's Melanie?"

"Yeah, she's good. Jon, why I've phoned you, apart from wanting to speak to my best mate in all the world—"

Jon interrupted, "Yeah, yeah, enough of your old bullshit. Spit it out, what are you after?"

"Well, bluntly and to the point, last time we spoke, your business was doing well, and as I am considering leaving the mob, have you got any jobs going?"

"Well, bugger me, Dutch French leaving the army, I never thought I would see the day. I always thought you would take your last breath in that uniform."

"That's what everyone said, but I'm not getting any younger, and unless you are an office *wallah*, it's a young man's game. I need to get a job which will take me to retirement, like you did."

"I get that. It happens to us all. What does Melanie think?"

"She won't be over the moon about it, as like me, it's all she's ever known, but she knows it's inevitable."

"Well, Dutch, me old mate, as usual, your luck is in. I have more work than I can handle at the moment. I'm even having to go out and get my hands dirty and that was never the plan. If you can get yourself housed in central Sussex, as most of my work is in the county or on its borders, I can give you plenty to do to keep even you occupied. But you will have to do it quick, as I need someone yesterday."

"Are you for real?"

"Your future and my business is not something I'd joke about."

"You are the man! I never thought for one moment that you would need someone immediately, you've almost caught me on the hop. If I give in my notice today, I can get some leave owing me and have a look around for housing. Would the Brighton area be okay? That would go a long way towards satisfying Melanie; as you know, her mum and dad live there."

"Brighton is good, you can get to most places quickly from there. You realise that you will have to do a bit of training because even though you will know the basics of the work, like everything, procedures and equipment have changed, and we have bloody health and safety to contend with in the real world—something that never used to bother us much when we last worked together."

"Yeah, I expected all that but you know me, I will knuckle down and do what must be done. I won't let you down."

"I know you won't, mate. You are the one person I could rely on, and it will be great to work together again. I know that you don't want to ask, but the rate of pay will be pretty good and as you will eventually be on emergency call out, I can let you have the permanent use of a van, which even has a CD and radio in it so you can play all your tunes to and fro jobs. How does that suit?"

Dutch laughingly replied, "That's not a perk. I expect the van is all logoed up, and I'll be advertising 24/7."

"You ungrateful bastard, that's where you are wrong. None of our transport has logo on because as most of our work is sub contacted, it would be confusing to the customers."

"Jesus, it all now seems strange. It's suddenly hit me that I am leaving the army after all these years, and it's a weird sensation knowing everything is going to change."

"Yeah, you are right, I know that feeling exactly, but there is life outside. It's a lot different, but you get used to it."

"Do you need official paperwork, like job application or CV?"

"Do I bollocks! I know you better than you know yourself. Just get things moving as fast as possible, and let me know as things progress. One good thing about having you, an immortal, on the payroll is when I tell my insurance company, my premium rate will go down."

"Wanker! I'm beginning to wish that I had never told you, you were honoured. Melanie is the only other person I've confided in about that. I'll sort it out quick and thanks. Can't wait to tell Melanie. By the way, how's Sal?"

"She'll do for now. I've started to call her the present Mrs Shipway to keep her on her toes. Now fuck off, get sorted, and get your arse down here. Every day you're not here, I have to get out of my office chair. By the way, have you heard anything from Skins since he left?"

"Yes, funnily enough, I saw him a few weeks back, he is still ducking and diving, doing as little work as possible. That CO was right when he called him a waste of skin. I told him you were still a miserable bastard."

"Cheers for that, I could always rely on you to enhance my reputation. If I was ever miserable, it was due to working with your bunch of tossers."

"Come off it, you loved it really."

"I would rather have had my dick cut off with a rusty knife than work with your mob again, lunatics and asylums spring to mind. One thing you will find different out here is that people expect you to call them by their real names, takes some getting used to."

"Yeah, that will be strange. I suppose you have heard that Crocket went out with PTSD?" (Post Traumatic Stress Disorder)

"No but not surprised as he never recovered from that ambush when poor old Dickie Bird lost his leg. When I can get some time off from this place we must go and see them."

"I'm definitely up for that. I did go and visit Dickie at Headley Court Rehab, but not sure where either of them are now though, but we can find out easily enough. Be in touch soon and thanks again."

"Don't keep thanking me, you silly bastard. If I had known you were thinking of leaving, you would have been the first person I would have offered the job to anyway. By the way, have you still got that stupid habit of singing what you considered to be an appropriate song in certain situations?"

On hearing the remark, Dutch started to sing, "You've got a friend in me, you've got a friend in me, when the road looks rough ahead and you're miles…"

Jon interrupted, "Christ, Dutch, no wonder you came to me for a job. You are never going to make a singer as long as you've got a hole in your arse. Get here as soon as you can and keep me in touch."

Jon put the phone down.

As Dutch rang off, he reflected on Jon's comments: immediately, on joining the regular army, they both became aware of the tradition of the practice of ascribing nicknames to almost everyone. Sometimes, regarding an individual trait but particularly, if more than one person in the unit had the same or a similar name. Amongst their colleagues, they had 'The Mole', who could dig a foxhole faster than anyone else; 'Sputnik', who had once been blown off his feet by an explosion, which was said to have almost sent him into orbit (though he was, remarkably, unhurt) and 'Mars Bar' as he was thought to love himself so much that if he was a chocolate bar, he would eat himself; their good friend, James Mallard, known as 'Quackers' and the obvious 'Jumbo' for the biggest guy in the regiment—the list was endless. But his favourite by far was 'Stewy', which derived from an occasion when this particular soldier was on leave together with colleagues in Bangkok where he met a pretty local girl in a bar. The pair ended up outside the premises where the soldier put his hand up the female's skirt and was confronted with, what he later described as, meat and two veg. The serviceman made the unfortunate error of telling his colleagues of the embarrassing experience, and he assumed the new name from that day. Due to the fact that Jon, when younger, was never far away from his flexible fibreglass vaulting pole, he rapidly became known as 'Jon, the Pole' in order to distinguish him from other Jon's or John's in the regiment. When it came to Dennis being dubbed Dutch, in terms of just exchanging his surname to another nationality, he considered himself lucky and relieved considering some of the disparaging names that could have been and were allocated.

Their particular allotted names regularly frustrated Jon and Dutch when newcomers to their units assumed that both men were of nationalities to which they had no connection with whatsoever, resulting in both Englishmen having to regularly explain the titles attributed to them. Dutch later found this practice almost infectious and he would mentally refer to many different people and their characteristics with his own nicknames.

Melanie was in the kitchen preparing their evening meal when she heard Dutch enter the front door. She had now grown accustomed to him keeping regular hours working in the training department and enjoyed the fact that their lives now had a regular routine—not like before when life was seldom routine.

Dutch came in, calling to her as he helped himself to a drink, and sank down in a chair. Melanie walked in through from the kitchen with a handful of cutlery and noticed that he hadn't changed into his running gear.

"Not heading out for a run?" she asked, surprised.

"No, I need to talk to you. It's important, the run will have to wait."

"Blimey, it must be serious if the run has got to wait. What's up?"

Melanie went over and flopped down in a chair opposite him.

"You know I've been looking to get out of the mob for a while now?"

"Yeah, I know you want out."

"Well, I've been talking to my old mate, Jon Shipway today and it seems like he can help me out."

"What do you mean, 'help you out'?"

"He's got a job for me. A proper, salaried job, working for the Water Board mainly, but he'd be my boss. Only thing is, I've got to get down there quick cos he needs someone as of yesterday."

"Down there?"

"Yeah, back into Sussex, perhaps the Brighton area, so that'd be ideal, wouldn't it? Near your parents and all our old friends and…"

"Hang on a minute," cut in Melanie, "it's not that simple though, is it? I mean, our life is set up here now, isn't it? We've got far more friends here than ever we did back in Brighton, and I will need to find another job and…"

"Whoa, whoa, yeah, I know but we've always known this is going to happen one day, and what could be better than to go back to somewhere we know? I mean, we can't stay right here, in army accommodation, no matter what I do, so we'd have to move out eventually anyway."

"But I thought that you were so happy with what you are doing now."

"I am very happy with our lives at the moment, but I can't get rid of the feeling of uncertainty that in a few years' time when I am forced to retire. If I don't act now, we will be faced with no home of our own and limited job prospects. This may be our only chance to change that."

"I know, I know but I just wasn't expecting it so suddenly." Melanie had her eyes fixed firmly on the floor, and she could feel hot tears pricking at her eyes, and she tried to blink them away without Dutch noticing. "I know it has to happen sometime, but I just don't feel ready yet."

"But will you ever feel ready? And besides, this kind of opportunity isn't likely to be repeated. I'd be mad to turn it down."

Dutch could see that Melanie was getting upset and he hated to be the cause of it.

"Look," he said, "I know this has come as a bit of a bolt out of the blue, but it really is a fantastic opportunity; we can get our own place and you can maybe look to do something new too? You're always on about working with children and there's bound to be lots of scope for that in a place like Brighton, and so long as we don't overstretch ourselves on property, we should be able to afford for you to go and do some re-training; it could be a whole new start for us."

"So, where's the money coming from for this big venture of yours?"

"It's not 'my venture', it's a step we've got to take and I've worked out that with our savings, my army pension and investments that will have matured by now, we should be in a reasonable position to only have a small mortgage."

"Sounds like you've got it all worked out."

"Not really, but I'm just being realistic. I know it's possible. What do you reckon?"

"I dunno, I need some time to think about it."

"Well, yes, but you need to think quick because I've, more or less, said yes to Jon already."

"You've what?"

"Sorry, Mel, but I didn't want him to think that I was anything less than really keen, and quite honestly, I can't see anything better than this coming up for us."

"Sounds like it's a done deal to me. I'm surprised you even bothered asking me."

"Aw, c'mon, you know it's not like that." Dutch got up and knelt down in front of Melanie, taking her hands in his. "You know you are my top priority, my number one girl. I'm just trying to secure a good future for us both, and I guess I got a bit excited and carried away with the conversation with Jon. If you want, I can call him back and say it's not a go-er."

Melanie let out a big sigh and lifted her eyes to meet Dutch's. She knew that he was ambitious and decisive and she loved that about him, but she also knew that he would never plan anything without considering her.

"It's okay. I suppose that I just need to get used to the idea but I really didn't expect it all to happen like this."

"Neither did I. I just rang Jon on the off chance but that makes me think it's all the more 'meant to be'."

"You and your superstition, Dutch," she said with a half-smile.

"I know it's in my blood, but I really do have a good feeling about this."

Lying in bed that night, listening to the incessant ticking of his alarm clock, he could not stop his mind from racing as he began making plans and contemplating all the different obstacles that needed to be overcome for them to begin a new life outside of the army. He was both apprehensive but excited to think that he would be returning to the Brighton area where he and his wife were originally from, just as his mother had done following his father's death. It would be good to return to some of his and Melanie's old stomping grounds and maybe even catch up with old friends and family, but equally, they were leaving behind a really good, established life, rooted in certainty and enhanced with many good colleagues and friends. His time in the mob had been pretty much all that he had hoped when he was a youngster and the experience had shaped his entire life. Like all occupations, he had experienced good and bad times over the years but, on the whole, had no regrets and considered that he had completed a worthwhile job, both as a combat soldier and in his capacity as a training instructor. Granted, it had been necessary for him to kill during his time in combat, and he was far from proud of these actions, but it was his duty and he was able to live with the knowledge that in each case, he felt it was justified as he was fighting for something he believed in; he had seen close colleagues die and permanently maimed. It was kill or be killed, such actions made less challenging when confronting those responsible for atrocities against defenceless innocent woman and children. He would only ever talk about such matters with the service shrinks or those who had been through similar experiences, as those outside of the armed forces wouldn't fully understand.

Despite Melanie's scepticism, he also took time to reflect on how fortunate it was that he was still standing, still walking the planet, as the "lives" that he had lost to date were stacking up, but hopefully, in the new peaceful environment that he had planned, there would be very few similar close encounters that he had experienced in the past. He was aware that had he not chosen the army for a career and instead pursued an everyday job, he would not be considering that he was regularly using up his nine life-changing moments. Was his late Nan right that day when she told him of the nine lives?

With that thought foremost in his mind, a feeling of contentment swept over him as he realised that he had joined as a satisfied soldier and was about to leave as one, a thought that assisted in a restful night's sleep.

Chapter 7

Bad Moon Rising (1969)
Artists: Creedence Clearwater Revival
Writer: Jon C. Fogerty

A low bank of sagging grey cloud loomed over the Downs, threatening showers; almost two years had elapsed since moving into their new home and life had settled into the kind of interesting but stable routine that Dutch had wanted. His new job, working for Jon Shipway, was working out even better than expected, and he was enjoying the variability of his new occupation and whilst the hours could sometimes be excessive, the overtime rate was excellent, and with no other ties, he still had plenty of time to do the other things in life that he enjoyed.

Melanie was also now more settled and happier; her job at the nursery school was going well, and she especially enjoyed the fact that she was usually home by 3.30 pm each day and had the entire weekend to herself. She made the most of her free time, walking the dog in the nearby countryside, shopping and spending time with her parents, who lived relatively close by. She could now see the advantage of this new regime for both of them as she felt better, both, mentally and physically than she had for a long time and could also sense that her husband was mellowing and felt more relaxed in their new south coast lifestyle.

As the late afternoon sun made a valiant effort to breach the clouds, Melanie eased on her trainers, picked up her waterproof coat and unhooked Jodie's lead from its hanging place beside the front door, triggering an immediate response from the apparently dormant dog. The nights were starting to draw in and light would give way to dark quickly, and as the dog had been in the flat for much of the day, Melanie didn't want to cheat Jodie out of a decent walk. She was aware that Dutch would be working late that evening so would have plenty of time to prepare their evening meal on her return. She considered the different routes that she could take and quickly decided that she could make it to nearby Ditchling Beacon in about ten minutes, the high vantage point extending the daylight left to them. Hastily securing the dog in the rear of her Fiat, she threw her bag and coat into the passenger seat and set off for the Ditchling Hill car park. As it had been a fine day up until then, she suspected that the main car park at the summit of the hill could be quite full, only leaving the roughest of car parking spaces on the rugged part of the chalk surface; with this in mind and limited time and daylight available to her, she pulled into a lay-by, about half a mile short of the beauty spot, where there was a public footpath each side of the road.

She had walked the dog at the spot before but not for some time and relished the change of scenery and thought that Jodie too may enjoy the new sights and smells. As she opened the boot, Jodie leapt out of the car and clearly recognising the location, ran into the small wooded area that led into the open fields. Both Melanie and Jodie enjoyed the exercise and fresh air and roamed longer than she had planned, without seeing another soul. Melanie imagined that the route was less popular with walkers due to the smallness of the lay-by, accommodating only two vehicles, with no other suitable parking close by, and although the countryside scenery was beautiful, the sights were not as spectacular as from the beacon itself.

As she returned to her car, the daylight was rapidly beginning to fade, and she could detect the dotted glint of the city lights in the far distance where the city met the sea. She opened the boot and Jodie leapt into the rear compartment between the door and the rear seats. The gap was only just big enough for the dog to sit or lay comfortably but she was never in the car for more than ten minutes. As Melanie pulled down the boot lid, making sure that Jodie was well clear of the closing door, she became aware of a large, white van, slowing down and indicating to pull into the lay-by and parking behind her. Jodie had already settled herself comfortably, and she didn't give the vehicle or its occupants a second look as she presumed it was just another dog walker, hiker or even a courier taking a break. As she walked from the rear of her car to the driver's door, holding her ignition key, she heard the sound of a door opening and a male voice calling out "Hello". As the voice was raised, she turned, presuming the greeting was meant for her attention, and as she did so, she was confronted by a man who was now only a few feet from her. Melanie noticed that the rear of the van was reversing to only a few yards from where she was standing in the small dirt lay-by. The man confronting her was wearing a hooded jacket with the hood up over his head, with its drawstring pulled quite tightly around his head only revealing a dark tanned face with heavy black stubble. She immediately thought this as being odd as it was still reasonably warm. He wore nondescript, dark clothing and gave the impression of being a manual worker. The man stepped up very close to her, making her feel uncomfortable and guarded but when he said in broken English,

"Can you help us? We are looking for the way to go towards London."

The simple question came as a relief, and Melanie realised that she had been holding her breath, having felt slightly intimidated by his rough appearance. Relaxing, she turned her back to him, pointing in the direction that he needed to travel. As she said, "Carry on down this road until you come to a roundabout, then turn right and that will take you to the A23." She was distracted as another similar looking man emerged from the driver's side of the now parked van, as if to listen to her directions. He was wearing a woollen or cotton hat pulled right down over his ears and forehead, which she thought odd as both had emerged from what would have been a warm vehicle.

The second man did not stop to ask any questions or even to so much as glance at Melanie; he strode directly to the rear of the van and immediately opened both doors and as the doors opened, Melanie felt herself engulfed in a bear hug from the other man who had positioned himself behind her.

Startled, she did not call out but immediately started to struggle, but with the advantage of both height and strength, he easily lifted her off the ground and hurried her towards the rear of the van. She started to kick backwards at her assailant's shins, shouting out for help, but she knew immediately that her soft trainers were having no effect and there was almost certainly no one around to hear her cries. As her arms were pinned to her body, she then tried to push her feet out against the rear bumper of the van, but she was lifted even higher, and both men helped to bundle her inside. Still shouting and struggling, she was pushed, sprawling face first, to the floor of the van and was immediately followed by both men and the doors were slammed behind them.

The passenger, wearing the hood, then turned her and pinned her on her back to the floor with one large hand around her throat.

Thrashing, she tried to claw at his hand and free herself, but he quickly sat astride her, putting his free hand over her mouth. As she attempted to free herself from the pressure of his right hand, she felt something odd about it as if one of his fingers was just a stub. She then started to rain punches in the direction of his head and upper body but most missed or had no effect, and in return, she received several punches to both sides of her own head that stunned her, and she immediately felt the side of her right eye swelling. The man who had opened the doors now knelt down beside them, and she could detect the alcohol on his breath when he said in an identical accent to the passenger,

"If you scream or fight, you get more." He then assisted in her restraint.

The man astride her, then pulled a knife from his pocket and opened the long narrow shiny blade pushing it towards her face to which Melanie screamed beneath the now more relaxed hand over her mouth.

"Please, don't do this, please, please, let me go, I beg you. If you stop now and go, nobody will know who you are. I won't even report it, I will say I fell over."

As she said this, she could feel her whole body trembling under the heavy weight of the man astride her with the knife. Both men ignored her plea and started forcefully pulling off her shoes and clothing; Melanie again started to scream and struggle, earning her an even heavier blow to the other side of her head, again stunning her. The man at her side then reached round to grab something from the floor; he picked up a small object and then began tearing off a piece of black tape from a reel which was then stuck over her mouth, restricting her breathing and forcing her to breathe through her nose, causing further panic. As he did this, she tried again to repel her attacker and the fingers of her flailing hand caught under his hat, pushing it off of his head, revealing his full face and what appeared to be in the dim light a crucifix earring on a short chain hanging from his right ear. Her actions prompted him to then administer more tape, this time over her eyes. A steady stream of tears and mucous had already started to course from her eyes and nose, and with the added binding of the tape, Melanie felt the sensation of drowning and consciously willed herself to try to stop crying, as she knew it would only make the situation worse.

The two men were talking to each other in a language she didn't understand or recognise and the tape over her eyes was disorientating, as well as uncomfortable. She could feel their hands tugging and tearing at her clothing as they wrenched off her light summer outfit of cropped trousers and a t-shirt and then her underwear. Both terrified and mortified, she realised that she was lying on some sort of coarse blanket, the rough weave harsh against her now naked skin. Helpless and alone, dazed and short of breath and acutely aware that the threat of the knife was almost certainly not for show, she decided her only hope of survival was to completely submit to them.

At one stage, Melanie heard a vehicle pass and was hoping, above all else, it would stop and notice the dog on her own, locked in the car, but quickly realised that no vehicle could stop as there was no more room in the lay-by, and no one would investigate the parked vehicles as it was usual to see empty cars parked there for long periods of time. In desperation, she made one last attempt to stop the men from forcing her legs apart by holding her knees together, but this defence was met by one of them lifting her head and slamming it backwards onto the floor, stunning her and sending her sliding into unconsciousness.

Chapter 8
Find Me (2002)
Artists and Songwriter: David Gates

The recent light drizzle and failing light had further frustrated a long hard day working with Liam and Pete, members of the small gang of Clearwater Revival employees. It had proved to be a difficult job in excavating and repairing a mains leak and then making good the road surface in the small street situated in the ancient town of Battle, East Sussex. Dutch was cold and damp from sweat and filthy from head to toe. He felt tired after his early morning emergency call out, and as he prepared to leave the site, he was looking forward to a long hot bath and the nice evening meal that Melanie had promised him earlier in the day. The day had seemed to be even longer due to the tension caused when the recently-employed Liam discovered that Dutch had served in the Army in Northern Ireland and the atmosphere suddenly became tense between them; it was obvious to Dutch that Liam had sympathy to the Republican cause. The situation wasn't detrimental to their work but the general camaraderie had ceased from that moment. Dutch wondered how long the Irishman would stick the job when, if he didn't know already, he discovered that his boss Jon had also been involved in the conflict. Although there was no big problem at present, he wasn't sure how he himself would react if Liam continued in this vein considering how his own father met his demise, but he was determined to attempt to avoid any conflict at work so as not to harm Jon's business in any way. As he climbed into his van, he pushed such thoughts to the back of his mind as the only consolation for the exhaustion he was feeling was that the Friday rush hour would be over by the time he got closer to home and traffic should be fairly light. Before leaving, he called his home number on his mobile; as there was no reply, he tried Melanie's mobile but again, no answer from her. It was unusual for her not to respond to either phone, so he tried her parents' home and their mobiles but again, no answer from either. During the hour-long drive home, he tried all numbers again but still no replies, so he left a message on each one asking them to contact him. He started to think that they may all be together somewhere and had had to turn their mobiles off for some reason. As he reached the boundaries of Brighton and Hove, he received a call from Melanie's father, Ken, who had received his answer phone message, having just returned home with Molly following a trip to the afternoon cinema and a meal; they had not seen or heard from Melanie at all that day.

Pulling up outside the flat, he immediately noticed that her car was not parked in the street, and as he entered the hallway, he felt that there was something amiss; neither his wife nor the dog were present, and having called and spoken with Melanie at lunchtime, she had informed him of exactly what she was going to prepare for their dinner, and she would wait to eat with him, but the kitchen bore no signs of any preparation for their evening meal. It then crossed his mind that something had disrupted her plans and she had driven to the nearby takeaway taking Jodie with her, so he decided to forget the bath and instead shower quickly and change before her return.

Having showered and changed into clean clothes, they had still not returned, and he grew more concerned by the minute as she was a creature of habit; if anything unusual came about, Melanie would leave him a note, call or text him. He looked out the windows to the front and rear of the property, it had now turned quiet, cold and dark outside so he called her mobile again and once more, it went to answerphone. Her phone did not ring in the flat so he concluded that she must have it with her.

He then decided to go and look for them both, so initially drove to the local shopping parade which housed the takeaway restaurants that they occasionally frequented. As there was no sign of Melanie or her Fiat parked near the shops or in the adjoining streets, he thought of the possibility that perhaps, she had taken Jodie onto the Downs, broken down, got lost, became ill or the dog had gone missing, and he knew if that was the case, she wouldn't come home without her—no matter what time or how dark it was—but surely, she would have made contact with someone by now even if she had a malfunction with her phone.

He tried her phone once more and again, no reply, so then, he decided to check out the two locations that she frequented up there. He immediately drove to her nearest regular walk at the Dyke, as he drove checking all possible places that she could have parked her car. With no sign of her or the vehicle, he ventured onto the road leading to the Beacon, and as he drove along the Ditchling road, he saw her car parked on the offside of the road in a small dirt lay-by with another saloon car parked immediately behind it. With no further space in the lay-by, he was forced to park at the side of the road. Leaving his engine running and hazard lights switched on, he hurried to Melanie's car, aided by the light of his dipped headlights. As he approached, his headlights picked out what he knew to be her key fob and ignition key on the ground next to the rear of her car. He picked them up and opened the unlocked driver's door and Jodie immediately came hurtling out from inside and in desperation, immediately urinated in the nearby grass. The dog was panting heavily and was obviously distressed but very pleased to see him but there was no sign of Melanie inside. His attention was then drawn to the remaining car in the lay-by; his thoughts turned to the barely comprehensible—could his wife be inside in the darkness and behind the steamed-up windows?

His mind and body went into overdrive as he tugged on the driver's door but it was locked. He tried to look inside and through the darkness and condensation, could vaguely see two figures laying on the rear seats, hiding their faces from the beams of spasmodic lighting from the lights of his van. He then heard the sound of whispering from inside and responded with a raised and angry voice,

"Melanie, are you in there? If so, you had better come out now, or I will break the window and drag both of you out."

There was no response to his statement, only further whispering between the occupants, so Dutch repeated the warning, this time louder, with more venom, to which a male voice replied,

"I don't know who you are but there's no Melanie in here, in fact there's no woman in here at all."

Dutch could feel his temper rising,

"I know you are not alone."

A different male voice then answered from inside,

"No, he's not. Now go away."

"Open up and let me see. My wife's car is parked in front…where else is she?"

Dutch repeatedly pulled at the handle, rapping sharply on the window, all the time asking, "Where is she?" his voice growing louder and more insistent.

"I've no idea. Now calm down and give us a minute, you're scaring us."

Dutch could see and hear movement from within and took the opportunity to sprint to his van to retrieve a torch, fearing the car may drive off.

After a short while, two smartly-dressed but dishevelled and slightly embarrassed looking middle-aged men appeared from the rear doors of the parked car. The taller of the two, still holding the door open, said to Dutch in an agitated tone,

"Now take a look for yourself, she's not in there."

Dutch checked inside by the light of the powerful torch and emerged saying,

"Where can she be then? Open up the boot."

"Are you serious?"

"Yes, open it up. I want to check."

The two men exchanged nervous glances. Dutch's frantic movements and palpable anxiety were becoming increasingly intimidating.

As the boot lid popped, Dutch immediately thrust the torch inside, scanning from side to side, seeing nothing other than a neatly folded car rug and a couple of supermarket shopping bags. He demanded,

"Was her car parked here when you arrived or did she get here after you?"

The shorter of the two answered,

"We got here about 20 minutes ago and it was here then. We did hear some moans and what sounded like a dog whimpering, and Simon said it was possibly a couple taking doggie style to a new level."

The taller man smirked slightly at this but seeing Dutch's expression, hastily added,

"We were just minding our own business. That your dog, is it?" he asked, motioning towards Jodie, who was now busily sniffing at the ground where the three men stood.

"Yes, the poor bugger was locked in the car but my wife's not there. She must be in the woods or fields then, but she wouldn't leave the dog unless there was something seriously wrong."

The taller man, who identified himself as Simon, then said in a now much more concerned tone,

"Perhaps the car has broken down and she's gone for help?"

"She has a mobile which I have called several times and even if she had no signal here, she would have eventually found one and phoned me or her family."

At the same time, he took the keys that he had found on the ground and turned on the engine to her car, which started immediately. He then turned the engine off and checked and saw that all four tyres were inflated. Dutch then walked to the edge of the wood and shone his torch inside where he saw Jodie nuzzling into the long grass at the base of a hedge, and he heard a low moaning sound emanating from the same area.

One of the men started to say something but Dutch immediately hushed him as the sound came again from where Jodie was standing, now nuzzling something and whimpering loudly. On shining the torch into the undergrowth below the hedge, he could see a blanket and something wrapped inside of it move slightly. Not knowing what to expect, Dutch inched closer, listening intently before stretching out his hand and carefully peeling back part of the blanket and was horrified at what lay before him—a naked leg and torso came into sight and the realisation that it was his wife. Melanie was completely naked on her back, with her clothing laying in a bundle beside her. She appeared to be semi-conscious and shivering violently with dried blood around her mouth and nose and a wide strip of black gaffer tape stuck across her eyes. He went to her, gently cradling her head and saying her name and asking her if she could hear him, but her intensive shivering made it impossible for him to understand what she was attempting to say.

Years of combat training enabled him to go onto automatic pilot, and his previous first aid training kicked in as he checked her airways and pulse and signs of any severe bleeding, but apart from being freezing cold, shocked and badly bruised, she did not appear to be in imminent danger. He then eased the sticky tape from the skin underneath both eyes just enough so that she could see, all the time being mindful not to cause her even more pain by pulling the tape against her eyebrows or eye lashes or the strands of her hair trapped under it. He was fully aware that this operation would need to be completed professionally.

The two men, who were still standing at the entrance to the woods, could see that Dutch had found someone and called out,

"Have you found her?"

Dutch, busy reassuring Melanie and placing her in the recovery position, shouted back,

"Yes, she's obviously been attacked, we need to get help."

Simon picked his way cautiously forward and said,

"What do you want us to do? Shall we call an ambulance?"

"Yes, but first, can one of you take this torch, go to my van and get the sleeping bag that's rolled up in the back and bring it back quickly; she's suffering from hypothermia and I need to get her temperature up. Can the other one of you telephone for the police and ambulance? Tell them that a woman has been attacked and injured."

"Okay, will do."

"Oh, and you may have to move around a bit to get a signal up here. I take it you know our precise location?"

"Yes, no problem, I do. I'll make the calls and I'll ask Adam to get you the sleeping bag."

Both men hurried onto the road. Adam returned quickly with the sleeping bag, and Dutch was reassured to hear Simon in the layby, obviously talking to the emergency services.

Dutch then said to Adam in a clear commanding voice, "Thanks for that, now can one of you manoeuvre your car so the headlights are shining through the hedge to where we are? Then perhaps, I can then see what I'm doing."

Simon, who was standing on the other side of the hedge, shouted back, "Got that, I'm doing it now."

Seconds later, the sound of a car engine broke the silence and immediately shafts of light penetrated the sparse hedge partially illuminating the unfortunate scene.

Dutch then gently positioned Melanie onto the fully opened sleeping bag which he had laid on flatter firmer ground. He was now able to examine her injuries more closely and could see matted blood in her hair at the back of her head. He was tempted to move her head gently forwards to examine the area, but he was aware that such manoeuvres should not be carried out as she may have a neck or spinal injury and unnecessary movement may cause further harm. Having carefully enclosed her in and zipping up the sleeping bag, he gently placed her head on the discarded blanket which he had made into a makeshift pillow. He so wanted to carry her and sit her in her car but he was not sure at that stage if he would do more harm than good, so he concentrated on consoling her and gradually warming her up.

Simon, having made the call and positioning the car, returned to Dutch and said,

"The police and ambulance are both on their way and shouldn't be long. What happened, do you know yet?"

"No, I've no idea. The only thing I can make out is that she has been attacked by two men in a white van. It's hard to make out what she's saying but I'm pretty certain that's what she means."

Adam replied, "I'm so sorry, we feel so guilty that we never found her before you came along. We heard the dog and the moans but we didn't really think anything of it; we had no idea that something had happened, I mean, we just, er, thought, well, you know…" he trailed off in a mumbled apology, clearly distressed and out of his depth.

"It's not your fault," Dutch cut in, "but are you sure that you saw nobody else here or a white van when you arrived?"

"No, nothing. Did we, Simon?"

"No, there was only the Fiat when we got here but then we weren't really here to take any notice of anyone else." He looked rather sheepish and added,

"As soon as the ambulance arrives, we are going to shoot off. We can't afford to be involved as neither of us should be here, if you know what I mean."

"You're joking, mate. How suspicious does that look? I don't think for one second that either of you are responsible, but if you disappear quick, the police will come looking for you tonight as they have a record of the mobile number you called them on."

"But we are both married and our partners have no idea about our relationship."

"I appreciate your predicament and it's up to you. I can't make you stay but I guarantee that they will find you if only for witness statements. It will be much more discreet if you deal with it now."

"I think we need to talk this over," Simon said, drawing Adam to one side.

"Talk it over all you like, but you'd better be quick about it because the police should be here soon, and I'm not going to be able to give them the full story regarding your arrival here."

"He's right," said Simon. "It'll only make it worse if we go now. We can tell our families that we were on our way to a pub in Ditchling when we stopped to check a tyre as I thought there was a problem with the steering, but we will have to be upfront with the police."

"OK, I don't like it but it appears that we have little choice."

At that moment, the distant wail of an ambulance siren could be heard, winding its way up along the country route and the two men waited nervously at the roadside to guide the response vehicles to the scene.

Further back in the woodland border, Dutch heard the sound of a telephone ringing nearby and on shining his torch into the grass and fallen twigs, saw what he knew to be Melanie's phone case. He picked it up and could see from the illuminated screen the display showing 'Mum'. At first, he thought about not answering the call but then thought how obviously worried they might now be upon hearing his voicemails, so he composed himself and answered, "Hello", in as normal a voice he could muster. Molly's softly-spoken voice said,

"Oh, Dutch, are you with Melanie now then? We were getting worried."

Dutch replied, tears pricking at his eyes as he spoke,

"Yes, I'm with her. Can I get back to you shortly? The signal here is very poor."

Molly, sounding somewhat confused, replied,

"Oh, yes, please do, speak soon," and ended the call. There was no way he could break the news to them at that stage as to what he had discovered, either for his sake or theirs.

During that ten-minute wait that seemed an eternity, Dutch stroked Melanie's head gently and continued to try to talk to and reassure her and was still only able to make out clearly the words 'rape', 'two men', 'big, white van' and 'Jodie', amongst the sobbing and tears.

At the almost simultaneous arrival of the police and ambulance, Dutch could not keep back his own tears; the anguish and rage he felt at Melanie's plight burned fiercely in the pit of his stomach, but he felt some relief when he saw that one of the paramedics was a woman and, once familiar with the situation, she took the lead role from her male colleague, and after a cursory examination of Melanie, carefully protected her modesty by extracting her from the sleeping bag, at the same time wrapping her in a hypothermic foil blanket.

Although Dutch hadn't wanted to leave her side, whilst Melanie was being attended to by the paramedics, he had briefly taken himself away into the field beyond the woods and found himself shouting and raging at the sky, lobbing curses and questions at the moon like a man deranged, asking the question if there was a God or Creator, how could he have let this happen. The injustice and callousness of the act coupled with the helplessness that he felt at his own ability to protect his wife, fuelled him with extreme outrage and despair, painfully reminding him of similar circumstances that he had witnessed years before in a foreign land when his actions then were far more severe than just shouting at the moon.

At the crime scene, whilst the police officers were initially speaking to Simon and Adam, they became aware of his shouting emanating from the field and became concerned at his highly agitated state. As Dutch continued to rage and shout, pacing along the perimeter of the field back to the lay-by, he became aware of torchlight on the edge of the trees; it was a moonlit silhouette figure of a uniformed policeman striding towards him. The officer intercepted him,

"Excuse me, sir, I gather you are the lady's husband?"

"Yes, that's right, I am. I just needed to let off some steam. I'm in a mess. Have you seen what they've done to her?"

"I have and I can fully understand your anger and frustration, sir, but we need to ask you some questions and establish some facts about how you came to find your wife. I have spoken briefly to your wife and the two gentlemen and have some idea as to what has happened, so if you wouldn't mind joining us back at the car now."

"Of course, I need to be with her…you need to find out who's done this, how it could have happened? It was two men, two men, she said, in a white van. How could this happen? To Melanie?"

Dutch was visibly shaken and riled, his fists were clenched and he was speaking very rapidly.

"You need to try and calm a bit, sir. We need to ask you a few routine questions and then you can see if they're ready to take your wife to the hospital."

"I've got to go with her!" he barked.

"I will need to check about that, but you definitely need to calm down a bit first, sir."

When they reached the roadside, the area was now illuminated by the headlights and blue beacons of both emergency vehicles.

Once they had established the facts from all present, the officer insisted that Dutch compose himself if he wished to accompany Melanie in the ambulance to the hospital. Dutch apologised, explaining that he was just trying to release some anger as privately as possible and managed to pull himself together realising that he was not helping Melanie, and as bitter as he felt towards her attackers, he had to remain strong and calm for her sake.

Before he left, an officer requested the keys for both, his van and Melanie's car, and for him to temporarily place Jodie in his van so as not to contaminate the scene further. He was reassured that they would look after the dog and vehicles as the site was now a crime scene. Whilst the PC was taking brief details from Dutch and the two witnesses, a WPC was using incident tape to prevent further access to the lay-by and vehicles parked there to maintain a sterile area around the blanket and Melanie's discarded clothing and mobile for the attention of the scene investigators that had been requested.

Following her treatment at the scene by paramedics, Dutch, together with the WPC, accompanied Melanie to the emergency department at Brighton County Hospital.

After her initial examination, medical staff decided that Melanie had no life-threatening injuries but would be required to undergo treatment and observations on her head injury. Shortly after her arrival, Dutch was permitted to speak with her briefly and now that she had warmed up, she was much more comprehensible and spoke softly, sobbing with tears streaming down her face.

"I feel that my whole body has been violated. Will you ever feel the same about me?"

"Of course, I do. You are the same person, aren't you? And it's not your fault."

"Perhaps, it is. I keep telling myself if only I had not gone for that walk, or gone somewhere else, or if I had been more suspicious when I first saw them and locked myself in the car, could I have done more to stop them." Melanie then burst into tears, crying loudly.

Dutch held her hand gently. "It's only natural for you to think about the what ifs but truth is, there's no way you could have stopped those two bastards because once they had decided to do something like that, someone was going to be in the wrong place at the wrong time and, unfortunately, it happened to be you and there's nothing you could have done about it. You obviously resisted them as much as possible that's why you are here battered and bruised. I know these words are of no comfort to you but it's happened, now all we can do is over time try and repair the damage that they have caused you."

"Why me again? I thought I have had my share of problems with the miscarriages."

"Melanie, I'm so, so sorry, what more can I say but, together, we will get through this. We've done it before and we will do it again, believe me. Now stop talking and rest. I will stay here until you go to sleep."

"Before I do, there is something I'm not clear about. Was that you shouting when the paramedics were treating me?"

"I'm afraid so,"

"Who on earth were you shouting at?"

"Just giving the moon and anyone or anything else out there in the great beyond a piece of my mind about the injustice of what has happened to you. It was the only way I could let off steam but it didn't help much."

"Another thing I need to ask you, when I was semi-conscious and confused, just before you found me, the first thing I can recall is you shouting at me, and if you knew I was in the field, why didn't you come to me straight away?"

"I didn't know you were behind the hedge. I thought that you were maybe in the car; it was Jodie who found you."

"What, my car?"

"No, the car parked behind yours. The one that the two guys were in."

"What guys? Why would you think that I would have been in a car with them?"

"There was another car parked next to yours in the lay-by. I didn't know who was in there, it was pitch black and the windows were all steamed up."

"You thought that I was in there with someone else, didn't you? That's why you were shouting so angrily. How could you think that? Oh my God, I don't believe it. How could you?" Already pale, bruised and dejected, Melanie now looked utterly crushed. Tears flooded her eyes, red and raw from protracted sobbing. She looked up at Dutch, both, bewildered and disappointed,

"How could you ever suspect me of doing something like that?"

"My head was all over the place. I didn't know what to think, what with your car parked there with Jodie alone inside, another car parked behind with steamed up windows? I wasn't thinking straight anyway. I was so worried, panicking, wondering what had happened to you." He reached over and tried to take her hand, but she pulled it away, tucking it back under the taut of the hospital sheet.

"Aw, c'mon, give me a break, I'm sure the same thing would have crossed your mind if the roles had been reversed."

"Really? I doubt it," she snapped. She looked away, hurt and angry, biting on her lower lip the way she always did when she was thinking things over.

"Melanie, please…"

"I don't know, I've always trusted you when you've been away and when you're out and about, and I'm disappointed you could even think that way about me."

Her comment gave Dutch a sudden pang of conscience as his mind raced back to his infidelity with Kerry in Warrington.

He composed himself saying, "It was just a moment's madness. I was panicking and thinking all sorts of things. Please, Mel don't let this come between us, especially not at a time like this."

"You did come looking for me…"

"Yes, and it was out of concern, not jealousy and thank God, I did. I only wish I could have been there sooner."

"So do I," she whispered, as more tears escaped and rolled down her cheeks.

"I'm so, so, sorry I wasn't there. Sorry, I jumped to conclusions and sorry, I've made a bad situation worse…it was just a natural reaction, not a character judgement," he added softly.

Melanie gave a weak smile.

"They have to catch the bastards that did this, and they have to pay one way or the other. No one does this to you and gets away with it."

The anger in his voice reverberated around the tiny room, and when he turned to face her, Melanie's distressed face instantly silenced him and he resumed his seat at her bedside.

"I'm sorry, I wasn't thinking, you don't need this now." He gently smoothed a strand of her hair back away from her face, noting as he did so that she winced slightly as he touched her. Her reaction triggered a bolt of deep fury within him, fury for what had been done to her and what had been taken away from them both.

At that moment, a doctor walked into the cubicle and after introducing himself said, "I come with good news; the results of the scan of your head reveal that apart from the cut and bruising, you have no further injury to your head."

"That's a relief, isn't it?" Dutch said, glancing at Melanie, who just looked at the doctor and asked,

"Have you any idea how long I will have to stay here?"

"As you lost consciousness, we will have to monitor you overnight but all well and good, you should be out in a day or two."

Having thanked the doctor, Dutch said to Melanie, "I will let your mum and dad know straight away. I spoke to Mum earlier and made an excuse so as not to worry them, but I will have to let them know that you are here. They will never forgive me if I don't."

"Don't tell them the full facts tonight, it will be too upsetting for them. Just tell them that I've been assaulted for the time being. They will find out exactly what happened soon enough."

"I agree. Leave it to me to sort out, but I know that they will want to come up here tonight to see you. I'll leave you to rest now, love," he said gently, but Melanie had already closed her eyes, sedated and exhausted and badly in need of an escape from her ordeal.

Dutch stepped out into the harshly-lit hospital corridor and made his way back to the entrance so that he could use his mobile again. Turning up his collar against the chill, wondering if he did smoke or had a drink, it would help take away his anger and the pain he was feeling for Melanie, but he soon dismissed such thoughts, realising that neither would give any relief to such devastating situation. He speed dialled his sister, who answered after a few rings.

"Hello, Jeannie, its Dennis, are you busy?"

"Hi, Den, not really, just catching up on the soaps."

"I hate to ask you this, I don't know who else to ask, but I am in too much of a state to do it myself and I am worried about their response."

"What or who are you talking about, Den? You alright? You sound weird and all over the place. What on earth is wrong?"

"It's Melanie, she's been attacked up at the Beacon. We are at the hospital now."

"Attacked? No! Oh my God, is she seriously hurt?"

"Bad enough, but she will be okay. Look, can you drive around to Melanie's parents? You remember where they live, don't you?"

"Yeah, I know, the bungalow where they had a party once, it's got a monkey puzzle tree in the front garden."

"That's the one. Break the news as gently as you can. They are sure to ask what happened, tell them not to panic. She's not in any serious danger, just cuts and bruises and concussion. Between me and you, she has been raped but you don't tell them that, they would die on the spot, so for the time being, tell them you think it was an assault

110

of some kind. . That's best at the moment; they are both elderly, and I am worried how they will take it."

"Oh Lord, no, what a nightmare for you both. I'm so sorry, Den, I don't know what else to say. I'll take Martin with me. Will they definitely be in?"

"Should be, they rang me, just as I found her."

"What did you tell them?"

"Nothing, I chickened out because they love her so much and I was worried how they would respond, so I told them I had a bad signal."

"Poor Melanie. Do they know who did it?"

"No, not yet. It was a couple of scumbags in a van. This will put Melanie back years, she is only just getting over the trauma of the miscarriages. But just give me five minutes with those fuckers."

"Yeah, well, you leave it to the law, Den. Don't worry, the police will catch the bastards. Which hospital are you at? I will give them a lift if they want one?"

"The Royal Sussex County; I'll meet you in A&E. I'm sorry to lumber you like this, but I don't want to leave her alone and the police have got my van and the car at the moment."

"We'll get off straight away, see you soon. I'm so sorry, Den.".

Following the call, Dennis was approached by a woman, who identified herself as Detective Constable, Sonia Shah, a sexual offences liaison officer who explained Melanie had earlier consented to forensic tests on her body, which under normal circumstances would have been completed at the sexual assault referral centre at Crawley hospital, but due to her injuries, it had been essential to convey her to the nearest A&E for immediate treatment, and the police examination would take place in the morning when she awoke if medically fit to do so.

Having obtained his personal details, she took a short written statement regarding his involvement in the discovery of Melanie. She informed Dutch that as both vehicles had now been photographed on site, it had been decided that as neither were of any evidential value, they had been removed to Brighton police station and could be collected there together with Jodie, who was now being looked after in the police dog pound.

Following the completion of the statement, he met with Jeanette, Martin, Molly and Ken in the A&E department. Both parents were visibly upset which took Dutch to the brink of crying again himself, but realising that he had to stay strong in the situation, he once again pulled himself together, thanked his sister and her partner for their help and promised to speak to them the following day. Dutch then escorted both parents to Melanie's bedside and was pleased to see that Melanie was asleep, so it would not be necessary for her to hide any facts from them, preventing any further upset to either party. She was looking so much better than when he had first discovered her, having now been cleaned up by the medical staff, but for the hideous large swelling on her face, which shocked both parents. Dutch was at least relieved that Melanie's arms were concealed under the sheets preventing them from seeing the rest of her bruised body.

Dutch, like Melanie, was fully aware that the entire truth of the attack should be kept from them both for the time being to prevent any mental anguish to the couple and played the incident as low key as possible, telling them that it was a random attack following a road rage disagreement with two men in a van following a traffic incident near Ditchling Beacon. He made no reference at all regarding any sexual violation. Fortunately, neither parent had contact with the investigating officers who may have revealed the fact. He was not entirely certain that they were convinced but in time, they would learn the full truth but now was not the occasion for them to do so.

As Melanie appeared settled in a sedated sleep, once the parents were convinced that she was in no imminent danger, Molly and Ken left in the early hours of the morning by taxi. Dutch, after further consultation with medical staff, walked to Brighton Police Station and collected both Jodie and his van, having arranged with the night duty staff that he would collect Melanie's car the following day.

Arriving home, despite the late hour and complete mental and physical exhaustion, he took Jodie for a long walk around Hove Park as he knew sleep was going to be very difficult that morning due to his state of mind, which was a mixture of bitter sadness and vengeance. During that sleep-deprived night, the evening's events brought a sudden and dramatic change in Dutch, which he felt, and others around him were soon to experience. The placid, mild-mannered man, who once only met aggression with aggression or violence with violence, had suddenly became consumed with bitterness and vengeance. He felt that some part of him had left him that night, he was now a hunter, a predator and his prey was human. If the police didn't snare those responsible before he did, then woe betide them both.

The new, agitated and less forgiving Dutch first manifested itself on his first day at work following Melanie's tragic experience, when Liam made a disparaging remark about the British army, in a deliberate attempt to wind him up. Before Liam knew it, he was laying in his own, newly-dug trench with Dutch standing on its edge looking over him, shovel in hand threatening to fill it in with him in it. Liam resigned from the company that day but Dutch was exonerated as Liam's dismissal was already on the cards, as Jon had regularly smelt alcohol on his breath and had regarded him as a liability. However, Jon too had noticed the change in his friend's general mood and demeanour since Melanie's ordeal and felt for them both, hoping that given time, both would, in some way, recover.

Chapter 9

Watching the Detectives (1977)

Performed and Written by Elvis Costello

Detective Chief Inspector, Anthony Byrne, checked his hair in the rear-view mirror before brushing down the shoulders of his jacket and reluctantly getting out of his car to dash through the rain into the Sussex and Surrey Serious Crime Unit. His usual place of work was a specially designed investigative and custody suite building situated on an outlying Brighton Industrial Park. Due to major renovation to this building, the unit had been temporary moved to offices at the large Haywards Heath Police Station in Mid Sussex. This move was of no inconvenience to the DI as he lived with his wife, Christine, on the western edge of the town of Uckfield and his journey to his temporary workplace was a simple 20 minute drive along the scenic A272.

Having notched up over 27 years' service, Tony Byrne was looking forward to a well-earned retirement in a few years, when he planned that he and Christine would travel together to the many places in the world that they had yet to visit. He was also looking forward to having more time to indulge in his favourite pastimes of sailing and fishing and hoped to have time to take trips to nearby coastal towns to experience his much-favoured fresh seafood. He was feeling very content in both his job and home life and had the comfort of his three children and five granddaughters, all living in easy reach in various parts of Sussex.

Having been bought up in South London, his association with Sussex began when at the age of 12, his parents made an unexpected but welcome move into the county when his father's job was transferred to what was then known as Crawley New Town. Tony quickly settled into his new life; a friendly, outgoing boy who had no difficulty making new friends, and when he left school, he worked in local journalism for a short period but always harboured the ambition of joining the police. At 17, he was accepted into the Sussex Police Service as a full-time cadet and joined the regulars at 19, doing his probationary training at Chichester, followed by a spell working in the small affluent market town of Petworth. He was ambitious and focussed and soon passed his Sergeant's examination and after a short period, was promoted to the rank and posted to the uniform section at Horsham Police Station situated in the north of the county.

Several years of successful police work ensured an easy transition into the CID, then further promotion to Detective Inspector at Gatwick Airport CID, where he ran successful operations against the vast numbers of unlicensed and unauthorised taxi touts that plagued the airport, ripping off unsuspecting overseas arrivals with vastly over inflated fares. He had further success in detecting in-house organised baggage thefts and theft from bonded warehouses. These achievements earned a further promotion and a place on the newly formed Sussex and Surrey Police Partnership.

An imposing figure, standing at 6'4", well-groomed and neatly turned out, he was well-liked, and he was renowned for setting high standards and paying minute attention to detail, which often yielded good results but made him rather unpopular with the less motivated within the force.

It had been a particularly interesting Friday, starting with the local intelligence officer informing the Chief Inspector that a Chinese restaurant within their policing district was under threat from a Triad controlled gang. Byrne showed immediate interest as he had never had any dealings with this particular criminal organisation before and certainly did not want them operating on his patch. The manager of the food outlet had apparently inadvertently acquired a loan from a Triad controlled business and the interest on the loan was raised so rapidly that he fell into debt, and in recompense, he had been forced by the gang to have a bank card reading device attached to the restaurant's own electronic card payment system—the rogue device also had the capability of recording each associated pin number. A member of the gang planned to return to collect the device, and it was believed that the fraudulently-gained information would be then decrypted and the details sent to China where the cards would be duplicated and returned to the UK in a very short time. The informant was very reluctant to give this information as he was extremely concerned about the consequences as this organisation had a fearsome reputation, especially amongst the Chinese community, but he did not wish to be a willing part of the scheme. Byrne dearly wanted to bring these people to justice himself but immediately realised that such a large and delicate operation needed to be carried out by a specialist unit from the Metropolitan Police. After gathering all of the facts, he passed this intelligence onto his colleagues in the Met and stressed that whatever action they took, they must protect the source of the information at all costs, as he didn't want a shop arson or much worse as a result. He suggested that they took the courier out by way of surveillance and an apparent routine roadside check, thereby preventing the device and card details reaching their intended destination and also protecting the source of the information. This would not be his ideal way of working as this would not nail the main players, but he had learnt that sometimes, it was not worth risking casualties, especially as there should now be enough intelligence for the squad to arrest the gang in future. His working day ended by clearing his in tray as he was on-call for the weekend, and hopefully, if not called out, he could return on Monday morning to start the week off with an unusually clear desk.

On his drive home, he stopped by at his local shop purchasing a few treats for Christine and himself, looking forward to settling down to a relaxing evening.

After a much appreciated evening meal and picking up a half-read novel, Tony plonked himself down in his favourite chair next to his wife, Christine, whilst she watched the latest episode of a cookery programme on the television. He was enjoying a small tumbler of his favourite scotch; it was the first and only drink that evening because he was on call for the unit; when the telephone rang, he felt sure that it was for a job because it was only his work that would usually call after 8 pm. His assumption was correct and he swiftly took in the details from a Brighton CID officer that there had been a serious abduction and rape near Ditchling Beacon. The victim, Mrs Melanie French, who had also been badly assaulted, was now at Brighton County Hospital as she had been found semi-conscious. The first police responders had only been able to obtain very brief details of the attack and possible perpetrators and this information had been widely circulated. The area where the offence took place and where her car was still parked had been secured and cordoned off and crime scene investigators had been alerted and were attending.

Armed with this information, Byrne telephoned Woman Detective Sergeant, Verna Cannan, an experienced DS, originally from Derbyshire, sharp and efficient and not known to mince her words. The two officers, who regularly worked together, had both, a good professional and jovial relationship, and Byrne, being somewhat of a perfectionist and dapper man, would regularly be seen adjusting his hair or bushing himself down causing his female colleague to break out in song with the words from *'You're So Vain'*. They arranged to meet at Haywards Heath Police Office as soon as possible. Christine, his second wife, was well used to such disruptions, having been a long serving police officer in the South Yorkshire force herself.

Having liaised with WDS Cannan, they drove to the well-known beauty spot, and after donning on their forensic overalls and overshoes, they liaised with the duty uniform Police Inspector and the scene investigators present at the layby. Having viewed the attack site, they were made fully aware of the circumstances as they were known so far and were shown the evidence bags containing items of woman's clothing, shoes, a blanket containing two strips of sticky tape and a sleeping bag, together with a mobile telephone. Arrangements were then made to secure the site with an overnight guard for a specialist search team to examine the area in daylight. Both detectives then attended Brighton Hospital, where the victim was being treated for her injuries and preparations were in hand to obtain intimate samples by a forensic nurse practitioner, once medical staff agreed she would be well enough to do so. Subsequently, they were permitted to ask her a few questions in order to establish any further description of a van and the two males responsible, who she believed to be of eastern European origin. Police mobile searches had been made in and around the immediate area but there was no trace of the van or men concerned.

Before making all other necessary arrangements for the preservation of evidence, including the interviewing of two male witnesses—Simon and Adam—he ensured that a full description of the men and the van were circulated both locally and nationally. He realised that giving such distinctive descriptions, which included a missing finger and a description of an earring, to the media would probably result in the two offenders concealing such identifying evidence, but this was necessary to apprehend the suspects as quickly as possible due to the levels of risk they posed to other members of the public whilst they remained at large. He needed to appeal to the public not only through the media but also to target particular sections of societies including Eastern European groups. Whilst he considered all of these necessary arrangements, WDS Cannan approached Mr Dennis French, the victim's husband, at the hospital and briefly spoke to him regarding the discovery of his wife following the attack.

Before leaving for what would be a few hours' sleep, Byrne made arrangements for an early morning team briefing and contacted the Police Press liaison officer in order for a press conference to take place the following day to appeal for any witnesses or for anyone to come forward who may have knowledge of the van or description of the offenders. Furthermore, he left messages regarding the incident for his Detective Superintendent and the Chief Constable of both forces.

At 9 am sharp, the following morning, a fully assembled team of detectives, scene investigators, crime analysts and an exhibits officer were present in an incident room at Brighton Police Station. Having greeted and thanked the group for attending the briefing at very short notice, DI Byrne addressed them,

"Last evening, as you are now all aware, a rape took place in a small layby, close to Ditchling Beacon. A map of the precise location of the offence, a description of both offenders and photographs of the scene are on the board over there." He gestured vaguely in the direction of the wall behind them and continued,

"The circumstances are that the victim, Mrs Melanie French, who resides with her husband in Hove, had just returned alone to her car, having walked her dog and was approached by two men in a van, supposedly requesting directions towards London. She was almost immediately bundled into the rear of the van where she was seriously assaulted, threatened with a knife and raped whilst unconscious due to the trauma and the fact that she had tape placed over both eyes and mouth. She was later discovered semi-conscious by her husband some two hours after the attack in a field close to the scene, completely naked, wrapped only in a blanket."

DI Byrne picked up a Styrofoam cup of coffee, immediately regretting it as it scalded his upper lip.

"Due to the seriousness of her injuries, she was obviously taken immediately to Brighton County instead of the forensic examination centre at Crawley where apart from a head wound and severe bruising, she is making a good physical recovery and is not in any immediate bodily danger, but understandably, the same cannot be said for her mental well-being. Before leaving her at the hospital last night, she was able to describe the van as being large, off-white in colour, quite old, in a rough condition; she thought it was the type that builders might use to carry their equipment. The only items that she could recall being in the rear were some plastic containers, cushions and blankets. She had no idea of any make or registration number."

Glancing at his notes, he continued in a more optimistic tone,

"The description that she gave of the passenger, who spoke to her in what she described as a Polish-type or eastern European-sounding accent, who left the stationary van and asked directions, was of a fairly large build, about 5'10" to 6', unshaven with a weather-beaten dark completion. He wore a hooded jacket with the hood over his head, drawn tight over a large part of his face, dark trousers, not sure about what type of shoes. She could smell from his breath that he had recently been drinking. She then described the man whom she believed to be the driver, although she never actually saw him in the driving seat, as being smaller in height and build to the passenger and also spoke in a similar accent to him. She was not able to give any further detail of his general description as he just suddenly appeared from the side of the van wearing a woolly type hat which was pulled tight to his face and over both ears, and as he did so, both men opened the doors and forcibly pushed her into the rear of the van."

Byrne reached for his coffee again and took a few tentative sips before resuming his outline of events.

"Being quite a fit woman who had, in the past, attended self-defence classes, she vigorously tried to fight off both men but once the passenger got on top of her, she was unable to resist them. At one stage during the struggle, she got hold of what she believed to be the passenger's right hand and as she did so, she felt what she thought was a stub of a finger. She remembers this as it felt very odd to the touch. Because she continued to resist, they started to slap and punch her and bang her head on the floor, but when she saw that the passenger was holding a knife to her face, she discontinued the struggle. At one stage during the attack, she managed to free an arm and lash out causing the drivers hat to fall from his head revealing, in the dim light, a crucifix style earing dangling from his right ear. The same man then placed some black sticky tape over her eyes and mouth and she then found difficulty in breathing. Shortly after this, due to a blow to her head, shock and breathing difficulties, she passed out and remembers nothing else before being discovered by her husband." He glanced around the assembled group. "So, are there questions before WDS Cannan hands out the assignments?"

DC Dave Mills straightened himself up from where he had been leaning in the doorway and asked,

"The victim described the van as possibly being the type of vehicle to carry builder's tools and stuff, but there was no mention of any tools, only blankets and cushions; could it be that the cushions are for some form of passenger transport, as there has been no mention of rear seats?"

"Perhaps," said Byrne, "we must bear in mind that a van with blankets and cushions in the rear as possibly workers transport, which would fit perhaps a group of migrant workers. The victim was asked about any further distinguishing points about the vehicle, such as any logos or amber roof lights, any side panelling, or a single or double wheel base vehicle but could add nothing further."

A general murmuring went around the group and then DC Howard Bostock, generally the joker of the pack but astute and always full of enthusiasm, chipped in,

"Guv, you say that she was found by her husband, how did he know where to find her if she had remained unconscious following the attack? Had she managed to phone him or something?"

"No, her phone was discarded nearby by the assailants and she was definitely in no condition to use it." He glanced over his shoulder, looking for WDS Cannan. "That reminds me, Verna, can you ensure that we get her telephone interrogated as to its use before and after the offence to ensure that what we have been told so far tallies up?"

Byrne continued, "When her husband returned from work, with no sign of his wife, her car or the dog, he unsuccessfully tried to phone her on several occasions and when it became dark, he became concerned and subsequently carried out a mobile search in the areas that he knew she frequented for dog walks, the Beacon being one of them. As he approached the site, he saw her car parked in the lay-by at the side of the road with another car parked behind it. He found their dog alone in her vehicle and with the assistance of the dog, located her behind a hedge just inside the field. All this has been confirmed by the two independent witnesses in the other car parked there, who then assisted him in raising the alarm."

DC Bostock interjected again, "From what you have said, I presume the two others parked there are unable to shed any more light on the offenders or their vehicle?"

"That's correct; the two gentleman concerned arrived after the offence took place and did not leave their car, having no idea that Mrs French was laying in the field close to them, and they are under no suspicion whatsoever concerning this offence."

"What were they doing there? Just sitting in a car at that time of the evening then?"

"Let's just say neither of them were found by Mr French to be occupying the front seats at the time and leave it like that."

The comment was met by quiet laughter and smiles from most of the assembly.

Indicating hush, Byrne said, "Verna, could you also designate officers to liaise with the SOCO and exhibits officer and see if there is anything special about that tape or the blanket, which might reveal its source without obviously contaminating any forensics it may contain."

Verna Cannan nodded and continued to make notes as the briefing continued.

"The victim stated that she smelt alcohol on their breath. I am not familiar with this area, are there any pubs near that Beacon?" asked Mills.

"No, not really. The two closest are in the small nearby village which uniform officers made enquiries at last night and they are certain that they didn't visit them as such descriptions would have certainly stood out in that particular environment. The closest after that are in the city and are numerous and, save for the missing digit, neither man would particularly stand out there. Apart from the descriptions, clues are pretty thin as there is obviously no CCTV for miles around, or though someone will be tasked to trawl through images taken from the nearest, more obvious routes to that location."

A local Intelligence Officer, PC Ian Hands, who had been assigned to the team for this particular investigation, held up his hand,

"At this stage, I presume we have an open mind as to if this pair was actually looking to get to London or not?"

"That's correct. They could have possibly been lost and took the opportunity to attack a lone female in a remote spot but chances are that it was just a ruse to gain her confidence and divert her attention as it's hard to believe that if one was travelling to London, you would find yourself in such a remote location."

"Yeah," Hands concurred, "given that they were partially disguised, had the tape and a knife in the van and were in an area where you could expect to see lone women walking at all times of the day gives the impression that they are local."

"Exactly; all those facts show that they were fully prepared for what happened and, at the very least, indicates they may have some local knowledge. That is why we will be concentrating our initial enquiries on immigrant work forces in our area, but we need to keep in mind that, with cushions and blankets in the rear, they could be travelling and sleeping rough."

PC Hands, an officer known for his interest in vehicle investigation, interjected,

"Bearing in mind the nationality of these two Herberts, I suppose this van could be on foreign plates?"

"Sorry," Byrne said, "should have mentioned that the aggrieved party says that the passenger alighted from its nearside when the vehicle was still reversing, so being right hand drive, we have to presume it's being driven on standard British plates, which is a pity because foreign ones on such a vehicle would stand out much more."

The PC nodded in acknowledgement to the answer to his question.

Further questions were fired and the officers present discussed their own theories and thoughts before being assigned their respective tasks, which included the searching of police records and liaising with immigration and border agencies.

Byrne knew that amongst all other offences committed, this had been close to a murder or manslaughter investigation, not only as a result of the injuries sustained but had they not wrapped the victim in the blanket on that cold night in such a remote location, she could have died from hypothermia, especially in her then poor physical condition, but he wondered if the offenders had done this not for her sake but just to disguise her and to make lifting and carrying her lifeless body from the van easier. Medical staff had also commented that had the persons responsible not removed the tape from her mouth, she could have died of asphyxia as her nostrils were blocked with dried blood and mucus, or had she vomited prior to them removing it, she would have choked to death. Whatever the reason when leaving her, they must have considered that if not found quickly, she would die there.

He voiced his thoughts to the enquiry team office manager, DS Hunter who responded in his soft Irish brogue.

"You're right, sir, but I can foresee that in defence of those points being put to them, they would say that that is why they removed the tape from her mouth and wrapped her in a blanket to protect her from the cold. They would further say that they had considered that her car and phone would assist in her being found quickly. You and I know that's a load of bollocks and as such that won't help their defence one little bit due to the severity of the attack. Let's face it, those two callous bastards didn't give a shit if she lived or died, it's just fortunate that her husband found her when he did."

The DI was aware that with no other visible distinguishing features and with so many similar vans to the one that Mrs French had described out on the roads every day, many of them containing two men of a general similar description, it would be like searching for the proverbial needle in a haystack. They had to hope that the van might come to notice for a road traffic offence or something similar, as it would not be until officers heard their accents, coupled with the descriptions, that they would then connect these two highly dangerous men to this crime. His best bet at this stage was for a member of the public to come forward, having recognised the descriptions circulated.

With this knowledge, arrangements were made by the major crime incident room for enquiries to be carried out at establishments within the Surrey and Sussex Police districts, where groups of eastern Europeans lived, or were employed, in an effort to trace the van or individuals, and with the immigration and border patrol departments, who were also alerted of the descriptions including the facts concerning the earring and missing finger. Under Byrne's instructions, all Surrey and Sussex divisions were to visit and check hotels, restaurants, car washes, agricultural sites and other likely locations in a search for the van and its occupants. These actions were carried out swiftly and dutifully by all divisions in both forces, but when eastern divisional local intelligence office compiled a list of such sites in their area, they were unaware of a new business premises having very recently commenced operating on the Riverside Industrial Estate in the ancient town of Lewes, East Sussex, which had not yet come to their notice. The negative results of all of these enquiries were forwarded to DI Byrne and his team.

Following her release from hospital, Melanie would be required to supply a full written statement and was re-visited on several occasions by specially trained officers from the sexual offences liaison unit and was given specific advice regarding the support available to her from not only the medical profession but also from various voluntary organisations. They assured her that she could contact them at any time with any concerns or if she remembered anything further which would assist the enquiry. In the meantime, hairs and foreign fibres collected from the blanket and tape left at the scene and scrapings taken from under Melanie's finger nails had been fast-tracked for DNA testing. Byrne was aware that these were the best opportunities to provide identification as the semen recovered from the aggrieved was possibly from both offenders which could complicate identification.

The early investigation showed no match with any similar crimes locally or nationally that involved a van and two occupants matching the given description. Byrne realised that he had some new kids on the block who were giving him great cause for concern; the brutality and callousness of the crime was a clear indication that these two sickening individuals needed apprehending and taking off the streets as soon as possible.

Chapter 10
Sad Song (2013)
Artist: We the Kings
Writers: T Clark/ K. Bard/D. Immerman

The police forensic examinations complete, it became imperative to obtain a fully detailed written statement from Melanie who, despite her shock and mental anguish, provided a comprehensive account in which she gave the police as much information as she could recall regarding the attackers' descriptions and the van they used. This limited additional information was circulated via police intelligence and the media. Major incident notices were placed in the area of the abduction and enquiries were carried out with dog walkers and drivers in the area for several days following the attack.

Although her physical injuries began to gradually heal, Melanie remained deeply traumatised, becoming withdrawn with fear and isolated from her social network. She was soon reliant entirely on her husband and parents and no longer engaged in any of her day to day activities. Everyday life was so different for the couple now; their peace and tranquillity had been turned into an existence of living within a nightmare, with neither of them being able to come to terms with the situation. Dutch was consumed with concern for Melanie and her parents, who had now been made aware of the full extent of their daughter's ordeal due to the media exposure. Despite being distraught, after explanation, they were understanding as to why the couple had initially kept the full facts from them.

Melanie's mental health had been delicate since her past miscarriages but had made a lot of improvement and through diligent self-management and good support, had regained much of her former confidence and spark. However, the attack had sent her spiralling once again into the depths of depression, haunted by flashbacks and intrusive thoughts, falsely believing that she was somehow complicit in the event as she had eventually had to submit to them even though

Dutch and the police liaison officers, who visited, after she had left the hospital, to provide support and to clarify certain points in her statement, constantly reassured her that she could have never resisted two strong men.

Dutch was, both, incensed and devastated by what had happened to his wife; especially as, after his unsettled upbringing, he had finally found happiness only for it to be taken away by the attack. Whilst he was trying his best to remain focussed on supporting Melanie and helping her to recover from her ordeal, his thoughts turned constantly to revenge; his mind meticulously picking over the sequence of events, trying to make sense of it and trying to identify any significant facts that the police may have missed, and he spent many sleepless nights reflecting about what he would like to do to the perpetrators. It had ignited a rage inside of him such as he had never felt before; how was it that a woman walking alone amongst so much natural beauty should not be safe from such a despicable act? The incident had a profound effect on him, reawakening all the sad memories of the life that he and his brother and sisters had had to endure during their childhood, and to a certain extent, still mentally affected them all now.

The last time he had felt such intense anger and sorrow was with the horrendous death of drummer and machine gunner, Lee Rigby, of the Royal Fusiliers, who in 2013, when walking back to his barracks on a southeast London street, wearing a 'Help the Heroes' logo hoodie, was run over and then hacked to death by two Muslim extremists for what they said was for the retaliation for British military presence in Islamic countries. The manner of this cowardly murder sickened Dutch, and he had so wished that he could, in some way, avenge such a barbaric act. Knowing from experience, the only opportunity for such reprisal was largely confined to the battle field itself. Although, as an infant, he was baptised into the Church of England faith, he was never a religious man but in times such as these, he did offer up prayers, and he prayed for his wife in a hope that she would fully recover soon. He always felt that although he was not a firm believer in God, it was worth hedging his bets with a prayer from time to time, just in case. His reasoning was that, including Atheism, there were over 4,000 different religions in the world and, as only one could be right, he found it difficult to truly believe in any.

As the police investigation continued, Dutch grew restless, anxious for news of developments and discoveries. Initially, all that was forthcoming was the news that there had been no similar crimes committed either locally or nationally, which could be linked to the incident and enquiries were being made with employers and facilities connected to the Eastern European communities. They further assured the couple that the descriptions Melanie had given had been widely publicised through numerous media sources and circulated to all police forces but so far, there had been very little response.

On her release from hospital, Melanie and Dutch were able to have their first intimate conversation.

"Jon's told me that I can take as much time off work as I need."

"That's good but you shouldn't have to be away too long as I have spoken with Mum and Dad, and as soon as you go back to work, I'm going to move in with them for a while."

"Why can't you stay here and we can all take turns in looking after you?"

"I can't be alone at the moment and what happens if you get called out on an emergency at night, I couldn't stand it."

"I could ask him to take me off the call out roster."

"No that's not fair on either Jon, you or our income. They have agreed that I can take Jodie with me and as they are at home most of the time and with you coming over whenever you can, it will be much better for me until I regain my confidence."

"Looking at it like that, I suppose you are right. It would be a lonely place here when I'm back at work."

Dutch was very understanding about her wishes and was determined in helping her in any way he could towards her physical and mental recovery, making him reluctant to quiz Melanie about her horrific ordeal, but her continued distress coupled with his own increasing rage and frustration eventually prompted him to risk asking her about that fateful evening.

"I know it's a stupid question, but how are you feeling now? Can we talk about what happened?"

He could see the fear envelop her, and he felt utterly heartless for even attempting to draw her out.

"I hurt all over," she whispered. "I'm a complete mess." She looked at him from big, scared eyes. "The cuts and bruises will heal but my mind won't. I'm trapped with my memories and they won't go away, not ever…" and she dissolved into tears.

Dutch leaned over and tentatively placed his hand on hers; he realised that he had become very reticent about touching her at all, he was so afraid of spooking her.

"I know," he said urgently, "but every day that passes will be another day away from the nightmare and hopefully, time will help."

She did not appear to have heard him and continued,

"What I remember most of all was how cold I was, I thought I was freezing to death."

"I've never seen anyone shiver like that. I'm so glad I had that sleeping bag handy."

She smiled weakly, seeming lost in thought and then suddenly said,

"Did I ever tell you, when I was a little girl and something or someone frightened me, I would pretend that I was a big, strong lioness and that seemed to somehow calm my fears?"

"No, what made you mention that?" he asked, bemused.

"Well, when they were attacking me in the back of that van, that image returned to me, and I fought as best as I could by scratching and biting," she chewed viciously at her lip. "That was before they put tape over my mouth and according to the crime scene investigator, she thinks that she has found some samples of skin under my nails."

"Oh, I see; I hope you are right as that should help no end to find out who did this." Dutch ran his hand across his face, rubbing tiredly at his eyes and then, suddenly, stood and paced across the room, alert and agitated again.

"Melanie, I've avoided talking to you at length as I know you've gone through it numerous times with the police, and I don't expect you to tell me all the gory details, and I imagine it is probably easier for you to tell that sort of thing to others outside of the family, but you must tell me as much as you know about those bastards that did this to you. At the moment, I could pass them in the street and not know it was them and that's not right."

He instantly regretted his outburst as he glanced up and saw that his wife was looking alarmed.

"I've already told you all I can remember about them."

"I know, I know and I don't want to upset you, but are you sure there's nothing else at all?"

Under his breath, he muttered,

"They're are not getting away with this, it's driving me insane."

Melanie remained silent for a while, twisting her hands in her lap and biting her lower lip with anxious chewing before saying,

"Well, there is something else I vaguely recalled last night, lying awake yet again for most of the night, having to endure it all over in my mind again."

"Yes? What is it? Will it help catch them?"

"That's the problem, I think it might."

"Problem? I'm sorry, I don't follow you."

"I've constantly been thinking about this and I don't want them caught now. If they were, that would mean me going to court and re-living it all over again."

"But that's how they will be brought to justice, it's a necessary evil."

"No, I'm not doing it; probably be called a liar by both them and some fancy barrister and all in public and all the intimate details being revealed to all and sundry. I won't do it, I can't. I'm not going to and that's final."

"I get that and I wouldn't let you go through that if that's how you feel, but if I don't do something, I might as well drop dead now because it will torment me all of my life if I don't try. They need to pay for what they have done to you and what if they do it again to someone else? I don't want that on my conscience and I'm sure you don't either…" he broke off abruptly, aware that he was ranting and that he was beginning to pressurise Melanie.

"I'm sorry, I didn't mean it. I just need to do something and I'm finding it bloody impossible sitting here twiddling my thumbs whilst those bastards are out there, having messed up our lives and got away with it."

"I know," she sniffed, "you are right, but I will never, never go to court and testify and you must understand that."

Dutch sighed, "I do. I want you to recover as best as you can from this, and I can see that bringing it all up again in the future is not going to help you in that process, but please, please tell me what you have now remembered."

"You must promise not to tell the police if I do? If you do then no matter how much I love you, I will never forgive you or ever trust you again."

"You have my word. You know I wouldn't sacrifice our relationship."

Melanie seemed still to hesitate but then took a deep breath and began,

"Well, you know about the van, the blankets and cushions inside, but what I've now remembered is that after I dislodged his hat and before he put the tape over my eyes, he released his grip, I guess, to re-adjust the hat, so I managed to arch my back and neck, look backwards and wriggle towards the front, towards some big plastic containers behind the seats. On one of these, I can now remember, there was a picture of a shield with a hand holding a sword. Why I remember this now is because I've been racking my brain as to what I had seen and where I had seen this crest before and I've finally got it; it was when we went to watch Colchester play Charlton in an FA cup game, and it was just like the one on their supporters' flags and banners. Do you remember?"

Dutch leaned forward, excitedly, "Yes, I do. Charlton are known as the 'Valiants'. I only know that because Fluff is a big Charlton fan, and he had that emblem on his locker door. Is that it? Was there any writing on these containers? Can you remember any other details?"

"I'm sure there were large printed letters on the blade of the sword and a label, but I wouldn't have been able to read it as, apart from fighting for my life, it was dark and all of the writing was upside down for me to remember."

"You did well to notice all that, considering what was happening to you. I'm not certain if you told the police about that, it would help to find them anyway." Dutch said, decisively.

Unconvinced, Melanie continued, "Probably not, but I've decided that if I remembered anything else, I am not telling them. I am not going to court, do you fully understand that?"

"I get the message loud and clear; if that's your decision, I will honour my promise on the condition that if you do recall any more, you will let me know."

"Actually, there is more, but again, it's only for your ears. You know that I told the police I believed that the passenger, the larger of the two, had a finger missing from his right hand and the other one had a crucifix earring in his right ear?"

"Yeah, go on."

"Well, thinking about it more carefully, I think it was two crosses on the earring, one smaller than the other. The other thing is a bit odd, just before tape was put over my eyes and I completely passed out, I can remember it suddenly appeared brighter as if the interior light had been switched on or something, and from what I could make out, I think they were using a camera."

"Why do you think that?"

"Because it became so bright and I am sure one of them said film or video. Why would they do that?"

Dawning realisation hit Dutch like a massive blow to the stomach.

"Because they are sick fuckers, that's why. Are you certain that you are not going to tell the police all of this new stuff? It may go a long way in identifying them?"

"I've already told you," she replied shrilly. "It's no longer up for discussion. I will confide in you and you only, but I have one more thing to tell you and I'm so embarrassed about it."

She looked so vulnerable and mortified—sitting there, struggling to tell him the details of what had been a cowardly, vicious attack on a defenceless woman—that Dutch could feel the bile rising in the back of his throat as he struggled to contain his bitterness.

"Go on, love, it's okay. You know you can tell me anything," he encouraged, trying his best to conceal his own distress.

"When the hospital had checked me over, they took some tests and discovered that one of those filthy bastards has given me an STD."

Dutch was speechless, put his head in his hands and said, "My God, I'm so sorry, for you, Melanie. You think it can't get any worse and then it does."

"That's everything now, you know everything. Absolutely everything," she added in a tone of desperation. "Do you think we can talk about something else please?"

She reached over to where Jodie was lying stretched out, dozing on the rug next to her—she found her presence comforting. As she stroked the dog's soft belly, she said softly,

"Y'know, I used to think that I would never get over the sadness of us not being able to have children; all those times we tried and I couldn't carry them full term. I felt such a failure and so alone and then we got this one," she gestured towards the dog, "I didn't believe at the time that it would really help much but I was so wrong; she helped me so much and being able to walk with her in the Downs was such a big positive in my life. It made me feel connected to something, the place, nature, just life, I suppose. Now it's gone, ruined, spoiled forever."

"What do you mean? We're not going to get rid of Jodie." Dutch tried to keep the alarm out of his voice.

"God, no!" Melanie replied, "I would never be without her but I wouldn't ever feel safe to go out walking her like that again."

"Maybe in time you will…" he ventured.

"No! I won't. I don't even want to try. I want to move away from here, from this flat, this area, everything that reminds me of what has happened. It will never be okay for me here, not now. They've ruined it, they've ruined it all."

"Yes," thought Dutch to himself, "they have, they've ruined it all."

Chapter 11
Car Wash (1976)
Artist: Rose Royce   Writer: Norman Whitfield

Later that evening, Dutch sat alone gazing at the lights of the distant highway, barely registering anything, deep in thought, replaying the conversation with Melanie. She was right of course, to go to court and give evidence and then be cross-examined and possibly accused of lying, only for her attackers to either receive short sentences or possibly deportation, if indeed they were convicted at all, whilst she would have to re-live the ordeal all over again and all the facts of the case would become public knowledge—it was a horror that he could not possibly expect her to contemplate. Conversely, for him to stand by and allow such a barbaric and devastating event that had altered the entire course of his and Melanie's life to go unpunished seemed equally untenable, and he knew that he would not be able to let the matter rest; his whole life's plan was unravelling and lay around him in disarray.

As he looked out at the familiar view, the reassuring thought of the concealed weapon came to mind and he immediately lost some of the feeling of powerlessness. He needed a plan. He must use all the information he had available to him to get ahead of the police and find a way to track down the perpetrators. The thought of having a clear goal settled his mind and he resolved to a make a start there and then. His sad thoughts then turned to Connie which prompted him to play her favourite CD, the one item that he had insisted he inherited from her, and as the smooth voice of Matt Munro played in the background, he flicked on his laptop and settled back in his chair, preparing himself for a long night's surfing session as he scoured the internet searching for anything that might lead him to discover the identity or whereabouts of his prey.

He started with the description that Melanie had given him regarding the badge or crest on the containers; entering many variations of the described image, searching for a combination of both the crest and large plastic containers, when after hours of trawling through the images, unable to find anything significant, he was finally rewarded by the discovery of a car cleaning chemicals website. The company emblem was a shield and within it was a hand-gripped sword with the brand name 'Pajzs' printed vertically down the blade, identical to the one Melanie had described. With the aid of his laptop, he translated the word into English, discovering it to be 'shield'. This large manufacturing company was based in Hungary and amongst images on this website, were those of large plastic containers of vehicle shampoo. This was exactly what Dutch had been looking for and he was overjoyed with his findings.

The description of two eastern European males, coupled with such large quantities of shampoo and the origin of the product, immediately made him think of the foreign-led car cleaning and valeting companies that had appeared over towns and cities in the UK over recent years. This theory was further enhanced when he carried out further research regarding the description of the earring and found the double crucifix that Melanie had described to be also called a Patriarchal Cross, a variation of the Christian Cross, a religious symbol of eastern European origin. He first thought that it would be impossible to visit and look around all of the car cleaning sites in the area for the men and van responsible, but when he considered the number of such units he knew in the Shoreham, Brighton and Hove area, he realised that there were only a handful and they were well publicised. He suspected that the men were probably operating locally as they appeared to have been drinking and so would probably not have wanted to chance driving too far and getting stopped by the police.

He compiled a list of all such car washes that he knew about in roughly a five-mile radius of Brighton and Hove, and he was aware of most because he travelled extensively in his work and would be able to visit them whilst operating within his usual work schedule. This would be made easier for him to do because due to his work locations in rural, often muddy areas, close to water, the vans were constantly dirty and often got stuck in mud, and Jon insisted that for the company image, they were cleaned regularly inside and out, either by the drivers themselves or in a hand car wash site, which was reimbursed by the company on the production of a receipt. When visiting such sites, Dutch planned that he would closely study each individual worker as they washed or vacuumed the van, looking out for the distinctive earring, the missing digit and the large white van.

His friend and employer, Jon, was very understanding of Dutch's home circumstances and allowed Dutch to take time off work whenever he felt that it was necessary, but he tried to ensure that he limited this as much as possible, only being absent when Melanie needed him and trying to fit his 'research' around his usual schedule wherever he could. He was acutely aware that he needed not to draw attention to himself by behaving in a way that would be considered out of character by anyone who knew him well, and he made sure that he regularly deleted his internet history and kept this computer files well-protected by passwords, even though he was the sole user of the laptop.

Dutch then attempted to structure his work timetable, as much as was possible, without arousing suspicion by visiting and briefly surveying the likely car wash facilities, and his diligence was rewarded when one late Friday afternoon, three weeks following Melanie's ordeal, Jon requested that he go to the Riverside Industrial Estate in the small ancient town of Lewes situated nine miles northeast of Brighton in order to collect a part required to repair a water pump from a factory premises before they closed for the weekend. After collecting the part, as he drove the van away from the factory, he noticed what appeared to be large new banners, advertising a car wash facility in one of the minor roads on the estate. Although he had visited this estate in the past, he had never noticed the banners before so. As the van was dirty inside and out, it presented the ideal opportunity to get the van cleaned and for him to investigate another such facility, even if it was only to eliminate from his list of possible sites.

He scrutinised the printed banners advertising the E-Zee Kleen Hand Car Wash; it looked pretty much like any other such operation and gave few details but they appeared to be professionally printed and clearly indicated the site of the premises. As he turned into the narrow road indicated by the banners and drove down the sloping concrete road that overlooked the site, he saw that the entire premises was protected by newly-erected, metal-spiked security fences and gates. As it was obviously still open, he drove the van through the open metal gates and at the side of one gate, he noticed a heavy duty open padlock hanging from a cross member of the fence by its securing arm. Once inside, he was immediately waved on by a man with a high-powered lance water jet and then signalled to stop as the man and another one who suddenly appeared, started to wash the vehicle. Dutch felt a wave of disappointment as each of them was wearing heavy duty, two-tone blue rubber gloves; therefore, he knew that he would be unable to determine if any of them had any fingers missing but did quickly establish that neither of them was wearing any earrings. One man engaged in applying the wheels with a cleaning solution and the other sprayed the body of the van with water; following shampooing the vehicle, they sprayed off the suds with a pressure hose—all usual procedures that he had been through many times before during his search and each time having studied every employee closely. He noticed that both men appeared by speech and description to be eastern Europeans but neither, as far as he was able to see, had the characteristics of the offenders for whom he was searching. He was then beckoned forward by a tall, well-built man with short dark hair, situated on the other side of a mechanical gantry that assists in drying by blasting hot air onto vehicles as they pass through. Dutch drove the van through the arched structure and as water was blown from the wind screen, he was instructed by the way of hand signals indicating him to increase his speed or slow down as he progressed through the drying machine; this man too was wearing identical gloves to his colleagues with no visible earring. After driving through the machine, the same man indicated for him to stop and then commenced to wipe away the majority of the remaining water from the glass and bodywork with a chamois leather, then asked in broken English if he required the inside of the van cleaned, and as Dutch confirmed that he did, he was directed to park in the interior cleaning area under the large, blue, heavy plastic canopy marked Bay 2, where he alighted from the van. Dutch was now attempting to study the two male workers accompanied by a female worker involved in the drying of a car in the adjoining bay, none of whom were wearing gloves. He hovered around the area as long as possible and both males appeared to have all fingers intact, one male having a stud only in his right ear lobe. Satisfied that he had eliminated both of these men, he fetched his expenses book from the van and was immediately approached by a man in his mid-twenties with a brown leather cash type bag over his shoulder with a strap running across his chest, which was carried in such a way that it was safe from theft and could not easily be left unattended.

He informed this man, who was also eastern European and appeared to be the cashier, of what he required. This man then indicated to the group of three, that were still engaged in drying, of the service the van required, and as he did so, Dutch took a visual note of his hands and ears.

The cashier then indicated for him to take a seat in the outside waiting area next to an old, white mobile home with the words 'office' hand-painted on a panel besides the door, every window of this unit had been covered over by thick metal panels, secured by screws on the exterior. It was evident that this unit was used regularly as it was connected with propane gas from a large, red, 47-kg Calor gas container situated at one side. As he sat and pondered, once again disappointed in yet another fruitless search, he started to take note of his surroundings. Because of his past post as a PTI responsible for health and safety issues at the regimental sports complex, he identified a huge fire risk within the compound. Spread about the perimeter of the yard, there were three, large, blue, metal, windowless cargo containers, each apart from the office was raised off of the ground by resting on metal adjustable stilts. The office was supported on a low brick wall with access gaps on each side and each unit was accessed by sets of portable steps. On one side of the unit marked 'office', there were three more identical free standing red 47-kg, metal, propane gas canisters and on the other side, on a pallet, inside of a large gauge steel security cage, was a 1000-litre plastic tank of traffic film remover marked with hazard stickers warning of flammable noxious liquid. It occurred to Dutch that how dangerous it was to have both of these items immediately alongside a structure that was made of only thin metal, plastic and plywood with various flammable items underneath, including an amount of prepared wood that appeared to have been left over from a large canopy construction, erected for cleaning the interiors of vehicles on wet days. It was an accident waiting to happen, like waiting for a bomb to go off. The health and safety executive obviously had not visited this new business yet. As he waited, he concluded that by the movements of the staff, that one container was the rest room, one was where various cleaning products were kept and the other appeared to be a toilet. He was interested and very familiar with such containers as the army had used them for secure storage, both abroad and in the UK. Dutch noticed that the door of the office had extra security by way of a large metal clasp and padlock. With all the security in place for an office, he began to wonder what it could contain.

Whilst waiting and observing, a new, very smart, silver Porsche drove into the compound and parked in front of the office. This car had the distinctive and obvious number plate of B00 5TAN. The male driver, who was alone, got out and walked towards the locked office door with a key in his hand. He was about six feet tall with a tanned complexion, medium built, in his early forties, had jet-black greased hair combed into a small pony tailback, wearing what appeared to be an expensive suit and two-tone crocodile skin shoes. Dutch considered that he also gave the appearance of being of Eastern European origin. After unlocking the padlock from its clasp, then unlocking the integral door lock, he entered the office taking the padlock with him. A short while after, a new gleaming red BMW pulled up and parked next to the Porsche. Both cars would have graced any executive vehicle showroom. A short, squat shaven-headed muscular man, who reminded him of a Turkish wrestler that he had once seen at a wrestling contest on Worthing Pier, exited the passenger door; whilst the driver, a slim, well-groomed, silver-haired man in his fifties, also alighted from the car and immediately opened the boot of the vehicle and took out a large heavy brief case. By his mannerisms, demeanour and the appearance of having a bodyguard, Dutch judged him to be the boss of the outfit, 'Billy Big Bollocks' as Dutch commonly referred to such people. Both men, also finely suited and booted, then entered the office and a short time later, the intimidating looking passenger emerged and made several trips from the office carrying and placing what appeared to be cases of spirits or similar into the boots of both pristine cars. As he did so, Dutch was able to glance through the open door of the office and saw that there was a large number of identical cardboard boxes stacked inside. After closing the boots, this man returned to the office closing the door behind him. Dutch noted the time as being a little after 5 pm.

A few minutes later, the door of the office opened, the driver of the Porsche shouted a foreign sounding name and the cashier hurried over to him; after an exchange in a foreign language, the cashier shouted to one of the valets,

"Jorge, go, see Mr Stan?"

One of the cleaners engaged in the vehicle cleaning walked over to the cabin and entered, closing the door behind him. The cashier then returned to his original position and a short time later, Dutch heard a commotion inside the office; after a few minutes, the door was opened and the cleaner exited by stumbling down the steps, obviously now in pain as he was slightly bent over and his face was now reddened as if he had been beaten. Before the office door was closed, Dutch could see and hear the 'Turk' laughing with the other two present and at the same time taking what appeared to be a metal, silver-coloured knuckle duster from his hand and putting it in his pocket. The injured cleaner slowly made his way to the mess hut holding a small brown envelope and painfully stumbled through an open cabin door. Shortly after this, the cashier indicated for another of the staff to go to the office containing the three men; on this occasion, the male cleaner wearing the ear stud entered and returned almost immediately passing Dutch, also holding a similar brown envelope. He was shortly followed by the female cleaner who also entered the cabin and at the same time, the person, who had waved Dutch through the hot air dryer, informed him that his van was ready. Dutch took a £20 note from his wallet and requested a receipt. The cleaner then pulled off his wet glove to take the note and as he reached for it with his outstretched right hand, three fingers and a stub of a finger became clearly visible. As the man took the note for a brief moment in time, Dutch French felt his body jolt as if thousands of volts had passed through him and remained motionless, not knowing quite what to do at that precise moment. His heart was pumping rapidly and he felt the hairs on the back of his head rise knowing that the man in front of him could be one of the men responsible for the attack that he was searching for. He felt an intense anger overpower him and all of his emotions must have been visible in his face as the person now holding the money was quizzically looking at him. Dutch felt like exploding, grabbing this man and interrogating him regarding the attack but in an instance thought if he were to confront this man, he was highly unlikely to admit to such an act there and then, and all element of surprise would be lost and if a confrontation ensued, he was heavily outnumbered by his fellow workers with little evidence to justify his suspicions at this stage. Thinking again, allowing his intense anger to subside, he then considered that the missing finger alone was not yet enough to be certain that he was his man as he was aware that many employees in such places had been through tough times in the past and it would be very easy to lose a finger in a war-torn country or poverty-stricken areas where many of them would have come from. Dutch was already aware from his travels that some

Eastern European gangs would cut off fingers or toes of people that they considered had crossed them, and furthermore, if he was responsible, where was the van and his partner with the earring? Having taken the payment to the cashier, the same man returned to Dutch and handed him a receipt, and he was glad that he could confirm that his eyes had not been playing tricks and this man did have a finger missing from the same right hand that Melanie had indicated. Although accepting the receipt, if this sighting panned out the way he hoped, he would be destroying any evidence that he had been present there, especially as to what was going through his mind. Before entering his van, he observed the female cleaner also leaving the building with an envelope and deduced from what he had seen that this was possibly pay day at the site—which may account for why this man, if found to be responsible, had been drinking on the Friday when his wife was attacked. Dutch surmised that the so-called office was not only being used for administration purposes but also as an illicit storeroom for bootleg booze and possibly other items, hence the extensive security of the building and that 'Turk' was not only Billy's minder but also the muscle present to quell any disagreement with staff wages. The roughed-up employee had possibly disputed his wages and had taken a beating for doing so.

As he drove out of the compound, as a result of what he has observed, he felt mixed emotions. On one hand, a sense of pride as his determination and patience had possibly paid off but on the other had been further incensed, not only for possibly locating one of the men responsible for ruining both, his wife and his life, but had now witnessed the three obnoxious thugs 'pitch up', show off their physical power and parade themselves around in their expensive clothes, cars and bling in front of their sorry-looking workforce, who had probably just received a pittance of a wage; this type of person, in his mind, fed off the misery they inflicted on people who were in no position to defend themselves. They were able to exploit the workers who wholly relied on the employment and had no choice but to be treated in this way as they probably had all manner of holds over them and therefore, could be subjected to blackmail or violence by such controlling gangs. These three were big time bullies. In his mind, he viewed them no better than leeches—similar to the blood sucking creatures that he had encountered in previous jungle expeditions. This behaviour brought back sad memories as it was identical to the bullying that he and his siblings had encountered in the past. He detested such people who went through life terrorising and using innocent people for their own pleasure with no regard to them or the destruction they leave behind. To combat this sort of person was exactly why he joined the army and why he tried to join the police. From time to time, when he had such bitter feelings towards such conceited people with wealth and power, he would question himself: was he, in fact, jealous of their position in life? But soon, came to the realisation that it was nothing of the sort, he had always had an intense dislike for bullying, arrogance and greed since childhood and would never wish to be remotely like them. Dutch thought from what he had witnessed, the driver of the Porsche deserved the derogatory response prompted by its registration mark. He was now desperate to possibly locate the van concerned and on leaving the premises, instead of turning right to join the main estate road, he turned his van left into a small adjoining business park. His search was fruitless until he drove into a secluded area, outside of a large storage unit business, where he saw a large, white Vauxhall Movano van, which was obscured from the view of personnel in the car wash compound by other buildings giving the impression as being hidden away. He parked his van a short distance from the larger van and approached the rear on foot immediately noticing several dents in the rear doors of a vehicle that had seen far better days. There was also damage to the rear door handle from which the integral locking cylinder was missing and the security of these doors had been substituted by a robust hasp, suitable for the use of a padlock, which was not attached. As a result of this, it was of no surprise to him that he found the rear doors unlocked. He wondered to himself what it was with these people and their apparent requirement for padlocks as he had encountered three in a short space of time, but fortunately they were not bothering to secure this particular one. When he was certain of being unobserved, he fully opened one of the rear doors and saw exactly what his wife had described. There were cushions and blankets on the floor and at the rear of the front seats, secured by bungee ropes, were two 35-litre plastic containers of vehicle shampoo, both labelled with an emblem of shield. In the centre of the shield, within a red circle, was a sword held in a gloved hand with 'Pajzs' printed vertically down the blade, identical to the image found on his computer research. The interior gave the impression of worker's transport, especially as there were very few vehicles parked inside or outside the car wash compound. He carefully closed the door in the knowledge that he now knew for certain that he has discovered at least one of the two responsible together with the vehicle involved in the abduction and rape of his wife but who was the other? Could it be that he did not work there, or could it possibly be the cleaner with the stud in his ear, having removed and concealed the very distinctive earing?

Before returning to his van, he took a special interest in reading the large yellow and blue printed banners affixed to the fence near the gate, which stated the prices of each size of vehicle cleaned and more importantly, as far as he was now concerned, the opening and closing times of the premises.

He was desperate to confront the man who he believed responsible, and he knew that any reasonable, sensible person would inform the police of his discovery and when presented with all of the evidence, they would have ample to arrest and possibly prosecute, but he was never known to be reasonable or sensible when it came to matters concerning the heart and principle. If they were to appear before a court, there was no guarantee of a guilty plea, therefore requiring his wife to attend and be a witness and he was not prepared for her to be forced to do this against her will when, as far as he was concerned, there were other methods that he had already in mind.

He then parked his vehicle in such a position where he could observe the Vauxhall van without him being visible from the site or to anyone returning to it, pondering as to his next move to fulfil the satisfaction that he required to give him peace within himself.

As he did so, perusing various solutions, he caught site of a man leaving the site, walking up the slope towards the main public road running through the estate. He could see by the persons gait that he was in some discomfort and recognised him as being the worker roughed up by the Turk.

As far as Dutch knew, this particular employee had no connection to Melanie's ordeal; in fact, he was on the rough end of the stick himself so perhaps, this may be an ideal opportunity to gain some information. Time to do some more homework, he thought, at the same time ensuring that there was nothing on display in the vehicle that could identify him or the company. As he drove towards him, he saw the man bending forward, holding his stomach, obviously in a distressed condition. Dutch pulled up alongside of him and saw the man was sweating, his face reddened with a large swelling on his left cheek with a straight deep cut in the centre of the contusion. His lower lip was split with an open cut that had obviously been bleeding heavily, judging from the stains on his shirt.

Both injuries were consistent with a knuckle duster, Dutch thought. By the way, he was holding his midriff—he had obviously received punishment on the lower part of his body as well.

Dutch wound down his window and said, "You look rough. Can I give you a lift somewhere?"

The injured man replied in good clear English with a European accent, "I need to get to Brighton."

"Your luck has just changed, that's where I am heading. Do you need the hospital?"

The man emphatically replied, "No, no, just Brighton, no hospital."

Dutch signalled for him to get in, which he did placing a heavy rucksack on his lap.

As soon as he was seated, the injured man said in a distressed voice, "Thank you, I didn't know how I was going to get there."

Dutch then commenced their short journey westwards on the A27 to Brighton.

"What happened back there? I was getting the van cleaned and saw most of it. Why did they do that?"

"Don't worry, it's not a problem now. They have told me to leave."

"What do you mean? Have they sacked you?"

"If you mean no more work, then yes, and I must leave their house in Brighton by tonight; otherwise, I will get more of this," pointing to his face.

"Did you do something really bad then?"

"No, they are just evil people who can do what they like. Nobody can touch them."

"You must have seriously pissed them off though."

"Do you know them?"

"No and what I've seen of them, I wouldn't want to. I was just passing through, saw the signs for the car wash and popped in. Never been here before."

"Then I will tell you. These people are big, you know big in all things, some very bad. They have forced my sister, Kristiyana, into prostitution, she can't resist them as we were smuggled here on the condition that we worked for them. They promised us, how you say, false identity cards but they won't give them to us until we pay more

143

money. We have no more, we gave them all we had to get here. My sister is now so depressed as she is frightened and hates what she is doing, so she is taking drugs to do it, which works well for them as she relies on them for supply, she is trapped. She was never like that until we met them."

"What's that got to do with what they have done to you?"

"Are you sure you don't know any of them? Are you telling me the truth?"

"Honestly, why would I lie to you?"

"Then I will tell you but you must never tell anyone else. Some of their workers just disappear, nobody knows where they go. They could find me, their network is big. Two of the three in the office are quite big in the organisation; the other bald man who hit me, is, how you say, 'enforcer' or 'muscle'. They all come here every Friday at this time to pay the wages, which is very little when they have taken our rent away. They can pay little as they have a threat of some sort on all of the staff here. Anyway, I had telephoned them and asked them to stop giving her drugs and get her away from what she is doing. They laughed at me and said that she was the prettiest girl they had who was making good money for them so things would remain as they were. So, when they came today, they called for me, and I protested with them about my sister and got angry and this is what happened."

"They sound a nasty bunch."

"They are all very bad men. I didn't like to work in this place but I had no choice. They promised my sister a job in a bar which was false. We both paid them to get us here from Kosovo and for false documents, for a better life, but it's far worse and now I have nothing—nowhere to live."

Dutch was almost tempted to mention his previous service in Kosovo where he had been part of a humanitarian and peacekeeping force, at the same time realising that the man in his presence would have been a teenager at that time and witnessed the atrocities of a bloody internal war, which must have had a profound effect on him. This was also the campaign where he had taken possession of the Walther, but the less this man knew about him, the better. Instead, he said,

"What's with all the bottles they have in there?"

"Vodka. It's very cheap, how you say, a 'dodgy' make."

"What do you do now then?"

"I don't know. I must get out tonight; otherwise, they beat me again and throw me into the street, but I must go back to get some of my clothes. I need to find my sister but what can I offer her to get her away from them? I must try and get to my brother in Newcastle, who has been given asylum there and see if he can help."

They further talked on the 20 minute journey with Dutch revealing nothing about his true self, even creating a false name if put on the spot, with the tried and tested method of using his first pet's name, which in this case was Sinbad's dog and his mother's maiden name. Using this practice he would be able to reply quickly and confidently and most importantly wouldn't forget it. Therefore, incognito he was Jack Furminger.

Dutch insisted for the benefit of the injured man, and for his own personal information, that he would take him to his doorstep and when on the outskirts of the city, he was directed down the Lewes road and then into a long street of terraced Victorian houses situated a short distance behind the Sussex University Campus.

His passenger indicated Dutch to stop outside of a large, poorly-maintained, terraced building, which immediately gave the appearance of that of rented rooms like so many in the area, as this street and those nearby were very popular cheap accommodation for the heavy student population studying nearby.

As Dutch engaged the handbrake of the van, he said, "Do all of the workers at the Lewes car wash live here?"

"Most of them."

"How do you all get to work?"

"We use a van."

The passenger then gestured a handshake, which Dutch engaged with and said, "I didn't catch your name, although I did hear one of them call it out."

He replied, "Jorge," at the same time thanking Dutch for the lift and, fortunately, not asking for his name in return.

As he exited the van, Dutch was pleased that as Jorge walked around the front of the van, he never looked down at the number plate. Why should he? As far as he was concerned, he had just been given a lift by a Good Samaritan. He then waited and watched him enter the distinctive red door, which made it easily recognisable for any future visits if required.

Dutch had, on the face of it, found him to be a pleasant, unfortunate character, who he sympathised with as he had once witnessed the immense problems within his country, but the city was full of such cases and at this time, he had problems of his own and wanted no distractions. He was pleased that he had given him the lift which revealed much useful information including where the majority of the workers were living, knowing what transport they used, the time the wash site closed giving him a good idea as to what time they would return. As much as he wanted to, he never once mentioned the two that he was really interested in because that would have made Jorge suspicious of his concern. Looking around, it was blatantly obvious to him that this particular site would never be a suitable location for his proposed intentions, and he would return soon and await a further opportunity when better prepared.

Chapter 12

Holding Out for a Hero (1984)

Artist: Bonnie Tyler
Writer(s): Jim Steinman and Dean Pitchford

Over the next few days, whilst travelling on the A259 Sussex coast road between Brighton and Newhaven, as part of a possible plan, Dutch, with the aid of a map, casually studied locations where vehicles could be driven close to the cliff edge where there were no fences or similar obstructions to preventing them plummeting hundreds of feet to the sea below without risk to any other person, only the occupants of the transport concerned.

On the Friday of that week, he took the opportunity to leave work early, having arranged with Jon that he would make the hours up for a specific task the following day which was rostered as his day off. On his arrival at the flat, he retrieved his hand gun from its hiding place and then changed into the appropriate clothing for his task in hand. Having dressed in black combat trousers, sweater and black trainers, he stepped into and pulled on a navy-blue, disposable, all-in-one boiler suit overall with a black ski mask rolled on to his head in the form of a beanie hat. He placed the Walther pistol with a full magazine inside of the manufactured reinforced weapon pocket of the trousers. On his trouser belt was attached a knife in a sheath and a small torch, another pocket contained a pair of thin plastic protective overshoes that were provided should he have to enter homes in relation to his work, his trusty Zippo lighter and a set of latex disposable gloves. He was also in possession of a nylon draw string shoulder bag containing a roll of securing tape and a number of plastic securing immobilising ties. His breast pocket contained 50 pounds in bank notes as he was unaware of where his final destination that night would be. The only personal identification that he had on his person was his dog tag, which also contained his medical information.

Life 6: As he adjusted the shoe string around his neck from which the tag hung, he cast his mind back as to the gratitude that he and others owed to this thin piece of woven material when during one of his tours in the Middle East, he was one of a forward foot patrol approaching a small village recently abandoned by Islamic state fighters, when he felt his boot loose on his foot. Remaining observant, he crouched down to tie it up and looking at an ancient, abandoned flatbed truck ahead of the advance, he noticed a suspicious looking device resting on top of the rear wheel under the protruding rubber wheel arch. He immediately halted his advancing colleagues and called for the bomb disposal officers and the device was found to be a large IED, all primed and ready for activation by the first unsuspecting soldier. There was no doubt in anybody's mind of those present that day that had Dutch not stooped down when he did, the device would not have been spotted at normal eyesight level and the result would have been catastrophic.

He telephoned Melanie to inform her that he would travel over to her parents later that evening and intended to treat them all to a take a way Chinese meal, requesting her not to telephone him on either telephone as he had some cleaning up to do. Melanie was not certain what he meant but knew it was best not to ask. He then left his mobile phone in the flat, leaving lights on and the television recording programmes whilst he was out. Before leaving the flat, he wondered if what he was about to do was worth the risk to satisfy his need for revenge for the humiliation and hurt caused to his wife and quickly decided that if he didn't go through with it, the constant reminders were too much to endure should he not take some decisive action. He then returned to the house that Jorge had been forced to vacate and eventually found a parking space in amongst the many cars parked on both sides of the street. He positioned himself so that he could watch the front of his target address without being obvious to anyone leaving or entering the property.

As he waited, he was unaware that only a few miles across the city lived a wife and mother, who were going about their normal, family-oriented day.

Having dropped off the kids for their fortnightly weekend stay at their father's home and expecting her present husband late back from the ritual Friday evening office drinks session, she was feeling somewhat bored and lonely.

"Come on, Belle, let's go," said the commanding voice of the pretty Cheryl Richardson, who looked younger than her 36 years with natural brown wavy hair and of average height and build. As she opened the rear door of her 4x4, the black and white collie leapt into the rear luggage compartment as if it had catapulted in by some mysterious force. Although she had not had a remarkable life, she had landed on her feet when she met and fell in love and married Luther, a black, high-flying company executive at the time but had now progressed to owning his own independent estate agents. They were both divorced when they first met at a mutual friend's birthday party. The family was now complete, with her two teenage children, Tom and Susie, Belle and a budgerigar named Lionel. They lived in a large detached house in the affluent Preston Park area of Brighton, near the edge of the city and close to the main arterial A23 London Road where mixed marriages, such as theirs, were unusual. Although there were parks close to their home, the largest being Preston Park, if Cheryl had time on her hands, she would drive, taking Belle in the 4x4 on the ten-minute journey to her favourite spot in the area on the Downs close to Devil's Dyke. As it was a fine, late summer's evening, she decided that due to all of the recent rainy days, she was going to take the opportunity to take a long walk in the country air as both her and Belle had been cooped up indoors for much of the preceding two days and both, dog and owner, were desperate for some fortifying exercise.

After driving a short distance north on the London road, she turned left, climbing up the steep Mill Hill and then onto Saddlescombe Road with Belle getting progressively excited as she anticipated their destination and the release from her confined space and inadequate exercise that she had recently been subjected to. On turning onto Devils Dyke road, Cheryl couldn't resist continually turning her head to the left, looking at the magnificent view of sea meeting land with the large ships on the horizon. Such a view was not always available at this time of year as sea mist and low cloud at this high point often obstructed the scene below. She was soon to indicate her intention to turn right into a small gravel car park, conveniently constructed for such visits as theirs. She was continuously conscious and grateful as to how after only a few minutes car journey, she could leave a busy world behind and find such peace and tranquillity; she preferred this particular spot rather than the more popular and busy location a mile ahead. Having stopped her car, she alighted quickly as the exuberant Belle was so excited that the noise inside was deafening, and as she opened the rear door, the dog exited in the same manner as she had entered, immediately running between a gap in the bushes onto the well-worn footpath of their usual choice. After locking the car and ensuring that she was in possession of her mobile phone, her thoughts of taking a cautionary umbrella were halted when realising that any wind on this summit would just turn it inside out, rendering it useless. As she strode towards Belle, who was now patiently waiting with her tail wagging frantically, Cheryl noticed that there were two other unoccupied cars parked there, the occupants being somewhere in the great expanse of rolling countryside. Following walking the short distance parallel to the minor road, they both then crossed it, joining the footpath where it was her general practice—depending on the anticipated weather conditions—to walk to a large pylon situated in the distance on one of the high peaks. She would only make the whole journey when being confident with the weather, as to get caught out in the rain and mist in such exposed conditions could prove very uncomfortable. The forecast had been reasonable, so off they both set.

Shortly before 6 pm, Dutch saw a large white van turn into the street; he immediately recognised it as being from the car wash site. The van was driven slowly up the street, moving alongside the parked vehicles, obviously searching for a parking space of which there were very few, especially not sufficient for a large van, but much to Dutch's surprise, the van did stop in front of a gap between two cars and started to reverse into it. Dutch, who remained in his discreet position, took great interest in how the vehicle was going to fit in, what he considered to be, a very tight space. After many attempts, the van eventually squeezed between the vehicles but not before bumping both cars heavily front and rear. Dutch saw the vehicle behind the van jolt as the tow bar, which he knew was attached to the rear of the van, came in contact with it. He was appalled at the ignorance of the driver, as any of its passengers could have alighted and assisted the driver in the manoeuvre. Once finished playing bumper cars, the driver and passenger climbed out of the van, and was delighted to see that even from a distance, he could identify the passenger as the worker with the missing finger. As both walked away from the van, neither gave the cars, they had obviously damaged, a second look. They were then joined by four persons who emerged from the rear of the van, when two of them, a man and a woman he also recognised from the site, gave farewell gestures to the remainder of the group and walked away leaving the remaining four, which included his target, to walk up the steps and through the red door.

About 30 minutes later, his suspect, together with the cleaner who he recognised as the male who he had seen at the site with the stud in his ear, appeared from the house, both in a change of clothing, and what was particularly striking was that 'Stubby' was now wearing a burgundy-hooded jogging top and 'Studdy' donned a black, cotton or woollen hat, both items identical to those described by Melanie. If Dutch had only been 99% sure that these were the men responsible, their attire had now made him 100% positive. Dutch, now certain in himself that the stud was a substitute for an earring that was, as a result of publicity, too distinctive to be on show. Both men entered the van which was manoeuvred out of the tight space by the same shunting method as used when parking. The vehicle was then driven off, immediately followed by Dutch who was pleased but not surprised there was still no padlock affixed to the clasp on the rear doors. After a journey of about three miles, the Vauxhall turned into Hangleton shopping parade, which was a very familiar location to Dutch with it being only approximately one mile from his flat, where he observed the vehicle park in the pub car park and the two enter the licensed premises. Dutch then parked his van behind the parade of shops, where he could see no sign of CCTV cameras; he then walked to the front of the parade wearing the ski mask in the form of a hat and the pair of tight-fitting latex gloves, appearing to any bystander as being a workman who had just finished work, going to the pub for a quick pint. As he strode across the car park, when he was sure that there was no one around, he seized the perfect opportunity to execute his plan and hurried to the Vauxhall van and entered the unlocked rear door, closing it behind him. Once inside, he peered over the top of the front seats and saw the words 'The Bombardier' emblazoned on the red white and blue pub sign. With the image of an artillery soldier from the Great War peering down directly on him, he thought how appropriate this was for this ex-soldier and the task in hand. He now realised that he was in a position to dictate where, when and how this scenario would end. At this stage, he had no idea how it would pan out, but if this mission was to fail in some way, he would, if necessary, always have the option to run and there would be little chance of anyone catching him, and as long as no one saw his face,

151

there would be no reason for him to be a suspect, hopefully leaving him to strike another day.

After pulling on the overshoes, he then waited cautiously whilst observing the main entrance to the public house.

On reaching their destination, Cheryl rewarded Belle with some of her favourite treats and for herself, a small chocolate bar which she thought the exercise would justify. After a short rest of taking in the sights, they both made their way back along the chalk paths, encountering the usual hiker or cyclist on the way, and as they progressed, she noticed that the renowned Downs' mist was starting to roll in and obstruct her view and was grateful that she had left it no later to make her return journey.

After an uncomfortable wait, despite the use of one of the cushions on the cold, ribbed metal floor, Dutch observed both men leave the licensed premises and commence walking towards the van. Dutch secreted himself by lying down at the rear of the seats alongside the two secured soap containers, at the same time, covering himself with a large blanket and cushions and pulling the ski mask down over his face, and now had his loaded weapon in his favoured right hand. The men entered the van talking loudly and laughing and speaking alternatively in English and their native tongue and soon, there was a strong smell of alcohol in the air. Dutch listened intently to their conversation trying to decipher the foreign language being spoken, at the same time, trying to keep his breathing as shallow and as quiet as he could. Dutch was aware that he was now in a position where there was no turning back and at the next opportunity, when the circumstances were in his favour, he would need to strike, as the element of surprise was essential and the longer he remained in the van, the more chance there was of him being discovered. Being unsure how events will now unfold or if he can actually kill in a cold blood non-combat situation despite his anger and desire for ultimate revenge, but by having the gun, he had the means to dictate the outcome from now on. This would not be the place to initially confront them as the van was too close to the pub, and he could hear voices in the smoking area outside.

As the van was driven out of the pub car park, both were still very talkative, almost excitable, discussing very crudely what they would like to do with a barmaid they had just encountered and obviously had no idea of his presence. Further chatting between the two was mainly in English, occasionally lapsing into their native tongue. He was pleased with their incessant talking and laughing, as it masked any sound of his breathing and any slight adjustment he was forced to make with his body due to the jarring of the uncomfortable, cold, metal flooring beneath his bony spine. As Dutch was so familiar with the area, he was able to trace, in his mind, exactly the roads they were travelling on despite him being in darkness under the blanket. He felt the van turn out of the pub car park and left onto Hangleton Road, then continue on down into the dip, close to his flat, before ascending the steep King George VI Avenue. On reaching the roundabout, the van took a left turn onto Sadlescombe Road and then another left turn onto Devil's Dyke Road. Dutch could visualise that to the left of the van was a view of the sea overlooking Hove and the town of Shoreham with its harbour and to the right were fields and hedges with the occasional lay by or small car park. After only a few minutes, the van stopped and then slowly turned around. By the conversation between the two, they were looking or waiting for someone. During the mumbled conversation, he heard one of the men say, "If we get more film, we ask Stan to pay more for it this time."

As Cheryl and Belle neared the end of their walk, they again crossed the road and walked down the adjacent grass footpath at the side of the road, where Cheryl could now see into the car park between the gaps in the bushes that only her car and one other remained, but she hardly took notice of the large, white, scruffy-looking van that slowly passed her and after turning around in the road behind her, entered the same car park where her vehicle awaited. As she entered the area through the gap, she approached the rear of her car, not fully aware of the same van parked nearby with its engine running. As she fumbled in her pockets with cold hands in search of her keys, the passenger door of the van opened and a man emerged, approached her and asked her in a foreign accent, "Can you direct us to the A23 road?"

Cheryl took an instant dislike to this man—he had a hood pulled tightly around his face, looked scruffy, unshaven, and she could smell that he had been drinking. She felt intense intimidation and suddenly recalled something Tony had told her a few weeks previously about a rape in the area involving two men in a white van, but she hadn't taken too much notice at the time because there was always some major crime going on in the city, but now she was scared and hurriedly attempted to locate her key to open the rear door to get Belle inside as quickly as she possibly could, at the same time, replying in an obviously panicked voice, "Just turn left out of here, then right, then turn left at the roundabout and you will come to it at the bottom of the hill." As she said this, the van was being slowly reversed and stopped closer to them when suddenly the passenger grabbed her arms forcibly; at the same time, the driver, who was wearing a black hat pulled low over his head, suddenly appeared from her blind side of the van and quickly opened the rear doors. She gave a loud shout causing Belle to snarl and bark, resulting in one of them aiming a kick at the dog, which must have connected as the dog gave out a loud agonising yelp. She started to scream and shout but there was no one in her sight; despite her struggling, both men pushed her forcibly into the rear of the van. As she fell in, the passenger followed her whilst the driver slammed the rear doors behind them both. As she fell to the floor on her back, the impact of which forced the air from her lungs leaving her panting for breath and facing the rear of the van, the man forced himself astride her, pinning her arms to the floor. Due to the natural light restriction caused by the design of the vehicle and the now overcast conditions, it was dark inside, and once she regained her breath, she again started to scream and as she did so, he let loose her left arm and pulled a knife from his jacket pocket and pulled out the blade from its handle; after putting the knife to her face, he placed his finger to his lips, indicating for her to be quiet. The weight of his body was hurting her chest, so she began an attempt to wriggle free, at the same time, grabbing out at anything to hold onto to assist the movement.

Dutch, who was still secreted under the blanket, although unable to see, was listening attentively to the alarming events taking place. Following the conversation outside the van, he had heard a dog yelp followed by a female protesting and screaming loudly, who had now been forcibly, against her will, placed in the rear of the van and was struggling with someone only a few feet from him; this was a scenario that he would never have envisaged when considering possible outcomes. The van then started to move slowly and aware of the advantage that there was now only one man in the rear, together with the realisation that Melanie's ordeal was going to be inflicted on yet another, he prepared himself to intervene.

As Cheryl desperately felt behind her for any object to grip onto, she felt some soft material on the van floor above her head, which she then pulled on, hoping it was secure enough to help release her from underneath his weight. As she pulled on the material with her now free, left, outstretched hand, it became lose, and she realised that it was just a blanket; at the same time, she saw the man kneeling over her suddenly divert his attention from herself to an area in the corner behind where she was laying. He then appeared to momentarily freeze as if studying something closely.

Dutch, who had readied his gun in his right gloved hand, suddenly felt the blanket covering him being pulled away, fully exposing him in the semi darkness. His vision was initially momentarily impaired due to the sudden emerging from the darkness beneath the blanket but became immediately aware that the passenger was now wearing the hood of his jacket up over his head and pulled tight around his face, astride a woman, just as his wife had described her ordeal, and this man was peering at him as in disbelief of what lay before him and was holding a knife to the woman's face. Before the hooded figure could say a word or make another move, Dutch raised the Walther and aimed it directly at the centre of his forehead; even at point blank range, Dutch realised that this has got to be his best shot ever, as this seemingly violent man was leaning over both of them with a knife in his raised hand, and if he missed his target, both of them would no doubt be stabbed to death as the perpetrators would not want any witnesses to the event. As Dutch pulled the trigger, the noise of the shot vibrated around the confined space and the bullet passed through the front of his hood and penetrated the centre of his forehead and a small, neat bloody hole appeared in the material; at the same time, Dutch was hoping that there would be no adverse bullet ricochet but was aware that the man's skull would largely reduce the velocity of the bullet. Another immediate concern was, as the assailant fell forward about to completely cover the female with his now limp body, that the knife may come in contact with either of them, but he was able, with his left hand, to grab the right wrist of the four-fingered hand holding the knife to prevent injury to either the trapped female or himself. He had been left with no choice, he had to take the shot—the man had a knife and Dutch was in no doubt that he was about to use it on one or both of them. He had shot and killed before, and had found himself in many life-threatening situations but never at so short range in such a confined space. The gun shot had been so loud that it appeared to render the woman silent, and she now remained still as the man's upper body went rigid for a second, and Dutch could see the whites of his eyes almost bulging from his head as he silently landed on her, As the knife fell from his grasp, Dutch released his grip from the man's wrist, at the same time, pushing the knife out of harm's way, immediately aware that any remote possibility of him relenting from his plan had disappeared. Following the shot fired, the driver swore loudly in English and then spoke in his native tongue expecting an answer, but as there was none, he stopped the slow manoeuvring van abruptly, applied the handbrake, unfastened his seat belt and at the same time, turned his body around and leant over the seats peering into the back of the van with his head and shoulders now immediately over top of Dutch, who had returned to his original prone position, then raised his weapon to an area between the driver's now fully-exposed chin and throat, then pulled the trigger and once again, the discharge was deafening. The driver, who now had his hat pulled low over his face, immediately fell heavily across the passenger seat, again like his accomplice without a murmur. There was no ricochet from the first bullet and Dutch thought this was probably due to the shell not exiting the skull but with the second shot, he had heard it hit the interior cab roof after penetrating softer tissue and bone.

Still wearing his mask, Dutch then pulled the passenger off the female and dragged the heavy body to the side of the van. He then immediately looked out through the front windows ensuring that there was nobody present, and once confident that the shots had not been heard, he slowly opened one of the rear doors slightly and peered out through the eyes holes of his mask, assured there were no persons in the vicinity, then fully opened the door and helped the distraught Cheryl onto the gravel surface and then assisted her in sitting onto a low grass bank that surrounded the car park.

She was shaking and crying, and it was then she realised that Belle was not present and started asking what was happening? The man in the mask didn't reply. He never spoke during the whole short incident, and she had no idea where he had come from. He then hurried away to the passenger door of the van, and shortly after he entered the driver's side, drove off in the direction of Devil's Dyke itself.

Cheryl, who still had the sound of the gunshots reverberating in her head, sat momentarily in total bewilderment as to what had occurred in those last few minutes during her shaking and sobbing; asking herself who were these people, who was the masked gunman and where had he appeared from? Was he originally a party to what was happening but relented and shot the other two involved?

Whoever and whatever he was, she was—at that moment in time—just glad that he had been there. The whole incident was insane and would be unbelievable had it not happened to her. Getting unsteadily to her feet, she had a quick look around for Belle, at the same time retrieving her mobile phone from her jacket pocket; as she did so, she spotted the dog at the side of the road about a 100 yards away. Frightened for her pet's safety in the now murky conditions, she ran towards her, calling her name. As she reached the dog, she held her tightly and dialled 999. Before the police arrived, the driver of the one remaining car, parked in the same car park as herself, arrived back with his dog. He could see that she was very distressed and helped her into her vehicle, where she waited with him until the arrival of the first police response vehicle. They arrived within ten minutes and after informing them of what had happened, and although declining hospital treatment, they informed her that in such cases, it was necessary to get her to a designated hospital as certain procedures had to be adhered to in cases such as this, and they would be requiring all the clothing that she was wearing for forensic examination. She was then conveyed to Brighton County Hospital where she was treated for the bruising to her arms and back, and able to make contact with Luther, informing him as to what had happened and requesting him to meet her at the hospital with a change of clothing. As he had been drinking Luther, now also somewhat bemused by this incredible information, called a taxi to convey him there, but before doing so made contact with his sister, Laura, requesting her to retrieve Belle from the care of police officers remaining at the car park. Following a medical examination at the hospital, Cheryl gave all of her clothing to the uniformed police officer that had accompanied her in the ambulance, commenting that she had no idea who the rescuer was or where he had come from, but was so grateful that he appeared when he did. The police were also puzzled at this strange event.

Chapter 13

Running Man (1978)

Artist: Lindisfarne   Writer: Alan Hull

Reluctantly but with no choice, he left the distressed woman sitting on the bank; then on looking through the bushes knew their position immediately as he could just make out, through the rapidly-forming mist, the lone, distant, tall chimney of the power station at Shoreham Harbour. Dutch thought to himself that in some respects, he was in the perfect location for what he had to now do, as he knew this area better than most, but on the other hand, perhaps he was too exposed and too close to home. He saw that there was an unoccupied, small saloon car parked close by, which meant that other people could suddenly appear so it required a quick exit. It was far from the type of location that he was hoping to choose, but if he was quick, all could still work out because he knew exactly what to do and his immediate destination. He then hurried back to the van, opened the passenger door and commenced to lift what he instantly knew was a dead body into the passenger side of the van, and as he did so, he noticed under the un-zipped jacket, the top buttons of the now blood-splattered shirt were undone, revealing a necklace from which hung a double crucifix earring. He felt a great sense of relief as his suspicions had now been confirmed, even though he had been fully confident that this was the other person responsible, as how many men were actually capable of such despicable acts? Having manoeuvred the body low into the passenger side so as not in view, he then entered the driver's compartment and immediately saw a mobile telephone in the centre console between the two front seats, and the penny suddenly dropped as he recollected their final conversation mentioning selling a film to Stan, and it was probably primed and ready for what they thought was going to be another similar film as to the one that Melanie suspected had been taken. This realisation hit Dutch like a dagger in his heart as he realised that it was highly likely that they had filmed Melanie's ordeal. The rape of his wife alone was enough for him to seek revenge, but this additional revelation that it probably was filmed took it to another level. Who else had these images? Who and how many had viewed them, and who the fuck was Stan? Then he remembered the personalised number plate. Thank God for show offs and personalised plates, he thought, as they had now made his task so much easier. He seized the telephone and placed it in his pocket.

The engine of the van had remained running so with a slight adjustment of the seat, he put the vehicle into motion; no need for a seat belt, he thought, as if it went bent, he may have to do a runner. As he turned right out of the car park northwards onto Devil's Dyke Road with the wheels of the van spinning on its gravel surface, he looked into the nearside wing mirror and saw the obviously distressed woman walking down the road in the opposite direction to himself towards a dog which he presumed was hers, the one he heard yelp. He disliked leaving her in that predicament but the longer he stayed with her, the more chance a walker or car would appear, and as she recovered her senses, there would be chance of her noticing and remembering some of his characteristics. He soon dismissed these negative thoughts by thinking that even now she was in a far, far better place than if he hadn't happened to be in the back of that van. In a far better place than his poor wife had been, and it was also fortunate that the two shots were immediately fatal with minimal bloodshed, neither man making any agonising sounds so as to alarm her even further.

Dutch was sure that having planned to be alone in that location, she was sure to have a mobile phone, so his time was extremely limited. He estimated that if she called the police immediately, they would probably take up to ten minutes to get to this rural location; on their arrival, they would certainly alert the force helicopter unit, but he was equally confident by his past experiences of travelling in helicopters that due to the fact that the Downs, at this point, were now covered in a dark and damp mist, if they did take off, they would only search the lower reaches of the hills due to the poor visibility, so he needed to get clear of the open ground and into the urban area as quickly as possible. If this was the case, hopefully, the van would not be located until the following day, giving him ample time to dispose of any incriminating items. He had not foreseen such circumstances where he would have so little time to make an exit from the situation. After a journey of less than half a mile, just before the road forked to either Devil's Dyke pub or the Dyke golf club, he arrived at a familiar dirt and rubble-filled track on the left-hand side of the road—one that he had passed through on many occasions when on one of his longer training runs. After a short distance, he came to the large, rusty, metal farm gate that led into a vast field, which sloped downwards from the side of the hill. The gate had never been locked in the past, and Dutch was more than thankful that he could see no securing chain to prevent entry; otherwise, he would just have to attempt to crash through it. He stopped, hurried from the van, unfastened and opened the gate, drove through, closing the gate behind him and then continued to drive the short distance onto the field and then ploughed through the thick surrounding undergrowth into the centre of a copse under a canopy of branches. As he drove deeper in, the sound of the branches scrapping on the roof and side panels of the van was deafening, but he bulldozed on until the vehicle could proceed no further due to the density of the natural obstructions. Out of site of the road and any buildings, Dutch then briefly, but calmly, searched through in his mind as to whether there was any possible evidence that he could be leaving behind—no fingerprints because he was wearing gloves; he wasn't bleeding so there was none of his blood, but he was certain to have traces of both of the deceased's blood on his clothing but that problem could be dealt with later, and there would be no sole prints because he was wearing overshoes. His attention now was drawn to the rear of the van where he needed to retrieve the two shell cases that had ejected from the gun following each discharge and find the mobile phone of the passenger. The retrieving of the shells was not vital because he had disposal plans for the weapon but why leave any evidence behind at all. He could leave the gun at the scene as he had no connection to it and its origin was untraceable, but due to the amount of times he had handled and cleaned it, he could not be sure that there was not a partial fingerprint or hair somewhere on the weapon or shell casings, and he wasn't willing to take any chances. As neither of the front doors of the van could now be opened due to them being wedged against the branches of the saplings surrounding the majority of the van, he climbed over the seat into the rear section. He couldn't immediately see the shell cases but as the rear doors were only just screened by light branches at the very perimeter of the wooded area, he was able to open them both and together with his torch, made the entire interior more visible. He picked up one blanket from the floor and as he did so, one shell case fell from it which he retrieved in his gloved hand. He then shook the remaining blanket in the hope that the other was tucked inside but it did not appear. Dutch then searched amongst the loose cushions that were now strewn about but nothing. He then decided to look under the corpse in the rear and as he turned him on his side avoiding a large pool of blood that had developed, he saw the remaining shell case under the area of the chest; he retrieved it and placed it in the zipper pocket of the overalls with the other, and then searched the pockets of the lifeless body and located the desired telephone. He then exited the van, closing the doors behind him. Dutch was confident that he had now left no DNA or other evidence so he would not have to torch the vehicle which was just as well, because if he had been required to do so, the van would have been found very quickly as the copse would have also ignited, giving him less time than he already had. He also required everything intact as he wanted the police to realise that this was the van and men responsible for the rape of his wife and the very recent attempted abduction, and from all the evidence found would certainly close both cases, and Melanie would never have to worry about being further interviewed or being required for court appearances. He did now, however, have to remove all data-containing cards from both phones in order to destroy any images they may have contained of his wife's ordeal. He was aware that only a phone itself could be tracked by its unique emitting signal, not standard data cards when removed from their housing, which due to his desperate hurry, he would not have time to interrogate for any images, so he removed the cards from both phones, placed them in his pocket and tossed the intact handsets into the rear of the van. Dutch realised that the police would soon discover the removal of the cards, but they would have no knowledge as to why this action had been taken. He now exited the area through the open field surrounding the copse and onto the wooded paths that led in and out of the valley below and hopefully, would remain unseen until he reached a built-up area. Once surrounded by trees, he quickly took off the gloves, mask and overshoes—all of which had remained in place throughout the entire incident—climbed out of the overall and placed them all together with the gun, knife and torch in the backpack, which he then slung over his shoulders.

He then commenced to run the three miles of his normal route from this point back towards his home, which he could have almost completed blindfolded, which at first was almost the case due to the heavy mist and fine rain surrounding the summit. As he ran to lower ground, the visibility improved, and he would have looked to any other rare users of these particular paths as just another runner using the down land footpath for exercise. As he ran, he briefly reflected on the shooting, and how grateful he was that the Walther had not given him a reoccurrence of the Mall moment as he and the woman had been in a perilous position when the passenger, armed with a knife, first saw him. Realising that if he became a suspect by the police, it was essential that all he was wearing is destroyed, especially the boiler suit, which was sure to have some traces of blood. During his flight, he thought as how both men had died instantly, not a murmur from either of them, which was the best outcome as he would not have wanted either moaning in pain, giving the abducted woman even more of a traumatic experience than she had already encountered. He continued to run through the grass and wooded areas skirting part of the Brighton and Hove golf course, and as he did so, he was already plotting the fate of Stan and his two cronies, but as incensed as he was, he knew that he had to be patient, hopefully remain undetected, let the heat die down and after careful planning, strike. On leaving the cover of the woods, he was vulnerable and exposed for a short period as he crossed the pedestrian bridge over the busy A27 dual carriageway and then diverted from his usual training route onto the Hangleton housing estate. On reaching a road and entering the built-up area, so as not to attract attention, he altered his running stride to brisk walk. As he made his way back towards the rear of the shopping parade and his own van, looking to his left to the other side of the valley that he had just traversed, on the horizon, he could see, in the mist, the dim-blue light of a fast-moving emergency vehicle travelling towards the car park that he had fled from. In those few minutes before reuniting with his van and driving the short distance home, he had a feeling of extreme nervousness and foreboding, as if he was discovered at that point with what he had in his possession, he would not have a leg to stand on. He had considered stashing the incriminating items but what if the van in the copse was located quickly, a police tracker dog was more than capable of following his scent and therefore, locating any discarded property. Although he realised that he needed to ditch the damming items quickly, but not in too much haste so as to make a mistake. He started to consider all options open to him and soon came to a decision.

On reaching his own transport, ensuring that he could not be seen, he broke down the gun and separated the contents of his bag depending on his planned method of disposal of each item. On his arrival at his home, before entering his flat, he unlocked his garage door and by the aid of a self-installed free-standing car battery lighting system, removed all items from the shoulder bag apart from the loaded pistol and the two shell cases. He then separated the overall and trainers, the remaining items—the torch, knife, tape and ties—he placed in his tool box, after removing the bullets that were secreted in its base. Dutch placed these bullets in the bag together with the gun and spent rounds, locked the garage door and entered his flat unobserved in stocking feet. Once inside following cutting up the telephone data cards, he placed the small pieces in a pocket of the soon to be discarded trousers together with other garments that he had been wearing into a plastic carrier bag. Even though he had been wearing gloves throughout, he vigorously washed his hands and showered, then changed into track top and bottoms. Following telephoning Melanie to make arrangements for their evening meal, he returned to the garage with the bag of clothing, then placing the overalls and trainers into the carrier bag with the discarded garments, which he in turn placed into his shoulder bag and into the van. He then drove to the outskirts of Shoreham, where a large long wooden pedestrian bridge crossed the River Adur. He walked to the centre of the bridge which was as usual deserted at that time of the evening and unobserved from his shoulder bag, he removed and threw the pieces of the now broken-down pistol, all of the bullets and the two spent rounds into the dark water below. He was aware that the river was tidal at this point, but there was always a constant stream of water in the centre of the channel where he had dropped them, and with his knowledge of this waterway, he knew that the metal objects would soon sink in the deep silt. He regretted having to dispose of it all, but he was aware that if he did, at any stage, become a suspect, the police would complete a wide search around the area of his home and they may come across the hide; it was one thing being caught in possession of an illegal weapon and entirely another being detected with one that had killed two people. On returning to the van, Dutch placed the bag containing the remaining clothing and trainers under the passenger seat and drove back to his flat where he collected his mobile phone, which if investigated by the police would show as being located in his flat at the time of the shootings. He then turned the TV recording off, which he planned to watch the following day should he be required to provide an alibi as to his whereabouts that evening. After making a visit to his local Chinese restaurant, he collected a meal for Melanie, her parents and himself, then drove to Woodingdean. On his way, he hid the bag and contents in bushes on the route that he planned to travel early in the morning, then spent the evening with Melanie, Jodie and the in-laws. When he got the opportunity, he informed his wife very briefly that he had been dealing with a situation; he told her no more at this time and she didn't ask as the true facts would have impaired her improving mental health. Dutch realised that they would have to discuss the circumstances when Melanie was in a better place. He returned home with Jodie for an early night as he needed an early start for work. He was unable to make up his mind if this outcome was a good or bad result; on the good side, the deed which he felt necessary had been completed and without his intervention, a further brutal rape would have taken place. The fact that the two were going to repeat their crime made what may have been a difficult decision far easier as he had no other choice to do what he did in the back of that van. On the down side, he had been forced to act in haste, not at all in the manner that he had foreseen; he had envisaged conducting the outcome at his pace, leaving the scene calmly and fully confident that he had covered his tracks. Because the situation had been frenzied and rushed, he was concerned that he may have left some vital clue but at that time couldn't think what that may be. Before going to sleep that night and as for every other night during his future planning, he would run through in his mind every little detail, no matter how small, that he had completed or needed to complete in order to avoid detection. If he ever thought he may have left any clues whatsoever, he would write it down at his bedside in a coded format as to what he needed to do to amend the situation and after doing so, destroyed the memorandum.

Chapter 14

The Self-Preservation Society (1969)

Artists: The Cast of the Italian Job Movie
Writer: Quincy Jones

Jake brought the eye-catching, pimped-up, red, 'Italian Job' styled Mini Cooper with the union flags he had painted neatly on its roof, boot lid and wing mirrors to a stop outside the tall, white-terraced Victorian Block. He was pleased that his friend was there, standing in his doorway ready to go. He hated it when Craig kept him waiting on that busy road, fearing that some unobservant, speeding motorist would plough into the rear of the motor he had invested so much time and money on—apart from the insurance. He had not declared the engine modification as the cost would have been prohibitive. Craig strode down his path towards the car, and Jake noticed that he was, once again, kitted out in new clothes. He was an only child to wealthy parents, who spoilt him in every way possible. He had no interest in cars or passing his driving test. Why should he when Jake or his parents conveyed him everywhere, and if neither were available, the cost of a taxi was no bother to him. It amazed Jake as to how a salesman in a phone shop, who spent most of his money on booze and weed, could still have all the luxuries in life. Craig got in the car and closed the door. Before any greetings between the two could be exchanged, he said excitedly, "I've rolled two fat doobies. Where are we going to smoke these big boys, the usual place?"

"Sounds good to me. What—then back to Black Rock and meet up with the rest of the crew? If there's no Bill around, I'll show them a few moves this baby can do, but we're not smoking in here from now on, not with these new seats. I don't want fag burns in them or reeking of weed."

"I find it odd that you'll thrash the guts out of the engine but are obsessive about the interior."

"These engines were made for high performance, but I don't want it looking or smelling like a doss house in here," Jake replied sternly.

Jake drove onto the Seven Dials roundabout and onto Dyke Road, making their way out of town, passing the mansions of the rich and famous on each side. At that time of the evening, their journey would only take a short time, unlike in daylight hours when traffic was stop and start.

They left the built-up area and climbed towards the Downs, entering the regular Downs mist of light beads of drizzle, which were now zigzagging across the windscreen.

"Fucking marvellous, s'raining now," griped Craig.

"We'll have to get a bit wet then, won't we? We can't light up in here—or are you afraid of messing up your hair?"

"Fuck off, it's not my hair I'm bothered about. I don't want to be in damp clothes all night."

"Yeah, right." Jake flipped his mate the finger, keeping his eyes fixed on the entrance to their destination ahead. He slowed the car and prepared to turn right from Devil's Dyke Road into the small car park surrounded by bushes. Blue-and-white police incident tape was strung across the only access and entry point, with a police's 'No Entry' sign in the centre of the gap.

"Well, that's fucked that plan up," he said, continuing to drive ahead.

"I wonder what happened there, then?" said Craig. "I don't know why we come all the way out here anyway—if we went into town, no one'd look twice anyway."

"If you hadn't noticed, you doughnut, this motor stands out a bit and the bill love to pull over people of our age, wind them up and search them for drugs and weapons. So why ask such stupid questions when you've got weed on you?"

"All right, all right, just relax, will you? OK, mastermind, where do we go now? You are in need of getting mighty chilled tonight, mate."

Jake didn't reply. He was becoming irritated, tired of these Friday night jaunts, tired of Craig, truth be told, and the crowd they hung out with, who had no interest in anything other than sitting around, talking crap and smoking weed. At college he'd recently met Pippa who was doing 'A' levels. Jake knew that she was way more clever than he was, and she had her future all mapped out—university, career, everything—but she seemed to really like him and was more understanding than most people he knew, and when the opportunity arose, he planned to ask her out. They'd started to meet up in college breaks, and she'd been the first person to suggest that he could be more ambitious for himself, although he had come a long way from being a prolific, illegal graffiti artist to now being an apprentice sponsored by a major bodywork specialist group. She had suggested that maybe he use his artistic abilities for something more than custom paint jobs on boy racers' cars and admiring the works of Banksy. There was no way he was going to mention her to Craig or that lot; he got enough flak from them for still being at college.

His thoughts were suddenly interrupted. "Oi, Jakey boy, pull over into that track ahead. I'm dying for a piss. It must be those few pints I had at lunchtime."

Jake didn't relish the thought of turning his pride and joy onto the stony surface, but as there was no other suitable stopping place on the mist-shrouded road ahead, he surrendered to the request of his desperate friend. He drove a short distance down the track, which snaked to the right where a large metal gate was positioned shut across the path.

Immediately, the Mini stopped; Craig darted out of his seat and ran over to urinate against the grey, rusty gate. As he did so, Jake continuously flashed his headlights at his vulnerable target, the two regular headlights plus the additional three spotlights illuminating him in the damp and misty night air.

Craig responded by shouting, "Pervert." He was enjoying a sense of great relief from his predicament when he noticed that the flashing headlights distinctly illuminate a pair of red rear-light reflectors of a vehicle in the wooded area in front of him on the other side of the gate. The rear of the vehicle was fairly exposed, and he could see that it was a large white van.

Hastily zipping his flies, he went to speak to Jake through the driver's side open window.

"There's a big old van parked in amongst the trees down there. It's probably the farmer's old run around—we could have a smoke in that."

"Don't be daft. It's probably locked anyway, or it could be someone shagging."

"No one would drive right in there like that just to have sex. It might have been nicked and abandoned. Let's go and have a look."

"Don't bother—you've had a piss, let's go."

"Give me a minute—I'm curious. Put your headlights on full beam so I can see."

"You know what curiosity did, don't you?"

With that, Craig opened the gate and pushed through the sparse vegetation at the edge of the wood. He approached the van; both front doors were hemmed in by branches and undergrowth and the only visible entrance and exit to the vehicle was via the rear doors. By simultaneously pulling the broken handle and hasp, Craig slowly and quietly opened both doors bit by bit and apprehensively peered inside. With the aid of the headlights, he could vaguely see two large plastic containers positioned behind the front seats, some cushions and what he first thought to be a bundle of clothing. This, he examined more closely. Feet and a hand were protruding—it was a person. He was about to close the door quietly so as not to wake the occupant, who he presumed was a vagrant, when the lights reflected the deep red of a large pool of blood on the floor around the body. Craig immediately let go of the door and ran back to his friend who was still sitting behind the wheel.

"Jake, you're not going to believe what's in there," he gasped.

"What the hell has spooked you? You look like you've seen a ghost."

"I just might have done—there's someone in there and they are either dead or injured, and there's loads of blood on the floor…"

"Stop pissing about and get in. If you're trying to freak me out, it's not working."

"No, Jake, I mean it. Look at me—I'm the one freaked out—look, I'm shaking."

"While you're shaking, shake the mud off your shoes, you've got crap all over them. You're not getting them on the mat."

"Fuck the mat, this is serious."

His actions and tone of voice got the attention he required of Jake.

"You're not kidding, are you? What did you see?"

"At first, I thought it was just clothes on the floor in the back, then I saw a hand and feet and blood. What shall we do? Shall we go back and check it out?"

"What do you mean 'we'? I'm not going near it."

"What shall we do then? They might be alive and bleeding to death!"

"If you're sure of what you've seen, then we have to call 999, inform them and get out of here."

"Yeah, the only problem there is that they will then have one of our phone numbers so we can't leave here; otherwise it will look like we had something to do with whatever has happened."

"Right. We have no choice but to stay here until someone comes, and you've got those joints on you."

"I'll chuck them."

"Wise up—if there's a body in there, they'll get a dog here and they'll find them, and who will they suspect of throwing them there?"

"How do we explain why we're here to the police and our families?"

"We'll just tell the truth, we went for a drive and I pulled in here for you to have a piss. The other alternative is to forget what you've seen. Or you go up onto the road, chuck the joints well into the bushes and we make the call."

"Bingo—that's the answer. We can't just leave it, we'd never forgive ourselves, but I'm not going back down there."

"Nor me. Go and chuck them. I'll call the police and ambulance if you're certain what you saw—remember the light's not good and it's misty."

"I know what I saw. I'll never forget it," said Craig. He left the car and hurried up the path towards the road, striking a match to light up one of the reefers.

Jake had obviously seen him. "Craig, don't be a prat! The police will be all over this place like a rash soon and if they smell that on you, we'll both get searched. We need to look whiter than white so we can get out of here as soon as possible."

"I suppose so. It just seems such a waste to throw them away."

Chapter 15

Cover Your Tracks (2012)

Artist: A Boy & His Kite   Writer: Dave Wilton

When he awoke early the next day, Dutch changed into his working clothes and boots, then drove and collected the rucksack and bag containing the garments and trainers that he wore at the time of the shooting from the bushes where he had secreted them the previous evening, then continued his journey to the village of Loxwood situated on the West Sussex/Surrey border where he had arranged with Jon to tidy the site and burn all of the remaining debris that the company had removed from the canal during a dredging operation the previous week where fallen branches from overhanging trees had been impeding the pleasure barges that used it. As he drove out of the city limits northwards on the A23, he looked to his left in the direction of the nearby Downs, half expecting to see the police helicopter searching the area of the Dyke below. As the sky was now clear and visibility was good, he wondered as that was not the case had the van and its contents been discovered already? If so, all the more reason to discard all incriminating evidence now back in his possession immediately. On reaching his village destination, he drove along a dirt track that ran adjacent to the Wey and Arun Canal until he reached a lock gate, close to where the work had taken place. Following the retrieving of the now dried, recovered branches, he chose an open space and placed them into a large pile at the same time reflecting on the incident in his past when without such a fallen obstacle, he would have surely drowned.

Life 7: He had been involved in a joint international military training exercise in Norway when a temporary pontoon bridge, on which he and other troops were crossing, was without warning hit by an ice pack, causing all on the bridge at the time to be jettisoned into the fast-flowing freezing river; with his heavy backpack and thick winter clothing, he was unable to swim in the fast current, managing to free himself from his baggage, he was just able to keep his head above the icy water which fortunately pushed him speedily towards the river bank and a large submerged fallen pine tree, which, with some difficulty, he was able to cling to until help arrived. He was found totally exhausted and suffering from hyperthermia, and it was estimated that only a few more minutes in the freezing conditions would have been fatal. Before being removed from the scene, he was able to request one of his rescuers to snap a small twig from the tree that saved him, and he retained the sprig in a box containing his service memorabilia, which signified yet another lucky escape. Two other soldiers swept away in the incident had not been so fortunate.

Dutch then took the bag from the van together with a can of petrol, which was always carried in every one of the work's vehicles for fuel for the mobile generators. Ensuring that he was not observed, he placed the rucksack and its contents into the wood stack, which he poured fuel over and ignited. When he had completed all the necessary burning and satisfied that the blaze had thoroughly destroyed the bag and all its contents and the fire fully extinguished, he shovelled up the ashes and scattered them about the barren area. Before finalising his work and leaving the site and returning home, he looked into the canal and was pleased that he hadn't decided to dispose of the gun parts there, as the water was quite shallow, and although the canal wouldn't be dredged again for some time, he didn't want the possibility of Jon's company employees finding it at a later date as Jon by then would probably have a good guess as to who put it there and why.

That afternoon, he visited Melanie and following a long walk on the beach with Jodie, they spent the early evening in the city before the couple were separated once again as Melanie still couldn't bring herself to be alone in the flat even for a short period. Throughout the day, Dutch was pleased that there appeared to be no public news about the findings of bodies on the Dyke, and he wondered if they had been discovered yet, but he certainly wasn't going to go anywhere near the place to investigate, he was aware that many offenders had made that mistake in the past.

Sunday was always a good day to visit London so he drove to Woodingdean early as planned, met with Melanie and her parents and it was decided that Dutch could drive them all in Ken's beloved, comfortable and roomy Jaguar. They journeyed to Greenwich, then took the Thames clipper boat service into the city where they spent the day in the Covent Garden area watching all the buskers and sideshows momentarily, bringing their lives back to normal for a short time, pushing the recent horrors to the backs of their minds. Nothing about that fateful night was ever mentioned when all together, it was only ever discussed on a one to one basis. Although not actually stated, the day's relaxation acted as a great relief to each and every one of them.

Early Monday morning, once again alone at the flat, Dutch received his early morning job message from the company office. He was required to go to the castle town of Arundel and inspect and report back on a suspected mains leak.

During that morning's work, he received a telephone call and saw that the screen of his mobile indicated Melanie; he was almost prepared as to what she was about to say as he was sure that a discovery had been made by now.

"Den, I have had a call from the police saying that at the weekend, they found two dead bodies in a van near Devil's Dyke and subject to forensic tests; they are sure it's the same two that attacked me. This sounds harsh but I hope it is them, and I can then stop worrying about ever seeing them again, but it's scary that they have been found so close to the flat."

"That's great news. It is probably them if the police are convinced enough to have contacted you. Don't you be worried about feeling pleased, anyone would after what they put you through. Did they say how they died?"

"No, they said it wasn't for public information yet, but they wanted me to know before I saw any publicity following their press release."

"I can't talk at length now, I'm halfway to fixing a pipeline. As soon as I've finished here, I have another job near Brighton, so I will pop in to see you. Will you be at your mum's?"

"Yeah, I will be here all day."

Later that day, Dutch stopped by Melanie's parents' home and spoke with his wife alone in the back garden.

Dutch swallowed heavily and steadied himself before saying,

"I don't know how to even start to tell you this but, Melanie love, I have done something very wrong in the eyes of the law. Not in my eyes but against the law and it's as serious as it gets, so much so that I will have to possibly leave the country for a while if not forever."

"What on earth are you talking about? What could you have done that bad apart from murder? Oh no, it wasn't you who found them and killed them, say you haven't?"

"I caught up with them and in the end, circumstances forced me to shoot and kill them both."

"Circumstances…what circumstances could have forced you to do that?"

"Yeah, I know that sounds weird, but I hid in the back of the same van they forced you into, not really knowing what I was going to do to settle the score; I just wanted revenge in some way. I was in there when they drove off onto Devil's Dyke and forced a woman walking her dog into the van, just as they had done to you."

"You're not serious, none of this is true. Why are you saying all this? It's fantasy, not funny."

"No, Melanie, I'm deadly serious, I couldn't have made this up in my wildest dreams. Now listen and try to keep calm. I know this is not easy for you. Anyway, while this woman was struggling with one of them, she pulled on the blanket that was covering me, and the one that had a missing finger was almost over me with a knife in his hand, so it was him or me and probably the woman too if he had done me, so I shot him. His pal was also about to get involved, and I couldn't take any chances as I didn't know if he had weapons or not, and I wasn't about to take the risk so he got the same."

"I can hardly believe this, but I can tell you are serious. You wouldn't say this to me if it wasn't, would you?"

"No, not after what you've been through and I'm sorry about putting you through another nightmare, but I've done it now and there's no going back."

"Are you sure it was the same ones?"

"No doubt about it. The police have even confirmed it to you. Eastern Europeans, identical van, plastic containers with the sword and shield on, blankets, cushions, missing finger; the lot. I was lucky to find him as he had gloves on, but I guess that he must have been right-handed and automatically took off the wet glove to take my money at a car wash. Although the other one didn't have the earring in his ear, there was a stud in the same right ear and the double crucifix earring was on his necklace. I reckon he changed that identifying piece of jewellery when he saw the press bulletins. How

173

many blokes are their around like that who would do that to you and try it again? It's certainly not a case of mistaken identity."

"I can honestly say I'm not in the slightest bit concerned for them, but I am worried about what might happen to you. What about that poor woman and what do you, or we, do now?"

"Luckily, she was relatively unharmed and ended up walking away. My intervention prevented it from going too far. As for us, I so hope we can still find a way to stay together."

"So you saved another woman from what happened to me?"

"Basically yes and now, unless I'm very careful, I could spend a very long time in jail."

"Dennis, what possessed you to get in their van, and how did you find them?"

"I discovered it all from your description of the shield on the containers which led me to a car shampoo imported from Hungary and believing that they were from an eastern European country, where that double crucifix has some meaning, gave me the idea of checking out some car cleaning sites, and when I visited one in Lewes, I found the two of them working there and the van exactly as you had described. Please don't ask why I didn't go to the police, because you made it abundantly clear that you wanted no involvement with any court proceedings, and I didn't want you to go through that anyway, so I did it my way. It's crazy, I know but what's done is done and I, hopefully we, will have to get away just in case I've slipped up but at present, I think I've covered my tracks, but I can't hang around too long to find out."

"Get away, to where?"

"A country where I can't be forced back from."

"If I do go with you, what about Mum and Dad?"

"You will not be wanted or under suspicion even if I am, you are the injured party. You will be free to come and go as you please, but I will have to wait to see how things develop when the police put all the facts together. I am sure that I will become a suspect but hopefully, if I'm smart enough, there will be no evidence to implicate me."

"So, this is what you have been up to when I haven't been able to get hold of you, and when you have told me you would be uncontactable for a while. I suspected you were up to something but I never envisaged this. Where did you get the gun anyway? Was it the one you had hidden? I always thought that was a bad idea."

174

"Yes, it was but it's disposed of now. I couldn't have the mobile on me at certain times because as you know the police can trace their locations."

"Things were bad enough, now it's got a whole lot worse."

"Melanie, you know me better than anyone and know I could have never have let what happened rest after what they did to you. How can I regret what I have done when they were going to do exactly the same thing again had I not been there, and they would have probably carried on doing more in the future? They were like a couple of wild animals with no boundaries, morals or regrets whatsoever."

"When did all this happen?"

"Three weeks after they attacked you, I found out that they worked at a car wash in Lewes and got paid there on a Friday evening, so I followed them the following Friday. You'll never guess where to?"

"You said, Devil's Dyke."

"No, the pub they first went to, where I climbed in the back."

"Haven't a clue."

"The Bombardier."

"What? The pub just down the road at Hangleton shopping parade!"

"Yes, unbelievable, isn't it? When they came out of there that night after a few drinks, they had one intention, one only, and that was to do the same thing as they did to you and so nearly did again."

"If you gave yourself up, surely as you saved that woman, the courts would be lenient on you?"

"That maybe so but can you imagine me doing time, cooped up all day for years, I would go off my tiny nut. That's not an option."

"No, you couldn't stand being locked up and wouldn't deserve it. You've done the world a favour really but the law won't see it that way."

"When this is all over and the dust has settled, I will tell you every last detail that you want to know, but the more you know now, the more likelihood you may slip up if interviewed by the police about me, so it's best you know nothing more. I've probably told you too much already. If they think that you know something, they might try some trick questions so be very careful as to what you say. If I can find a safe haven, will you come with me wherever it is?"

175

"I will have to think long and hard about that, but I do believe I need to get away from this area for a while with its bad memories— a new start in a new place may help me clear this nightmare from my mind, and I certainly don't want to lose you. I feel partly responsible because if I hadn't been so frightened to go to court, this would have never happened."

"Don't go blaming yourself again, even if they had gone to court and got a few years and extradited, I would have still not been satisfied. Who's to say that if you had told the police all the information that they would have caught them before they struck again? After all, I had a lot of luck in finding them."

"If Mum and Dad and Jodie are all going to be OK, there's nothing really stopping me coming with you, I suppose."

"Right, perfect. Give me a bit of time and I will see what I can come up with. So if I do find something suitable, no matter where, you would consider joining me once I'm sorted?"

"As long as I can come home and visit my parents now and again."

"That shouldn't be a problem, leave it to me. I may have to leave a bit sharpish but will have to appear to carry on as normal so as not to alert suspicion."

"Oh, Dennis, I'm finding all of this hard to take in. I knew you wouldn't let it drop, but I never expected this situation."

"No, me neither, but there's no going back for me now. I've started something that I must now finish. There's one more job I must do."

"What do you mean?"

"I will explain all some other time; as I said, the more you know, the greater risk of letting the cat out of the bag so to speak."

"What have we both done so wrong along the way to deserve our bad luck? It's as if we have been cursed!"

"Admittedly, we have had some bad luck over recent years but on the whole, we have been very happy and lucky, and who am I to say that I've been cursed, I should have died by rights many times, years ago."

Soon after, he travelled to the historic area of the city called the Lanes which contained many small, independent shops. Within the small pedestrian passage ways, there were a vast amount of quirky and unusual business's—some of which were jewellers and second-hand shops with past reputations as being establishments for the disposal and acquisition of 'dodgy' goods. After a brief search, Dutch located the small specialist magazine shop where he had purchased sports and military magazines in the past. On entering, he was confronted with the rows and rows of glossy magazines, all neatly displayed in different categories. As he trawled through the racks, searching for his particular title, he came across the adult section, and as he was the only customer in the shop at the time, he couldn't resist having a crafty peek at one or two of the magazines that caught his eye. Following the distraction, he then soon located the section that contained a large amount of various military magazines. He ignored the standard issues as he was aware that they would not contain the type of matter that he was seeking. From the remainder, he selected a magazine entitled 'New Deployment'—a monthly issued, well-presented, periodical—which he was aware specialised in re-uniting ex-armed service colleagues and advertising worldwide employment opportunities for such members. He then browsed through the various articles including such topics as recent war and combat technology, forums with advice from supposed experts in pensions and financial matters, together with the many adverts for combat clothing and accessories. He finally located the situations vacant column; the jobs on offer in most cases were aimed at ex-service personnel, which in the majority agencies were requiring security workers and some for mercenaries to serve in various parts of the world. It was in this column that a particular advert caught his eye and was so relevant to his personal situation that he purchased it immediately and returned to his flat.

Following this discovery, he checked out the present time in Texas where the particular employment agency was situated; as it was within working hours and as the advertised post was titled urgent, he decided to telephone them rather than email to get the application underway immediately. The telephone was answered by a very polite female with a strong American twang, who informed him that although the magazine article was fairly recent, the application period was only open for a few more days so he would be required to email all of his particulars very quickly. Dutch thanked the lady immediately and after contacting the Venezuelan Embassy in London, met with Melanie as he was reluctant to discuss the matter over the telephone.

"Melanie, you know I'm always banging on about my running hero, Alf Shrubb, and about having Alf moments. I think we have just had one."

"Den, you and your superstitions and Alf moments. What now?"

"Well, as you know, Alf was a lucky individual, unjustifiably forced to emigrate in order to continue the life he wished to live, and it proved to be the best move he ever made, and he carved out a great career. Well, I am hoping, with what I have discovered, we could both have a similar experience."

"That's a ridiculous comparison. The difference is, Dennis, he hadn't killed anyone and wasn't running from the police, was he?"

"I'm not running from the police as you put it. Well, not yet anyway, a move is purely insurance just in case. Anyway, I went into town and bought a magazine and in it, there is a job advertised for both a personal security officer and a child's teacher for an oil company official."

"Where? The mention of oil sounds far away?"

"South America."

"South America? Where in South America? It's a big place."

"Venezuela."

"Venezuela…why on earth would we want to go there?"

"Why because not only are the jobs tailor-made for us, but if I have made any errors in covering my tracks, there is no extradition agreement between Venezuela and the UK. In other words, even if they do obtain any evidence against me, this country could not demand me back for trial."

"It all sounds perfect but I know nothing about Venezuela, do you?"

"No, only that it is a mainly Spanish-speaking country, but I don't think that matters too much. If we are successful and get the jobs, our work contracts would be for three years, and we would be living in our own accommodation in the oil companies own, private-purpose built complex, which apparently has all its own facilities so no need to venture out. You would be teaching the official's two children, amongst other subjects, English as he is American and will eventually move back to the States. I would be looking after him with others as he apparently is a target for kidnappers and the like. How do you feel about it?"

"It all sounds interesting apart from the mention of kidnappers and someone needing protection."

"I won't lie to you. Venezuela is a dangerous country but it shouldn't affect you in a secure building. I would go out first and check it out and make sure that it's safe for you."

"It sounds interesting. If we get the jobs and security, it's OK; when would we start?"

"Soon as, apparently the person who I am replacing left suddenly, and they need someone quickly, but they would be prepared to wait a little for you as the children are only just at schooling age. I have also contacted the Venezuelan Embassy, and they say from receiving the applications to granting the visa and work permits should only take a week."

"You must agree that it looks very odd; if we leave so suddenly, the police and my parents will suspect something is wrong."

"Of course, it will but just odd won't get me found guilty of anything. Just tell your parents that we've been offered the jobs from a pal of mine out there and the opportunities are too good to miss, the police need not know until we've gone. The money is really good and with little or no expenses, you would be able to travel home several times during the three years."

"Putting it like that, it sounds quite good. What about the flat? Would we sell it or rent it out?"

"I was thinking renting it out as I know a bloke called Colin who is trustworthy and has a small rental and property maintenance company. We could leave an account open for rent to be paid into, the mortgage and facility bills could be paid out of the same account. As our small mortgage is less than a standard rental charge for a similar property, we will have a decent amount of savings after three years plus the flat which will help towards another place when hopefully we come back, if you still don't want to live there. If there are any problems, your dad with all his previous accounting experience is perfectly capable of handling any unforeseen difficulties together with Colin."

"I will have to eventually run it past my dad."

"Of course. I think he may enjoy the responsibility now he's fully retired."

"You've put a lot of thought into this, haven't you?"

"I've had to, we need to do this quickly. I don't know how much time I have before I crop up on the police radar."

"OK, Den, you seem to have it all planned out and I must admit that under the circumstances, it sounds as good as it's going to get. If you go out there first, I will trust your judgement as to if it's going to be suitable for me or not. In the meantime, let's apply then."

"I'm so glad you can now see this working out for us. Don't say a word to anyone about this until we know if we have the jobs or not as it would look suspicious to the police if they became aware, but I am very hopeful, as how many other couples would fit all of the particular requirements?"

"True, it does seem to fit us perfectly but I won't say a word. Do we need to learn any Spanish?"

"We could start learning some basic words as it won't harm even if we are not accepted. If you can get your CV together ASAP, I will send it off with mine to the agency in Texas."

"I've got an up-to-date one with a copy of my certificates from when I was thinking of changing schools."

"I will knock one out myself today and get it sent with my military papers. I have a feeling we will know fairly quickly as it sounds as if they are desperate to fill the posts."

"You will miss your music out there."

"I will miss going to the occasional gig but it's all on the internet now. You did often say that you would follow me to the end of the earth, now you may have to."

"Yes maybe so, but I would never in a million years envisaged it being under these circumstances."

Within a week, Dutch received the reply that he was hoping for—their applications had been accepted. He wasn't particularly surprised at this response and how quickly a decision had been made as there could have been very few couples that would fit the criteria and skills that were essential for both jobs. On receipt of the acceptance, the couple quickly made the necessary arrangements to visit the Venezuelan Embassy in London to obtain their visas and work permits and at the same time, investigate air travel to the country.

Despite the consequences and upheaval caused to Melanie and himself by his vengeful action taken against the men responsible for such a despicable act, which had resulted in ruining their formerly happily married life and causing Melanie lasting mental anguish and the need to move, he could not fully regret his behaviour as it not only had satisfied his need for some form of justice but without his presence, they were about to carry out and film the same act once again. He was further infuriated that as a result of the conversation in the van between the two now dead men, at least one, if not all three

180

men who appeared to employ these people, have viewed the brutal rape of his wife and as far as he is concerned, are almost equally responsible and are without doubt involved in other similar depraved criminal activity. It had been his life time occupation to protect the weak and oppressed and coupled with the likelihood that they possess the images of his wife's ordeal more than justified his hatred and intentions towards them.

Before disposing of the gun, he had played with the idea of cornering all three men together and at gunpoint, persuade them all to hand over their phones, but he did not think for one second that they would do this passively. They certainly didn't look the sort who would just roll over and give up devices that probably held very useful and dubious contact numbers. In addition, one or all were probably armed and if not, there was a good chance there was a weapon inside that well secured office structure. Dutch had a plan in mind but to remain undetected, he would have to think it through thoroughly.

The first opportunity that he had to obtain articles to support his scheme was when on route to repair a water pump at the River Mole near Gatwick Airport. As Dutch had recently smashed a rear light housing cover on the van when reversing and sliding into a tree on a muddy track, Jon had suggested that as he was passing a vehicle salvage yard located close to the A23 just south of Crawley, he remove and purchase one from an identical van. He turned off this main London to Brighton Road onto a minor road leading to a large, tarmacked, surfaced car park of a vehicle salvage depot which was ringed with high security fences stretching out into the distance. Amongst the cars already parked, there was obviously on the spot repairs taking place with customers replacing recently recovered parts to their defective vehicles. Dutch had never visited this site before, he only knew of it as Jon advised his drivers to purchase minor defective parts for the vans there as not only was it cheaper but also quicker than if a garage had to order the part, therefore keeping his fleet on the road. Having parked the van, Dutch removed his toolbox from the rear and entered the site through the main gates where the site office was situated. As he turned the corner and the area containing the defective cars came into his view, he was astounded as to how many cars and vans were scattered over a vast area. Although they had been placed in neat rows, the scene reminded him of car bomb blasts that he had attended in his past deployments in the Middle East. The more popular makes and models were mere shells having been stripped of every conceivable part, whereby the less common makes remained in more of their original condition. Dutch then commenced his search through this tangled, metal cemetery of pre-loved conveyances and soon found an identical van to his own, and was pleasantly surprised to see the light cover he required was in place and undamaged. Taking his screwdriver and putting on gloves, he unscrewed the required unit, followed by both front and rear number plates, and having done so, placed them inside the obsolete vehicle. He then went to the passenger compartment and when certain that the seat suited his purpose, he removed it from its mountings with a spanner from his tool box, then placed the seat on the ground. When sure that he was unobserved by any fellow salvage scavengers, he pushed both plates out of sight in an opening at the rear of the seat between the cushioning and outer lining of the seat cover. Having done this, he walked to the payment point at the main gate and presented the seat and plastic lamp unit to the cashier, who hardly gave the items a glance before stating the cost. Dutch was surprised at what he considered was an extortionate price for scrap, made worse as he didn't even require the larger item. Dutch paid the man in cash and declined a receipt, he wouldn't be looking for reimbursement on this occasion, as he wished for no paper trail. He then continued to the car park where he pulled the number plates from inside of the recovered seat and replaced them in an identical manner in the passenger seat of his van. Once he had replaced the defective light cluster, he then neatly placed the unwanted seat and broken plastic unit against the security fence with other discarded and defective parts that other visitors had left. He again had the problem of possibly having been picked up on CCTV when in the office area, but what was more innocent than someone purchasing a seat and then dumping it because it was not suitable for purpose. On a lighter note, in his mind, he satisfied himself that although he had committed a minor theft of the plates, it was of an item that nobody would have been allowed or wanted to purchase anyway, and to compensate, he had paid for an expensive unwanted seat, which he had returned and would, no doubt, be re-sold. There was no way of legally obtaining index plates without showing forms of ID, and he certainly couldn't do that with what he had in mind. Following testing the newly-obtained rear light housing, he then continued his journey to Gatwick, mentally ticking the number plates from his list.

On one occasion, whilst working on a drainage system on a building site near the village of Barns Green near Horsham, he saw a site that charged his imagination. A caravan that had once been used as a mess hut for the site workers had been completely destroyed by fire and close to the burnt remains of wood, metal and plastic were a number of badly burned gas cylinders that appeared to have been removed from the intense heat before exploding, a rescue act that he hoped would not be repeated in perhaps a future forthcoming event that had just entered his mind. Now with a definite plan, he had a feeling of contentment.

Melanie, who was still suffering from spells of deep depression, was not yet prepared to return home, so they decided it would be best for her to remain with her parents with the additional company of Jodie until their future plans were complete. Following discussions, it was decided that Melanie, with the aid of her father, would arrange the letting of the flat whilst he would continue to work and live in the temporary accommodation that was available at his work depot whilst negotiations concerning the rental of the property took place. Before his final departure, Dutch had one last act to carry out. Their lives had been ruined by certain individuals, two had been accounted for but some had not. As he was no longer in possession of his pistol, he would now have to rely on other resources at his disposal; therefore, he carried out studies concerning the ingredients of certain chemicals and gases and their reaction to the elements and as to the volatility of large quantities of high alcohol content spirits.

Dutch continued his work with Jon, having told his friend that due to the memory of the attack, Melanie would, when better, need to move from the area and he had put their flat on the rental market. Jon regretted this news but informed Dutch that the living quarters at the depot was there for him as long as he required it, and within days, Dutch took up residence which was situated at the side of the company's large workshop and depot at a large converted stable block situated on the outskirts of the small village of Sharpthorne near East Grinstead, West Sussex. Dutch was able to live and sleep there quite comfortably as Jon had built his own man cave within the property where he kept all of his army memorabilia and relics from his youth. There was a toilet and a shower as well, but Jon had seldom slept there overnight only if he worked very late into the night. As far as Dutch knew, the police were unaware of his new temporary address but still took the opportunity to once again use the retrieved tremble sticks by placing them strategically around the workshop and monitoring them during the night.

Chapter 16
There Are More Questions than Answers
(1972)
Artist: Johnny Nash   Writer: Johnny Nash

During one overcast Friday evening, four weeks following the rape of Melanie French, DI Byrne and his wife, Christine, had taken the twenty nine-mile road trip from their home to their favourite fish and chip restaurant situated opposite the seafront in the old town district of Hastings. They had nearly consumed what they considered was another delicious meal provided by this establishment when he received a text message requesting him to telephone WDS Cannan. On doing so, he was informed by the officer that there had been an attempt abduction earlier that evening in a car park near Devil's Dyke and the van and offenders appeared to be identical to those involved in the rape at Ditchling Beacon, but on this occasion, they were thwarted by a gunman who appeared from nowhere and shot both men whilst they attacked the woman that they had forced into the back of their van. After the shootings, the mystery gunman assisted the woman from the van, then drove off in the same van together with the two men who were believed to be dead or badly injured, and neither the vehicle nor occupants had been seen since. Byrne could hardly believe what he was hearing; if it had been certain officers that he knew well, he would have considered that they were having a prank, but Verna was not one to do such a thing in matters as serious as this. After asking her to clarify what she had said, because it appeared to be such an outlandish story, he found it hard to believe. Once reassured, he questioned her as to what procedures had been put into place. She assured him that the first officers at the scene had secured the entire attack site and had taken a statement from a dog walker, who had first come across the victim on returning to his car in the same car park where the attack had taken place. The victim was virtually unharmed apart from bruising but was obviously suffering from the shock; she had declined hospital treatment but had been persuaded to go to Brighton Hospital and scene investigators were on route to both locations. Procedures were in hand to contact a specialist medical examiner to attend to the victim. The description of the van had been circulated and armed patrols were alerted as a firearm was used. Due to the heavy mist and poor visibility, it had not been possible for the national police air service helicopter to assist in a search at this time. From what the victim had said, there was little likelihood of any evidence being found at the attack site and a cursory search under torch light had confirmed this, but the car park was sealed off for an examination by specialist search units the following morning.

Byrne congratulated the detective for getting things moving so quickly and after arranging to meet her at the hospital, drove via his home address to drop off his wife. Following their meeting, both officers spoke with the victim, Mrs Richardson, and her husband who was now in attendance and after she had been examined by doctors and forensic samples taken from her by the scene investigator, her clothing was placed in exhibit bags. After this, Mrs Richardson returned home with her husband followed by Byrne and the WDS. On arrival at their home, both—Cheryl and Luther—expressed more than once how so relieved they were that the children were not present at this occasion.

The couple were delighted to be re-united with Belle who had been collected from the scene by Luther's sister and appeared to be uninjured from the ordeal.

Feeling sufficiently recovered, Cheryl again relayed the version of events to the police officers, whom, following taking notes, both—Byrne and Cannan—participated in a welcome cup of tea before leaving Cheryl with other detectives to take her full written statement regarding the incident. Before leaving, they assured the couple that their car, which was still at the attack site, would be photographed in place and as it was not of any evidential value and would be returned soon. Both Byrne and Cannan then went to Devil's Dyke and spoke to the senior scene investigator. As it was now dark and the only possible evidence to be found at the scene was going to be on the surface of the car park, it was decided for the area to remain sealed off preventing any destruction or contamination of evidence. Following making these arrangements with the uniform duty inspector who was present, the three plain clothes officers made contact with other officers from the unit for an early morning briefing at Haywards Heath. They then left the area to inform the necessary departments of the incident and to prepare themselves for what they believed would be a long following day.

Whilst in the course of circulating all necessary details, Byrne and Cannan were informed that a van containing two deceased males had been located hidden in woods close to the scene of the attack. They both immediately returned to the area and the new scene, where two teenagers had located the van only a short distance from the car park where the attempted abduction had taken place, which could only be accessed from a narrow farm track leading from the Devil's Dyke Road. From the immediate arrival of the first response officers, who had confirmed the finding of the bodies, the scene had been preserved until the arrival of personnel from specialist departments. Initial photography of the static van was carried out; once completed, entry was gained to the front doors of the vehicle by the removal of branches and saplings, revealing the macabre scene inside. Once again, the DCI and WDS donned their protective overalls and shoe covers and approached the van via the muddy track on which scene investigators had marked a corridor to protect any useful imprints. After speaking with both scene guards and investigators, they approached the vehicle via the difficult terrain and inside of the open passenger door, they saw a male with the lower half of his body in the passenger foot well with his chest and head facing the floor. The scene photographer, with the aid of a portable lighting system, then took numerous photographs of this body, and when he had completed this particular task, a further scene investigator manoeuvred the head of the corpse backwards in order that a small round hole could be seen under his chin near his windpipe and a large amount of congealed blood was evident around his throat and chest. Further photographs were then taken of the fatal injury. Both the DCI and WDS knowingly glanced at each other when they both noticed the hat that he was wearing and a prominent necklace around his neck with what appeared to be a crucifix earring attached to it. All the officers present then went to the rear of the van and looked inside through the now open doors, where they saw the body of a man lying face down on the floor of the vehicle with a large pool of congealed blood around his hidden face and chest; the photographer was then given space to complete his work and whilst doing so, removed a tight-fitting jacket hood that covered the head of the deceased. Once completed, the scene investigator entered the rear and, in the same manner as before, lifted this man's head to the side until a small round hole surrounded by dried blood was visible in the centre of his forehead and images of this were again taken by the photographer. Byrne then requested the scene examiner to hold up the dead man's right hand and neither Byrne nor Cannan were surprised that it only contained four full fingers. They were both now aware that it would be a simple job in establishing that the two deceased were those responsible for the abduction and rape of Mrs French but now had another complex case to take its place. On looking around the entire rear interior of the vehicle, the officers noticed that there were cushions and blankets strewn about and two large plastic containers attached to the rear of the front seats by elasticated ropes. One of the scene investigators then pointed out the vicious looking blade of a bone-handled knife and also showed both officers the two mobile telephones found in the van, both with their battery covers removed and the sim and data cards missing. Neither deceased were found to be in possession of any paper work revealing their identities. Once the DCI had established that all procedures required were in place, the WDS and he, after speaking with the two young men who had discovered the van, left the scene leaving the investigators to complete their work. Once the deaths had been certified by a GP, Byrne then made contact with the coroner's officer to attend the scene and to make arrangements for the bodies to be removed to the mortuary. After being given clearance, a police tracker dog which after some initial confusion due to the recent footfall between the van and the road, traced a scent from the abandoned van onto a downhill track through fields and woodland from one side of the valley to the opposite side, around the perimeter of a golf course until it reached a point where the scent was lost close to a nearby housing estate, thought possibly due to dog walkers having walked over the same ground since the fugitive.

Byrne then requested the uniform duty inspector to organise a roster for officers to speak with drivers and pedestrians using the Devil's Dyke area and Hangleton estate on specific times and days and for information notices regarding the incident to be placed in strategic positions in the surrounding area.

As it was obvious that the two deceased were responsible for the initial rape and abduction, the investigation would now be considered closed, but some officers were retained to complete and eventually file the case as a detected crime.

In the early stages of this new investigation, it came to Byrne's notice that officers involved had nicknamed the killer the 'boiler-suited crusader'—a pseudonym for Batman—the caped crusader and some wit had also drawn a cartoon figure of a faceless man wearing red Y fronts over the trouser section of his attire, and although he could see the humour and significance, he was forced to pass out a memorandum to inform the unit to cease referring to this name as if it reached the press, it may glorify what was a double murder, as he already had an anti-hero on his hands. He was in no doubt that the media would, in time, invent all manner of bizarre theories regarding the mystery liberator, from the sublime to the ridiculous, but he did not wish such practice being attributed to any of his officers.

As with any undetected crime, an investigating officer looks at a suspect for means, opportunity and motive. The only positive clue the offender had left at the scene was imprints of a size nine shoe in the mud, the sole of which appeared to have been covered leaving no tread imprint for a future comparison.

Byrne had come to the conclusion that he was dealing with a very cunning and resourceful individual. To carry out what they had done and in the manner that they had completed, it showed a person with skill and commitment, but why? How did they arrive there at that moment with a hand gun, and what was the motive? He had no idea as to the answer to any of these questions as at present, there was no suspect but he needed to examine a possible motive closely as this, if found, could steer him to the offender—could it be love, hate, jealousy or revenge? It certainly wasn't theft as both of the deceased had a small amount of cash remaining on them and would not have been expected to have any kind of further wealth judging by their visual circumstances; the van had not been permanently stolen by the gunman, and the female was actually assisted, not harmed. From enquiries made with the work colleagues of the two deceased, it did not appear that there were any homosexual tendencies; in fact, quite the opposite, as apparently, they would regularly discuss females to an unhealthy extent. To confirm this, the lone female worker at the site later stated that both men had made unwanted sexual remarks and advances to her on many occasions in the past, and it was not until her new boyfriend started work for the same company that it had stopped after he had strong words with them both. Therefore, motive

189

had to be his first point of investigation, if he could discover someone with that; he could then use any forensic or outstanding DNA evidence, if found, to establish if they were the killer. Were the telephones, which had been established belonged to the deceased pair, tampered with and the data cards removed because they contained details of contacts in the drugs or criminal world for instance? Why in the second attack were they going to drive from the scene with the victim on board, but on the first involving Mrs French, did they remain at the point of abduction? He could only surmise that they had been confident at not being disturbed during the first attack, but not in the more popular car park where other cars were parked nearby. The fact that both sim cards had been taken, possibly interrogated and destroyed, indicated that one or both of them were in possession of some highly important details concerning someone or something that the killer did not want to come to notice, important enough to kill two people and for the assailant to take valuable time out in their escape to remove the items. At first appearance, it gave the impression of an organised criminal hit by a gang, perhaps using a professional assassin. Fingerprints lifted from the van were only those of the two deceased and some of the car wash workers, who were regular passengers, likewise with the blood. Ballistic examination of the two bullets recovered from the bodies revealed that both were fired from the same 9mm handgun and specific marks on the bullets could be matched to the weapon responsible if located.

Byrne was flummoxed as to where the killer had appeared from, and how was it that he was so efficient with a gun—it was as if a superhero had descended from nowhere with fatal results. These killings had the hallmarks of a professional assassin but why would two car cleaners be dealt with in such a way? Was it something they had seen or done, or had they double-crossed someone in the underworld? The questions at this moment were endless. The second female victim had told the police that she had no idea from where the gunman had appeared from, if he had entered the van during her struggle or was already in the vehicle. She became first aware of him when he fired the first shot shortly after she clutched onto a loose blanket. Byrne began to ask himself if the mystery man could have been secreted under the blanket present in the van, but if so, where and when did he enter the vehicle. Byrne was aware that the rear door handle and lock of the van was broken so he could have entered anywhere.

Both victims had indicated that their assailants had smelt of alcohol and the post-mortem examination confirmed that both deceased had consumed alcohol shortly before their death. As there was no trace of any alcohol containers in the van, Byrne instructed that visits were to be made to all public houses in a five-mile radius of the scene and the descriptions of the offenders shown to staff working on the evening in question. Byrne's opinion of their drinking prior to both the offences was probably to give them some 'Dutch courage', not realising the enormous significance there was to this thought.

As a direct result of these enquiries, officers were informed by the licensee of The Bombardier pub that his staff remembered the two men described as visitors to the pub on the evening of the incident as they had made suggestive remarks to a barmaid and had been required to leave. During interviewing the staff, it was discovered that the pub's CCTV system was defective at the time concerned, causing officers to enquire at all shop premises situated opposite the pub, and its car park in search of any useful CCTV, but after examination of images, results proved negative for the night in question.

The registration number of the transit van revealed the owners to be a car wash company of an address in Folkestone, Kent. The company official, who was also of eastern European origin, was at first evasive when asked about the van and his workers, but realising the seriousness of the matter, eventually gave details supplied to the company by the two deceased as being Victor Kardos and Istvan Vida, both Romanian. As both had been living in a Brighton flat rented by the company for their employees, members of the incident team searched their respective room and paperwork confirmed both identities. Further liaison with Interpol established that both men had a string of previous criminal convictions and were, at present, wanted in their homeland of Romania where they had been identified by fingerprints for burglary and sexual assault but had immediately fled to the UK. Immigration records showed them entering the country shortly after the offence in Romania, where a European arrest warrant had since been issued, resulting in various attempts by British authorities to locate the pair but to no avail.

Armed with this knowledge, comparison tests from the fingernail scrapings taken from Mrs French were compared with the DNA held by the Romanian authorities and matched that of Kardos, and both deceased were subsequently identified by photograph and DNA samples.

The two bodies were formally identified at the mortuary by one of the two managers, a Mr Ivan Stanescu; Byrne did not like him one little bit as he was all flash—suit and bling, with ridiculous crocodile-skin shoes and ponytail, who had a surly superior attitude about him and certainly showed no sympathy whatsoever for his two dead workers. Unsurprisingly, to Byrne, the company had no record of the next of kin, so it would be a task of his team to trace any relatives and arrange repatriation. Byrne instructed that this man and others involved in this car wash business were all to be subject of investigation, as at this stage of the enquiry, the information contained on the missing sim cards could have been relevant to any one of them.

Byrne instructed the two crime analysts assigned to the team to make contact with the obvious websites in an effort to investigate any social media activity by the two deceased, including both straight and gay dating sites and reminded any of his team that had been drawn in from outside of the area to have in mind that this was Brighton—the most sexually-liberated capital of the UK where amongst some, anything is acceptable so they may have to think outside of the box, even at a reason that may appear to be truly bizarre.

Chapter 17

A View to a Kill (1985)

Artist: Duran Duran
Writers: John Barry/Duran Duran

Inside of the workshop, there was a box that contained various padlocks together with keys that Jon had collected over the years for securing the gates and metal fences at temporary work sites. Dutch selected a strong ancient padlock and key, which he transferred to the toolbox carried in his van, in the knowledge that Jon would not have objected to him removing it, but may have disproved had he known of what Dutch intended to use it for. He could not take a chance buying a modern padlock as its source could be traced through serial numbers right down to the retailer; he was positive that the one he had selected by its age would be untraceable. He then filled a glass bottle with petrol and replaced the bottle cap before securing it in an upright position in the van. Dutch went to great lengths to make sure in keeping anything to do with his intentions well-hidden, because if Jon saw any unusual behaviour on his part, he would realise that he was up to something. Although he trusted Jon implicitly, he did not want to involve him in his personal issues, and furthermore, he thought his friend might try to dissuade him from his planned intentions which he felt were necessary to carry out to bring closure to his mission. For his friend's sake, he would be certain not to leave any traces behind so as not to incriminate him in anyway whatsoever. At a later date, he thanked Jon for all his help and gave in his notice, which Jon had been expecting but such haste took him completely by surprise. Dutch informed him in confidence that he had been offered very lucrative employment abroad and due to her horrendous experience, Melanie needed to get far away for a while. Jon accepted the hurried move and explanation as good reason. As Jon lived in excess of 25 miles from Brighton and hardly had any interest in newspapers or television, he had no real knowledge of what further incidents had occurred in the Brighton area, and even if he had, there was no reason for him to connect Dutch at this stage. Dutch felt that so far, he was not on the police radar as being a suspect but in case he had become a police surveillance target, he commenced to take anti-surveillance measures when taking actions or journeys surrounding his future plans. He was now in possession of all the documents required for Melanie and himself to move on with their lives together, so it was now time to implement his final planned action.

Dutch was due to leave the country late on Friday night and with the consent of Jon, worked on a small job in the morning and then spent the early afternoon cleaning work's equipment and packing before Jon accompanied him to the airport. During that late afternoon, having completed all of his planned tasks, he set the same cautionary procedures with his mobile phone as he had done on a previous Friday night encounter and returned to the riverside car wash site, again dressed in a protective overall. For precautionary reasons, he had replaced the true registration plates of his work's van with those taken from the breakers yard, as he knew if things went to plan, the police would trawl through video footage for miles around. He had considered parking on the outskirts of the trading estate and walking to the car wash site but people were seldom seen walking in this industrial area—lorries and vans were the most common of the road users—and furthermore, he would need to make a swift exit as what he had planned would bring attention to the area extremely quickly. As he again drove down the slope, passing the wash site gates on his nearside, he was pleased to see that the padlock was once again hanging loose on the metal fencing, therefore not requiring him to use the padlock that he had placed in his tool box. Once at the site of his previous vantage position, he observed the same three men arrive and enter the office as they had done before, and once more, he witnessed boxes of vodka being loaded into the two pristine parked cars. Following this, shortly before the premises was due to close, the same procedure involving workers entering and leaving the office with their pay took place.

Dutch was sitting and observing when all of a sudden, he saw a sudden movement to his right, near to a large hole in the fence separating the trading estate from the railway goods yard sidings.

The movement had been quick—was it a rat, fox or other animal as he couldn't see it now. Then he saw further movement in the semi-darkness behind a stack of wooden pallets close to his van. He looked carefully into the area in an effort to identify its form when he saw the face of Jorge. Dutch immediately pushed his spine and head hard against the back of his seat in an effort to hide himself behind part of the side panel of the van. After a few seconds, he inched forwards to see if he had been seen and as he did so, he saw Jorge was very much aware of his presence, as he was staring right back at him in disbelief.

Dutch immediately thought about driving off as he had now been seen so could not therefore go through with his plan, but he was due to leave the country in a few hours and he didn't want to leave unfinished business. What on earth was he doing skulking about in the shadows? Only one way to find out, Dutch thought, he would speak to him and weigh up the pros and cons as to his next move. He wound down his window and quietly beckoned him over. As Jorge approached the van stooping, keeping his upper body low and apparently, not wishing to be observed by anyone in the immediate area, Dutch saw that he was hiding something heavy behind his back.

Jorge was the first to speak in a quiet tone through the open window, "What are you doing here?"

"I could ask you the same. What are you doing, and what's that you're hiding behind your back?"

"Don't worry, I'm just watching those three bastards. You know I told you about my twin sister. Well, before I got to see her, she killed herself with drugs. It will be said to be an accident, but I know how depressed they had made her. As we were smuggled in, she had no way out but to carry on what they made her do."

"I'm so sorry to hear that. They really are a bunch of vicious fuckers who want sorting out. So, if you are just watching, why are you hiding something?"

"It's nothing."

"You are being very careful hiding nothing. Are you going to try and do something to me?" At the same time, Dutch prepared himself to take some evasive action, not knowing his intentions or the identity of the hidden item.

"No, I wouldn't do that. You are a good man, not like those evil bastards."

With that, he produced from behind his back a red plastic 10-litre container, and Dutch could see by its weight that it was full and could immediately smell the distinctive petrol fumes.

"What do you propose to do with that?" glancing in the direction of the site as he said it, watching for any movement.

"I'm going to throw it inside, light it."

"If that doesn't work, they will be straight out after you, and you will get far worse than what you got before."

"They leave the lock to the gates on the fence, I will use that to keep them in."

"You have thought about this seriously, haven't you?" This being the same method as Dutch was about to use to prohibit any escape from the office.

Dutch couldn't believe what he was hearing—here was two men who hardly knew each other at a chance meeting, fully armed with the same murderous intentions. What now, does he try to persuade him to go, get physical with him if he wouldn't? He seemed hell-bent on going through with it; that would create a commotion that would probably be seen or heard at the car wash. On one hand, Dutch knew that he should abandon his intentions, leave and be satisfied of what he had achieved thus far, but on the other hand, he so wanted to complete the task and rid the world of what he considered pure evil, but another pair of hands would be very useful in moving the heavy gas cylinders. He envisaged that if left alone, Jorge would fail to pull it off, getting caught or killed by the mob inside. Could such an unlikely alliance succeed and get away with such an extraordinary crime?

"Are you serious that alone will not burn the place down quick enough? They could rush you before you got the lock on, or even if you did lock them in that petrol alone may not be enough to do the job."

"This is all I have. I have to do this. They have caused my sister to die, ruined my life also. I have nothing left. They probably killed Istvan and Victor, who I have heard were found shot in their van near Brighton."

"Probably," said Dutch, winching as he said so.

"Are you sure that you can go through with this?"

"Of course, why do you think? I have been living in the railway for days, waiting for Friday to come."

Dutch then thought about scaring him off as he wasn't going to leave, not after all his preparation and anyway, what right had he to deny Jorge of the retribution he so craved himself? After all, he still had Melanie no matter how damaged she was, Jorge did not now have his sister.

"Are you really sure? You will spend most of your life in prison if you are caught."

"Yes. It's all I've been thinking about since I found out she was dead."

Dutch could tell by his eyes and expressions that he was determined and deadly serious. Was he now to embark on the biggest gamble that he had ever undertaken?

He then made an immediate decision, saying,

"It's hard to believe but I am here to do the same as you but I have a better plan."

A surprised-looking Jorge said, "You also want to kill them. Why did they do something to you or your van?"

Dutch almost laughed, "There's a lot more to it than that. You needn't know all the details other than they've caused a lot of hurt, bad enough to want the same result as you. If we do this together, you must do exactly what I say because I doubt if your way will do a proper job, hopefully mine will. Haven't you any belongings with you?"

"I only have what I have left in a bag by the fence." At the same time, pointing to the hole in the metal-mesh fence from where he had emerged from.

"Go and get it because we will have to leave here quickly."

Jorge went to the fence, picked up a rucksack and at Dutch's instruction, placed it in the rear of the van.

Once this was done, Dutch said,

"Get in and I will explain what we will do."

Dutch, realising he was taking a big risk, leant over and opened the passenger door, at the same time saying, "You can leave that petrol out there."

Having quietly closed the door, both men were discussing their roles when the premises closed for business, and they watched a small group of workers emerge from the site, go to a smaller van and an old small car, which were both driven away from the site. Dutch thought that it was interesting that this van, unlike the previous larger work's transport, was not tucked away—seemingly the new driver had nothing to hide. As the two vehicles drove up the road adjacent to the site, the 'Turk' appeared from the office, approached the gates and pushed them shut exactly as before and re-entered the same cabin. As soon as the door had closed, Dutch drove the van closer to the gates, took a pair of disposable gloves from the ever-present box, put them on, ensuring Jorge did the same. Dutch then retrieved the bottle containing the petrol from the van and both stealthily entered the yard on foot. After unhooking the padlock from the fence, Dutch hurried with it to the office door. Whilst doing so, Jorge, with his petrol container, was commencing to project the fuel into some of the voids in the brickwork supporting the office, generously splashing the fluid over the various assortment of wood and sheets of tarpaulin stored underneath, and when the container was empty, he also placed that under the construction as Dutch had firmly instructed.

Swiftly and quietly, Dutch placed the securing arm through the eye of the clasp on the door and pushed it into the locked position. As he did so, he could hear the men talking loudly and laughing inside. With no other doors or windows accessible, the three men were now incarcerated inside, and even if they became aware and alerted their predicament by telephone, any would-be rescuers would hopefully not arrive in time to prevent their intentions. Having placed the bottle on the ground, Dutch then approached the gas cylinder that was attached by a feed pipe to the side of the building and following his confirming, the gas feed was in the on position; he went to the three heavy propane gas cylinders that were still standing close to the side of the office where he had initially seen them, and following confirmation that they too were full, he was joined by Jorge and together, they quickly and as quietly as possible lifted each one— which Dutch was aware through his diligent research, when full, weighed 150 lbs—to different sides of the office. Once the cylinders were in the desired positions, they lowered them onto their sides with the release taps inside the voids between the gaps in the supporting brick walls around the cabin. It was impossible to move these heavy, cumbersome, metal objects across the concrete surface without some noise, and he could hear sudden movement from inside. Once in their desired position, they then, in rotation, turned each of the now horizontal containers to the full emission release position and each one, in turn, emitted a deafeningly-loud hissing sound as the pressurised heavy gas escaped underneath the building. The loud noise of escaping pressurised propane and the discovery of their imprisonment had now made the three inside aware of their plight and were shouting and hammering on the door, but not as loudly as perhaps they would have done if they could have witnessed the scene outside. Not only had they made the cabin difficult to break into, but it was proving to be just as difficult to exit. Dutch shut the sound that they were creating from his mind and hurried to the steel pallet cage, reached through, then pulled and twisted the plastic tap away from the almost-full tank holding the flammable traffic film remover, which immediately gushed out and flowed down the slight incline of the concrete surface through a void of the supporting office wall soaking the ground and the now petrol-soaked articles stored beneath. With the procedure now complete, they both moved back to the front of the building to where Dutch judged was a safe distance; he reached into his pocket from which he removed his trusted Zippo lighter that had served him for many years together with a prepared piece of cloth. Removing the top of the bottle containing the petrol, he positioned the cloth into the neck of the bottle making the Molotov cocktail complete. He had experience of such improvised devices, having had a number of them thrown in his direction when in various conflict situations around the world. Dutch was about to strike the lighter when Jorge indicated that he wished to throw it. Dutch could see by his facial expression that he was desperate to do so and with some deliberation, passed him the bottle. Dutch then lit the material protruding from the neck of the bottle and once it was burning, Jorge immediately and accurately tossed the bottle underneath the centre of the building into the void in the front supporting wall, and as he did so, Dutch heard him say "For Kristiyana". As the bottle hit the ground and shattered, its flame immediately ignited the gas and petrol, together with the liquid still flowing underneath. There was an immediate almighty whooshing sound and flames leapt out in every direction, it was now time for them to leg it. As they ran towards the exit, they could hear the fire roaring behind them in the quiet evening air, obliterating the shouts and banging from inside, and as they both climbed into the van, they saw the inferno that they had created before them. Dutch's immediate thoughts were that not only did the fire look sufficient enough to destroy the scumbags inside but also any mobile phones or computers in the building that may have held images of Melanie, but if by any chance those devices evaded destruction, at least it would now only be the police who had possession of their contents. The weather conditions were in their favour with no or little wind which would have blown the exiting gas away from the base of the cabin, and he became increasingly confident that no human could survive the now intense fire and thick acrid smoke occurring both inside and outside of the blazing building.

As he started the engine of the van, he briefly thought to himself that the last time he had run from a similar scene that he had set in this manner, he received a medal from Royalty, but the only royal recognition if caught for this would be time in her Majesty's prison. He then drove up the gradient and just as he reached the main estate road, he looked into his offside wing mirror and could see the flames leaping into the evening air below and the smell of burning materials was already prominent. He had no concern for the pond life inside of the burning building, but he did think it was a shame that both of the desirable cars parked close to the fire would also be destroyed. He then left the estate by the shortest possible route to avoid as many possible CCTV cameras situated in and on factory premises. Dutch then commenced his return journey, avoiding the main roads and at a normal speed so as not to bring attention to the van, which was still exhibiting incorrect number plates. Following an on-route discussion between the two men, Dutch drove the 26 miles to Three Bridges, a suburb of nearby town of Crawley which was close to his temporary home, where the railway station facilitated a fast and frequent train service between London and Brighton.

Once parked in a housing estate close to the station, Dutch pulled out his wallet and handed Jorge some notes saying, "There's enough money there to get you to Newcastle. The police will be looking as to why someone should want to kill these people and my name and your name might well come up, because we both have reasons to hate them. If they do eventually find you and speak to you, say nothing as I don't think they will have any evidence, so destroy your train ticket after use and think of a story as to where you were tonight. If you are going to be living at the other end of the country with your brother, they will hopefully never find you anyway. Understand?"

Jorge smiled, "Not one person here knows my real name as I have no documents and have been using a false Bulgarian name."

"That's good, but what happens if you get stopped by the police or immigration people and they ask for any identification?"

"As I have no documents, I will have to tell them who I really am and ask for asylum like my brother; I think they will send me back, but I won't care. Our journey was a big mistake costing my sister her life."

"If that happens, make sure you don't tell them about what you have been doing here or about Stan and his gang as they will then connect you to what we have done."

"No, not if I want to live. They boast that they have many eyes and ears and can get you wherever you are in the world and I believe that is so. We will both be hunted by them if they find we did this."

"You will have to stop using the name 'Jorge', because I'm sure the police will get that name from the car wash workers. If you drop that name, as far as I can see, nobody has a clue who you are. Am I right?"

"Yes, everyone here only knows me as Jorge."

"Have anyone got any photographs of you?"

"No, nothing like that."

"Have you a mobile phone?"

"Yes," at the same time, tapping at the breast pocket of his jacket.

"You will need to get rid of that as soon as possible as your whereabouts tonight could be traced."

"Yes, of course. I will do that before I get to my brother's."

"Right. As soon as you get on that station, go to the washroom and wash your hands thoroughly just in case, and swap some of your clothes over as you may have petrol on them, and when you get to your brother's, destroy or wash everything you have. I can't think of anything we have missed but if you do ever get arrested for this, I repeat, say nothing because I don't believe that the police will have any evidence to support any charges against you. Are you sure you are understanding all of this? It's important for both of us that you do this, right? Do you understand?"

"Yes, but what should I do about my sister's body?"

"There's not a lot you can do immediately as that may start a chain of events that lead back to you, understand?"

"Yes, but it's difficult as the rest of my family are in Kosovo."

"Thinking about it, to ensure that she gets treated properly, get your family to contact the coroner's office in Hastings but you must emphasise to them not to mention you."

"I will have to be careful how I do this as I can't tell my brother what we have done. I will just tell him that I have heard she has died in Hastings Hospital, and as I should not be here, he must deal with it, not letting them know about me."

"That sounds the best bet, you just stay out of the way, keep your head down," at the same time, ducking to indicate his meaning.

"How about you? What will you do?"

"Don't worry, I won't be hanging around either. We need to make a pact, a promise between us both," pointing to Jorge and himself as he said it. "If one of us does happen to get arrested for this, we will not mention the other's involvement because we were going to do it on our own anyway; neither of us encouraged nor pushed the other to do anything that they didn't want to. I swear that I will keep my promise, will you do the same?"

"Yes, I understand all that you say. I will inform no person about you as you have only helped me in what I had to do."

Dutch suddenly said, "What's your name?"

Looking at him quizzically, the man then paused and replied, "I will have to think of a new one."

Dutch then released his seat belt and offered the person he only knew as Jorge his outstretched right hand; the other man went to shake it, then realising that in his haste, he had forgotten to take either of his gloves off. Both men chuckled as he peeled them off and at Dutch's instruction, placed them on the passenger floor well together with his discarded pair.

Having shaken hands, he left the van with Dutch wishing him good luck, at the same time finding it hard to believe as to what had just happened during the past hour. Truth is far greater than fiction, he thought, no one could have dreamed of such a scenario. His recent violent actions, on the face of it, could give the appearance that he had a particular dislike to people from eastern European countries, but almost as if to prove otherwise, together with a citizen from that part of the world, he had just committed the most serious of crimes and put complete trust in him.

As Dutch watched the man who he had collaborated with in causing three deaths retrieve his rucksack from the rear of the van and walk towards the railway terminal, he realised that neither of them knew each other's true name and it was perfect that they didn't. As much as he sympathised with his predicament, he hoped that he would never see him again because as far as he was aware, he was the only person who could implicate him in his completed mission, but under the circumstances, he had very little choice, and for the first time since the commencement of his scheme, he felt a sense of vulnerability, as this was an aspect he had no control over, and he didn't like it. He was aware that he would always wonder the fate of his anonymous accomplice.

Dutch then continued the remainder of his return journey to the workshop and his temporary lodging at Sharpthorne, where he immediately commenced his evacuation process by firstly replacing the registration plates with the correct set, at the same time wiping any fingerprints from them and the bodywork underneath. With the further aid of petrol, he accelerated the destruction of the bogus plates in the onsite incinerator together with the two pairs of gloves, his shoes and all clothing that he was wearing and other combustible articles that he would no longer require. When the heat of the incinerator had completed its work and the small fire had destroyed all inside, he cooled the ashes with water and removed the charred remains of the two plastic plates which he then collected together with his knife, tremble sticks, torch, and other non-buoyant articles that would be prohibited on his journey. Being fully aware that if he is or becomes a suspect, police would trace this location and would possibly put a sniffer dog to work in the area searching for any burning or burial sites or to detect any movements, so with this in mind, Dutch bagged the articles, walked the short distance from the workshop in the fading evening light to his planned destination by crossing the road and walking on the public footpath passing the opposite side of the road to his intended destination until he reached a small wooden pedestrian gate that led into a large field. Again, bearing in mind the possibility of a tracker dog, he entered the field and walked a short distance in and then immediately backtracked his trail to the road. He then crossed the road where he reached a secure large wooden five bar gate and entered a wide lush green field by climbing over it, avoiding the strand of barbed wire stapled across the length of the top of the structure and proceeded to the centre of the field towards a large circle of tall trees containing a pond. This small, dark, still expanse of water was surrounded by high grass banks and large oak trees with a mist just above the water line around the entire circumference. He had recently learnt local legend told that a young boy had drowned there many years ago, and the mist was a halo depicting his young, innocent life. There was something eerie about the place, thought Dutch, the dark murky water looked very deep and the couple of times he had been there, he had never seen any sign of fish or bird life; there was no weed or water plants and very few insects and the mist had been present on each of his visits, probably because the sunlight could never burn it off as the branches of the trees kept out much of the natural light. It certainly presented a sinister aura and rightfully held its given ghostly reputation. It crossed his mind that his late grandmother, Connie, would have been very interested in this place. He then threw his unwanted articles into the

203

centre of the pond, causing splashes and a small wave effect across the water. As the ripples on the surface ceased from the disturbance of the jettisoned incriminating property, there, in one short second, it happened—one of the most hair-raising incidents of a life that had been littered with many shocking moments. As in that now dark, calm water, he saw the reflection of a young boy—not in colour—in black and white, like an old photograph. It happened so quickly but so clear. The head and shoulders image showed a good-looking, healthy boy with dark hair that was meticulously combed with an exaggerated quiff; the ears, nose and mouth were clearly visible with the expressionless face looking straight into Dutch's eyes, who was visibly shaken as to what he believed he had just witnessed. So much so that he had to take a deep breath as his heart appeared to be pounding outside of his chest. In an instant, the image had gone leaving Dutch to remain motionless for a short time. Convinced as to what he had seen, he gathered up some small stones from the field and tossed them into the same spot of water almost expecting a repeat of the image but to his relief, it did not appear again as he wanted it to be just a trick of the light and surrounding mist as he had enough problems with Melanie and Jon knowing of his one mystic obsession. He couldn't imagine how they would react if he was truly convinced as to what he had just witnessed.

He searched his mind as to where he had seen a similar face to the one he had pictured in the water, and he recalled that it had been shown on an old enamel advertising sign that once hung in Connie's scullery, illustrating a chocolate bar that originated in the early 1900s. As a child, he had taken a particular interest in this sign as he thought it being named 'Five Boys' was an odd title for a piece of confectionary. The wrapper of which depicted five separate images of a young boy with different facial expressions. This was the image that he had so convincingly seen in the water and it crossed his mind as to whether the boy whose demise took place there looked similar but instantly knew it was best that he would never get to find out, because if it did, such an episode could turn a person insane.

This incident made Dutch feel uneasy as he was already in perilous situation and this incident worried him; he wondered if it was some kind of signal that his actions had displeased some mystic force, which was to thwart his immediate future plans. He calmed himself from the strange ghostly experience with the comforting thought it was just his grandmother's past influence and continued with his well-rehearsed exit from the area.

The incident, however, did have a profound effect on him as Dutch felt saddened that the young lad had not been lucky enough to have been blessed with more lives such as he appeared to have been allocated. He then returned to the workshop and cleaned the van thoroughly inside and out in case any particles from the fire or scene had been transferred to the vehicle, and furthermore, he wished to return a clean vehicle and tools back into the custody of his friend. Better not use a car wash this time, he thought.

After showering, he packed all his remaining belongings, then changed into more appropriate clothing which would suit his destination and commenced the final drive in the vehicle that had given him such good service during his employment. He then made the short journey to Jon's home. On his arrival, his friend was ready for the pre-arranged meeting and following saying his goodbyes to Jon's wife, Sally, they left the village driving to their destination via the M23 and M25.

During the hour-long journey, the conversation between the two consisted of the usual banter but on occasions, was interrupted by bouts of silence when Dutch unwittingly reflected on that evenings devastating proceedings. He so wished that he could tell Jon of what he had done, but he did not wish his friend in anyway involved and that included lying to the police, which he knew he would do if it became necessary to protect him.

At one stage, Jon became aware that something was troubling his good friend and colleague.

"Is everything okay? You seem to be mulling something over. Are you having second thoughts about this move?"

"No, not really, just wondering what it will be like there."

"Since you told me where you were heading, I've been having a look into the background of Venezuela, and it looks a bit dodgy out there. You came out of the army for a quieter life and now you are going to live in a fairly lawless and corrupt environment. Isn't it a bit like going from the frying pan into the fire?"

"I know it seems odd but I have my reasons, and I think a move far away will help Melanie's recovery. I will certainly make sure that nothing harms her again, and anyway, I'll be getting paid a lot more than my previous miserly boss paid me".

"You cheeky bastard, but are you sure that's all there is to this? Because I've had a feeling that ever since you first dropped this bomb shell that's there's something more."

"OK, I'll be honest with you. There is, but I can't tell you now, but I promise that I will one day. The least you know, the better but I swear that I have done nothing to harm your business, I would never do that, not after how you helped me out."

"You are worrying me now, Dutch. This is sounding on the serious side."

"Don't worry, mate, you know I'll see this through and you of all people will understand why I took a certain course of action. Let's leave it there."

"Fair enough, I won't push you for anymore answers. I'm sure you know exactly what you are doing, you always have."

Both men continued with general conversation until their arrival at the set down area outside of Terminal 2 at Heathrow airport.

Before departing, Dutch thanked Jon for giving him the opportunity for work and apologised, once again, for leaving in such a fashion. His loyal friend was sorry to lose not only a good friend but a good worker; though he understood that there were both mysterious and unfortunate circumstances that were causing the departure of Dutch and his wife. Dutch assured him that as soon as they were settled, he would let him know of his whereabouts; he would be able to keep in contact via his laptop and hopefully, they would meet again at the termination of his new contract. After saying their final goodbyes, Dutch entered the terminal for the night time flight making his way to the Lufthansa airline check-in desk.

Chapter 18

Somebody's Watching Me (1984)

Artist: Rockwell
Writer: Kennedy 'Rockwell' Gordy

By the time the fire brigade arrived at the scene, the roof had collapsed and the front, rear and a side wall were completely destroyed, leaving one sidewall standing, giving the impression of a large gravestone or memorial overlooking the charred and burning contents at its base. The fire officers were initially concerned about the propane gas cylinders situated around the four sides of the burnt-out structure but soon discovered that all the taps were open and fully exhausted of the gas. The blaze had been so fierce due to the accelerants used that there was little material remaining to burn, therefore, it took only a short time for the fire crew to douse the flames that remained. Once the site was safe and the scene could be examined, the three burnt bodies were discovered underneath the remains of the fallen roof and walls and as a result, the police and a fire investigation officer were called to the scene immediately. Whilst officers were engaged in securing the scene, they quickly realised that they were dealing with an arson when it was discovered that the remains of the only door to the building had a locked padlock affixed to the outside, which was subsequently left undisturbed for the examination of scene investigating officers and photographers.

As a result of the scene examination, it became obvious to all police officers involved that due to what was found amongst the debris of the office, they were dealing with an international crime organisation. Through recovered, scorched documents found inside of a locked metal cabinet, they found evidence of false passports and identification fraud together with a loaded pistol. The scene was also littered with a vast amount of broken bottles of bootleg vodka. There was further evidence of crime in the nearby fire-damaged vehicles owned by two of the deceased; in one was found a hidden pistol and ammunition and in the other a large amount of cocaine. The burnt remains of clothing worn by all three revealed that each one was in possession of large amounts of money.

During his visit to the scene, Byrne was unable to positively identify any of the three charred bodies but did notice the remnants of a pair of unusual shoes worn by one individual and a blackened fire-damaged Porsche with heat-blistered paintwork bearing distinctive number plates.

Throughout his career, he had always been thankful to self-promoting individuals who, through either their preferred tattoos, jewellery or distinctive clothing, assisted in identification and Stanescu was proving to be no exception. He had taken an instant disliking to this man but would not allow his personal feelings to influence the investigation by passing his opinion to the forum at a hastily called briefing on the morning following the fire. After fully describing the scene, Byrne addressed the assembled group of detectives, some of whom for continuity purposes had remained involved in all three of the suspected connected crimes.

"These three executions could be linked to the deaths of two workers of the same car wash company who were shot dead at Devil's Dyke only three weeks ago whilst attempting to abduct a Mrs Richardson, a case that a number of you here worked on and are aware that beyond all doubt, the two deceased were responsible for the rape of Mrs French only weeks previous to that. As at present we have no motive for last night's killings but as all five dead men appear to be foreign nationals, could there possibly be a racial motive or have we got a random serial killer on our hands, both of these theories throw up the possibility that more murders may follow but at this stage, it appears that all five had possibly some thing or some information that a third party required or did not want revealed. The initial rape, the abduction and shootings, now these most recent deaths, all occurred on a Friday evening, which is the only day that the deceased managers visited the site to pay the wages so this may have some relevance to all these crimes. Both instances, where people died, were carried out in such a way and so efficiently and forensically aware, leaving no clues whatsoever that I am still led to believe that we are looking for a professional assassin or someone with a military background, as these actions are beyond the capability of the normal man in the street."

As soon as he had made this statement, the hand of Woman Detective Constable, Sonia Shah, seconded to the investigation and assigned to look after Melanie French's welfare, was quick to raise her hand in the air and once she was acknowledged by Byrne, said,

"With reference to your mentioning the military, all of our interviews with Melanie have been carried out at her parents' home in Woodingdean, apart from yesterday when we saw her at her flat in Hove where she had gone to collect some of her belongings as they are about to let the property. She says that she needs to get away from the area because the offence took place so close to her home. Whilst talking to her, I noticed a photograph on the wall showing her with a soldier who was in full, what appeared to be, army uniform with him holding a medal. Out of curiosity, I asked her about it and she told me that it was her husband who had been awarded a bravery award. I was interested in finding out the story behind it, as I had recently taken a statement from him regarding finding his wife after the attack, but she appeared reluctant to tell me so I didn't pursue it due to her present frail state."

Byrne: "Do you believe that she was holding something back then?"

Shah: "No, not necessarily. Sometimes she is reluctant to talk much, not surprisingly as to what happened to her, she can be very vague from time to time. There is no doubt that she is genuinely freaked out about staying there and is living with her parents at the moment."

Byrne: "So her husband was previously in the armed forces. Do we know what regiment?"

Shah: "He was wearing a red beret, so I presume the Parachute Regiment. As I said, we have to tread very carefully with her, if she doesn't want to talk about a subject we back off."

Byrne then turned to WDS Cannan, "Who is her husband and what does he do for a living?"

She picked up a large file of papers from the nearby desk and after several minutes of sifting through them, replied, "His name is Dennis French, 42 years of age and works for a water board contractor."

Byrne, "Do we know anything about his previous employments?"

"No, sir, there has been no reason to ask up until now."

Byrne, "Have we got his date and place of birth?"

"Yes, sir. Those were obtained from him in a statement taken by Sonia at the hospital on the night of the attack."

·   Byrne: "Right," indicating DC Mills, who he knew to have experience in the armed forces, "David, I would like you to carry out all the usual person searches on Mr French, then I want you to liaise with the army in an effort to establish if Dennis French has ever had a military career. I don't want anyone to approach his wife or him on the subject, because if he has got the ability of being our offender, I do not want to alert him as we have no evidence to put to him yet. He is certainly the only person that we have come across so far who could have the motive and possibly the expertise. Also check the firearms data base to see if he is the holder of a firearms certificate."

The Crime Analyst, Julie Ransome, then raised her hand and after a nod from Byrne in her direction said, "There is no doubt at all that the two men shot in the van were the persons responsible for the rape of Melanie French, so if her husband does become a suspect and is responsible, how did he discover that they were the offenders, as we had very little knowledge about them?"

Byrne: "That's a very good question. There are a number of scenarios that come to mind, amongst which are: did he just come across them by chance, or did his wife tell him something she never told us? Either way, I don't plan on speaking to either of them until we have done our homework on his background."

Byrne, having confirmed that they were in possession of his telephone numbers, instructed the analyst to investigate both his landline and mobile telephone numbers to establish any links there may be to the deceased persons or the car wash company, including the location of his mobile phone at the time when all the fatalities occurred.

Another member of the team, DC Howard Bostock then asked, "If this Dennis French is responsible for the death of the two, who obviously carried out the rape of his wife, are we thinking that he may also be responsible for this triple murder?"

"It's got to be looked at as a possibility, five deaths involving the same one company in a matter of weeks would be one hell of a coincidence. At this moment in time, as he is our only viable suspect, let's see if we can obtain as much detail on the man as possible that includes any fingerprints or photographs available from any source, either police or military. Also, without alerting him, we need to find out what vehicle he drives as it may be necessary to set up some surveillance."

DS Greg Hunter, the incident office manager, who had hurriedly been noting down his DCI's instructions, indicated his wish to speak and following acknowledgement from Byrne, announced to the gathering, "When the work force arrived this morning unaware of what happened overnight, on seeing uniformed officers, one of the staff ran off; he was quickly apprehended and found to be an illegal. I am also told that some of the identification produced by some of the others is suspect and in view of what's been found so far, we may find he is not the only one."

The DCI looked around at his audience, "That comes as no surprise, these people and the whole car wash appears to be just a front for numerous criminal activities and possibly a money laundering operation." Also be mindful when interviewing any workers we need to investigate any offences covered by the modern day slavery act. Looking at DS Hunter, he added, "Anything further of interest from the staff?"

Hunter responded, following shuffling through a pile of papers, "I have just finished reading through the brief statements made by the workers this morning as it seems most speak fairly good English, and a couple of them made mention of an incident that took place there the previous Friday when one of the staff who they only knew as Jorge, who they didn't know much about as he kept himself to himself, had a physical dispute with one of last night's victims and left the company immediately. He was living with them in a company rented house in Brighton, but he left the same day and has not been seen or heard of since. I am told, not surprisingly, they are all very reluctant to discuss anything regarding their managers, or ex-managers as they are now, or any suspicions they had regarding what was going on behind the scenes. The only useful info was the incident involving Jorge who they thought not to be Bulgarian as he claimed."

"Right. Thanks for that, Greg; allocate someone to find out who this bloke is and what that falling out was about, and see if it could also have anything to do with the two who copped it at the Dyke. It may have been a serious matter that involved all six of them, which would certainly throw up a motive. Also, can you alert the Home Office Immigration enforcement team that assisted on the Dyke job, inform them of this latest event, and tell them I will make contact later today when I have more details available?"

D.C Moore, known as Major to his close colleagues, a nickname attributed to him by an adversary who mistakenly believed him to be a former military intelligence officer, raised his arm. "Guv, as you haven't yet mentioned any CCTV, I take it that it was not fitted, or it was destroyed in the fire?"

"That's correct Mick there was no CCTV installed and you can understand why as the only skulduggery taking place there was by themselves. To record it would have been like shooting themselves in the foot. As you have flagged this up I will nominate you to check the surrounding cameras covering the entrances and exits to that estate."

Moore raising his eyebrows and smiling responded, "Cheers for that Guv, I always get the good jobs."

His gesture and remark were met with amusement by the assembled officers who then left the room following being designated their individual tasks. When the respective residences of the two managers were searched, there was ample evidence to show that they, and the organisation that they were working for, were involved in almost every conceivable crime known to man, including drug and people trafficking, the distribution of pornographic material, gun crime and custom tax avoidance. It transpired that Stanescu had been running a similar operation in the Midlands but had recently moved south when he suspected that he had come to the attention of the authorities. Written coded accounts were deciphered revealing transactions from a brothel situated in Hastings, where a young, unidentified eastern European female had recently died of a drugs overdose. A computer at one address, which was examined by analysts, contained video film of what appeared to be a rape committed by two men, showing detailed, explicit, vivid sexual acts on the defenceless woman. Due to the poor light quality and the wide black tape affixed across the woman's eyes and mouth, it was difficult to identify the victim's face, but when Byrne and his team scrutinised the short video, they could clearly identify the white-panel floor of a van and a number of cushions and blankets identical to those found in the offender's transport. It was established that this video had been sent via what remained of the now burnt and melted computer that now sat in the charred remains of a portakabin and had originated from a mobile telephone once belonging to Istvan Vida. It all now became clear to Byrne as to why the sim cards had been destroyed; one of the two deceased had filmed the rape of Melanie French on a mobile phone. It had then been downloaded to the portakabin computer and then forwarded to the one situated in the deceased property. Now he had a new motive as to why all these deaths had occurred. Perhaps they did not originate from a malicious gang feud or the mysterious Jorge but from the friends or family of Melanie French, who not only sought revenge but also wished to eliminate the images and the persons responsible, but how were they able to locate and identify the rapists, and if they had done so, who could have carried out all five executions so efficiently? Perhaps her husband or an associate had seen them by chance and decided to deal with it themselves, as Byrne was well aware that Melanie was certainly not relishing any future possible court proceedings. On the other hand, had Melanie held something back and passed the information to a third party who had carried out the acts? Melanie would have to be spoken to but very carefully, he considered, because if she had no knowledge of these facts, it could take her over the edge.

Following the fatal fire, detectives examined CCTV footage from cameras situated on the adjacent industrial estate and discovered from one of the factories grainy images showing a small, white van leaving the area at the time of the incident. Part of the registration number was visible and after police tested various possible combinations of the letters and numbers available, all except one was eliminated due to the remaining having logos on the vans or they had been parked and secure at the time. The only outstanding number showed a scrapped marker and when the previous owner was contacted, it was eventually traced to a salvage yard in Crawley. On visiting the yard, the police discovered that the van in question had since been crushed. By now, the team was aware that the husband of the rape victim, Mr Dennis French, had the use of an identical white van and it was decided by Byrne that following the imminent pending interview with an army officer concerning French's previous career, he was to be arrested. In the absence of a confession, a short interview was anticipated as there was no realistic evidence to connect him with any of the murders, only tentative circumstantial links such as possible motive and use of a similar van captured on film at a scene, which all considered, made him a viable suspect but without further primary evidence, a charge could not be considered. He hoped that the enquiry with the military would reveal more regarding his suspect.

The enquiries allocated to DC Mills had revealed that Dennis French had neither a police record or was the holder of a firearms certificate, and when it was established that he was a retired soldier,

Mills and Cannan attended an appointment at his former regimental headquarters at Colchester Barracks and spoke to a very smart and affable Captain Adjutant Robin Philips, who remembered the former soldier and at their request, was now in possession of his previous military record.

Following the introductions, the army officer began the conversation,

"I had a lot of time for Sergeant French as he was a likeable, reliable, solid interesting character, who was a born soldier. Were you aware that his father, also named Dennis, was a former soldier killed in action during the conflict in Northern Ireland?"

WDS Cannan: "No, I don't think we were. So, he was following in his father's footsteps?"

"Yes, and French junior, like his father, had an exemplary record and was thought of as basically a decent person with high moral standards—a first-class, fearless, combat soldier—and when given a mission, would carry it through until the relevant result was achieved. This attitude was prevalent when he was requested to head up the army's anti- sexist and anti-bullying campaign here, the duties of which he carried out with a passion. If there was a hint of this type of behaviour, he swiftly snuffed it out. He inferred to me that his particular commitment to this task was as a result of experiences during his early life. Another aspect to this was when he and his wife instigated a children's charity which they called Cuckoo, an acronym for Colchester Underprivileged Children's (Kids) Outings Organisation, aptly named like the bird which is notorious for being a bad parent, by leaving their young to be raised by others which was very appropriate with some of the families concerned. The organisation arranged for children from local children's homes, the less fortunate kids in the borough, and children that had come to notice of social services to go on trips, either in this country or abroad. They also arranged an annual Christmas party for them at a local hotel with a decent present, something I know was a must for Dennis as he knew what it felt like to have received little in the way of presents as a child. He was always able to persuade coach companies, taxi drivers, even airlines to convey the kids for free, and local businesses would provide food, drink and sweets also without cost. Any help required would come from voluntary off-duty personnel on the base; I even got involved myself on a couple of occasions. He had a charm about him and could be very persuasive. I had nothing but admiration for them both. Again, this was a result of demons from his childhood as he didn't want kids to go without as he had. He would also speak to the older kids about the dangers of involvement in crime and drugs use. I felt that as a couple, they did all this with so much passion and enthusiasm to help compensate for their personal misfortunes regarding childbirth.

"I also felt that his bravery and commitment were a need to demonstrate that he was equal or better than others, again due to his adolescent life. Although senior officers tried to persuade him to apply for promotion when he was younger, he refused, and in fact, when it came to appraisals, I, at his request, marked him down on his ability to lead; otherwise, he would be repeatedly called up to the promotion board, and he didn't wish to do this and explain each time why he did not wish to put himself forward."

DC Mills: "He did eventually get promoted, didn't he?"

"Yes, later in his career, but in his younger days, he just wanted to be in the front line—the sharp end as he called it—first in on all the action. He felt that moving up the ranks involved time, supervising others or extra paperwork which would take him away from that. As he became more senior in service, he did apply and was promoted and eventually saw himself not only as a PTI but also as a father figure to the junior soldiers under his command. He was admired by most of his men as he was seen as fair as he would without bias admonish and praise—a trait that served him well in that full-time training position. Despite his lack of formal education, he was intelligent and was a natural survivor. Like so many of the personnel here, adversity has made them stronger and more resilient to what life throws at them. He was also a qualified sniper but once again, he turned down a permanent position because he wanted to fight side by side with his unit. We did all that we could, myself included, to persuade him to stay on and continue as an instructor either as service personnel or in a civilian role in order for him to pass on his experience to others, but he was adamant that he wanted a complete change of lifestyle in a more peaceful environment. He had come close to death on a number of occasions, and I know because of this, he was thought by many who served with him on the front line as an indomitable soldier."

DC Mills: "I believe he was decorated. What was that for?"

"Yes, he received the Military Cross for what was typical of him. He risked his life to allow the successful liberation of captives held by a foreign terrorist organisation. When he was given a task or set himself a target, he would always, to the best of his ability, carry it through to the bitter end. If you were in tight spot, he would be the man you would wish to be by your side."

WDS Cannan then intervened, "His record suggests that he was the perfect soldier. Was his disciplinary record so good?"

Capt. Philips flicked through the thin file in his possession, eventually stopping and reading a page. After doing so, responded,

"The only contentious issue I can find in his personal record are comments regarding he and others being suspected of carrying out retribution during an overseas hostile situation involving—what they described as—pure evil, opposition forces, who had committed terrible atrocities against the innocent civilian population. As I understand it, a patrol he was leading discovered a group that had recently raped, murdered and terrorised women and children, which resulted in the perpetrators being shot and killed by the patrol, but there was suspicion by higher command that they could have been captured alive. The incident was thoroughly investigated but, as the deceased were all heavily armed and the victims refused to co-operate with the investigating officers, only to praise the soldiers concerned all of whom denied any wrong doing, no further action was taken regarding the matter. DC Mills, who had been listening intently to this statement responded "Will any of your remaining records show his shoe size?"

"That's an odd question. Is this investigation that serious?"

WDS Cannan: "We are not at liberty to say, let's hope not."

The officer again browsed through a manila file containing computer print outs and after a short time, said, "You're in luck, size 9."

Both officers thanked the captain for his assistance, immediately passing the information on to a very interested and inspired DCI, who now knowing of his suspect's outstanding courage and military expertise, coupled with the questionable incident, and identical shoe size of the offender, felt sure that he was looking at the right man for all of the killings. Although having the same shoe size was not damming evidence, it was another small part on to which to build a case. He decided that French should now be arrested on suspicion of murder and searches carried out at any properties connected to him to secure any possible firearm or evidence.

Simultaneous actions to arrest and search were carried out at both his flat and place of employment. When the flat was found to be unoccupied, the officers concerned, diverted their search to the address of Melanie's parents where it was immediately established that French was not present and had not been staying there.

Melanie informed officers that her husband had left the country, having taken a three-year contract of employment as a security officer in Venezuela. She was questioned as to any knowledge that she may have had regarding her husband's possible involvement in the killings, which she answered sparingly and gave nothing away. Neither her parents nor Melanie mentioned her imminent travel plans, knowing that the police may have considered that she had some motive for her hasty departure as well, not appreciating that her only reasons were to be with and support her husband who had jeopardised his liberty for her and her need to temporarily escape an area that held nightmarish memories. Both parents now became aware that their son-in-law was under suspicion for causing the deaths of Melanie's assailants, but as much as this shocked them, they had sympathy for his cause, having no concerns for their daughter's safety in his presence, because despite these suggestions, they knew that he deeply cared for her, so much so was why this situation had developed. Melanie then accompanied officers to the flat where a diligent but fruitless search of the premises and garage were carried out.

Following the initial contact by the police, Jon Shipway realised what his pal had possibly done, but before then had no idea whatsoever of his intentions; the only clue being that sometimes, Dutch appeared to be pre-occupied in his thoughts but had put that down to his concerns about the condition of his wife following the rape. His immediate reaction was to protect his friend as much as he could from the police investigation. When the enquiry revealed that French had been residing at the premises, thorough and extensive searches were carried out on the van, workshop, the entire grounds and temporary living quarters.

Amongst paperwork that officers retrieved from the Clearwater Revival Office were company tax records, which included a large number of car wash receipts—some for the van allocated to Dennis French—but none of these were in respect of the riverside car wash site, but the receipt issued and signed by him for the purchase of the water pump on the same estate did come to their notice. Jon, protecting his friend, pointed out that he himself instigated that particular visit to the factory and if his employee had cause to clean his van there, then he, as always as in the past, would have submitted a receipt, making the visit purely circumstantial and surely could not be regarded as incriminating evidence. Further receipts were found regarding purchases at the breakers yard located near Crawley but again, none of these related to French or the van used by him.

When asked regarding the last time he had seen his absent friend, Jon, knowing that Dutch was long gone and both the journey and their movements at the airport would be available on numerous CCTV cameras, revealed only the barest of information regarding their route and final conversation, never mentioning his own concerns or suspicions.

When police examined the company van allocated to French, certain aspects gave suspicion that the plates had recently been removed and replaced but no fingerprints were located in that area of the van, or other significant evidence in or on the vehicle apart from a box containing an assortment of disposable gloves, overshoes and navy blue overalls, which at first appeared to be of some significance to the investigation until officers discovered each of the Clearwater vehicles were equipped with identical protective coverings as were so many other business vehicles involved in similar working practices. The searches carried out of the building and grounds revealed nothing to indicate any involvement in the killings, and his mobile telephone records indicated that the device was at his flat and workplace at the time of each incident.

Despite exhausting all evidential and forensic procedures, no firm evidence was discovered at either murder scene except the offender at the double shooting wore size nine shoes and as he had not spoken, even his nationality remained unknown. Taking into consideration the numerous serious crimes that all five men were suspected of having committed in the past, they would have been sure to have numerous enemies, some, no doubt, as equally or more vicious as themselves, but the only credible suspects Byrne had was a former cleaner who had, according to staff, recently left following a dispute at the Lewes wash site and a former soldier, the husband of the first victim. All efforts were carried out to trace the missing employee, who was believed to be an eastern European named Jorge—whose full name and whereabouts remained unknown.

For Melanie, it would be a big wrench to leave her beloved parents and Jodie behind, but she assured them that she would visit home several times over their contract period—after all, they were both fairly fit and well and Jodie, on their return, would still be a reasonably young dog. As Molly and Ken enjoyed the company of Jodie, they were more than happy to care for her, as not only did they have a large garden but also enjoyed walking the dog on the public open spaces situated behind their home. The emigrating couple could not consider taking the dog with them due to their newly proposed confined living environment with little expectation of safe walking in the seemingly hostile surroundings.

Police enquiries confirmed with Lufthansa Airlines that Dennis French had left the UK via Heathrow Airport on a flight bound for Venezuela only hours after the arson attack, and despite numerous enquiries, the man only known as Jorge had not been traced and it was thought from further interviewing his fellow workers that he was an illegal immigrant from an unknown country. With no fingerprints or photograph found at the multi-occupied staff accommodation to confirm his identity, the hunt for this man had been exhausted.

When Byrne was told of the destination of his major suspect, he was immediately aware by a past experience that there was no extradition agreement between the two countries and coupled with his haste to depart, surely this man was responsible for the carnage, which had resulted from the rape of his wife. Despite initial concerns that perhaps one person alone was not capable of carrying out the arson and resulting deaths, now knowing the full history and tenacity of his suspect ,Byrne now believed that he could have the ability to be solely responsible. Fire investigation officers had confirmed that the inferno had been initially ignited by a Molotov cocktail, an improvised weapon that a former soldier would be fully aware of, the remains of which were found to be a commonly manufactured bottle with a residue of standard petrol, giving no clues to their origin. This together with the use of the gas and liquid accelerant also indicated a practical person with savvy as most of the essential materials to commit the crime were on site, not requiring the offender to purchase or transport the majority of the necessary items. French, not only had the motive due to the violent rape of his wife and the discovery of the images taken, but also had the expertise and skill. Together with the facts that he was now known to have recently visited the vicinity of the car wash site, had knowledge of the salvage premises, drove an identical van to one known to have been in the area at the time of the fire, he realised that his prey had slipped the net, but amongst these tenuous facts, there was still no concrete evidence to support a realist charge.

Byrne's thoughts turned to the shoeprint, which was the only clue to be found that gave some indication of the person responsible for at least two of the deaths—the same size shoe worn by Dennis French. There was no clear and identifiable tread marking left for evidential purposes, but he was in little doubt that the feet responsible for those indentations were now treading on South American soil.

Byrne had an excellent reputation for the high-detection rate and carried the nickname of the 'Mountie' as he invariably got his man with most of the cases he was presented with, but on this occasion, the most complex investigation of his career, secretly in the back of his mind and never to be discussed, he was not hugely disappointed. If Dennis French was to return to the UK in three years, he would be retired from the police, and unless something very spectacular was forthcoming, he could not foresee enough evidence to convict him for any of the offences he believed him to be responsible for. His own father had served in the army in Northern Ireland and now knowing of his adversary's background, had empathy for him. How would he himself have felt if someone close to him had been subjected to a similar horrific attack which had scarred them mentally for life, with the further knowledge that some sick people were in possession of a film of their torment? Although the images of this act of depravity would be required to be preserved for any future evidential purpose, he hoped that they would remain on file—never to be viewed again. He was sure that if his suspect did ever appear before a court and the full facts of the case became known to the public, of both his wife's ordeal, and his intervention in preventing a further identical crime, French would be equally regarded as much an injured party and good Samaritan, as a vengeful killer . Using a term from one of his favourite hobbies, Dennis French was the big one that got away. Byrne, who had spent his entire working life attempting to eradicate crime, believed that French had committed all five killings, and he didn't get a sniff of the culprit until it was too late, but due to all of the circumstances surrounding the case, he would only ever admit it to his wife and very close friends that he hoped the Englishman, with the name French and known as Dutch, would never be brought to justice.

Chapter 19

The Final Countdown (1986)
Artist: Europe Writer: Joey Tempest

As he lay there mentally exhausted, the sound of his activating battery alarm clock reminded him of his 8 am meeting with his new boss followed by a further briefing including George and Bo. Having managed to revitalise himself by way of a tepid shower, he made his way to the rest room and bar where Claudia, in comprehensible broken English, introduced herself and offered him coffee and breakfast. Dutch, still not being sure of what was eaten yet in this part of the world, erred on the side of caution and plumped for what he understood may have been similar to croissants and some kind of preserve, which reminded him to request Melanie to bring out as much Marmite as she could possibly get in her luggage. Following a polite, somewhat difficult conversation with much sign language, Claudia left the room to prepare his order, and Dutch could understand why George would be attracted to such a pleasant, good-looking lady and was already eagerly awaiting to meet the house keeper, the other party in the alleged love triangle.

Following his breakfast, Dutch reported to the small briefing room situated in the corner of the complex. As he was early for the meet, the door was locked. So he awaited for the arrival of his new boss, who arrived in a smartly-pressed, open-neck, white shirt with yellow and blue polka dot cravat, white slacks, together with his brilliant white beard and hair creating an almost blinding image, making Dutch feel ridiculously underdressed in his sweat top, khaki combat trousers and highly-polished boots. His boss, from what he was wearing, was obviously not himself going to be in contact with any oil that day, immediately handed him a large bunch of his own personal set of keys, all marked for various buildings and alarm systems within the complex. After exchanging early morning pleasantries, Dutch located the necessary key and entered the room where his employer set to work in explaining the duties that Dutch and his team were expected to perform. He now learnt, somewhat surprisingly, that he would be responsible for not only personal security together with the additional security staff who cover the two plants 24 hours a day, but also in charge of their shift rosters, hiring and firing together with a small armoury, communications, firearms training and tactics covering possible confrontational situations. Dutch was quietly taken aback as this was revealed to him as he thought that he was going to be employed as basically a bodyguard, but at the same time excited with this additional responsibility, as it would break up the anticipated everyday close protection role that he had expected, and after all, there was nothing he had been allocated that he couldn't handle.

Following the hour-long conversation, George and Bo entered the room simultaneously and were immediately given their duties for the day by the boss, who explained to Dutch that this would be his role when settled in. All four then studied a large map affixed to the wall and discussed as to what route to take to the land locked refinery that day, as the route was never exactly the same each day, in an attempt to prevent an organised ambush. After drawing weapons from the small but well-stocked armoury, they set out to their destination in two vehicles. Bo was alone in the pickup with George driving the SUV; alongside him was Dutch with the boss in the rear. Whilst on route, the two vehicles, which both contained assault rifles and ammunition in secure metal cabinets, would constantly change as lead vehicle communicating by way of personal radios. Dutch, now armed with a handgun concealed under a gilet matching his two colleagues, was impressed with the planning, equipment and alertness of his two colleagues but also suggesting to his boss that the acquisition of smoke grenades and flash flares would be desirable should they ever find themselves in a perilous situation. He further suggested the purchase of some of his beloved tremble sticks, as secondary to the security already in place protecting the aircraft outside of the building, and after explaining their function, the boss appeared impressed and told him that he would attempt to supply all of the items mentioned.

Some months later following Melanie's arrival and both enjoying their new lifestyles and occupations, only a few miles from The White House, a small well-armed and informed gang were plotting their next criminal venture by sitting around a dated computer and screen, studying a map together with a photograph of a white-haired, goatee-bearded oil representative. There was a buzz of anticipation about the group due to their recent acquiring and testing of a high-powered .50 calibre rifle and armour piercing bullets, which they now believed would enable them to execute a long-awaited plot. At the same time, a three-strong security team were planning their daily duties with their superstitious team leader assuming, in a land of high crime rate where life was cheap, that he still had two remaining lives of the nine that he believed he had been blessed with.

Life 8: He was completely unaware that in a flat above the shops on Hangleton Parade, 15-year-old Theo, his parents and neighbours had become so frustrated at being disturbed some weekends by youths rowdy behaviour ,he was regularly recording CCTV footage from a camera discreetly situated in his bedroom window. The camera scanned both, the front of the shopping parade and a portion of the Bombardier pub car park situated opposite in order to capture the images of the nuisance caused. The tenants' objective was to prepare a dossier to present to the local environmental health authority and local police in an attempt to curtail the situation. The camera, which was on a timed mode, was of good quality with a night-time vision facility. On one Friday evening, weeks previously, this equipment had captured a strange incident when a lone male, wearing a hat whose face was clearly visible, wearing a boiler type suit, walked from the parade to a large, white van parked in the pub car park. This man surreptitiously and quickly entered the rear of this van. When the driver and passenger returned, they drove away with the man remaining inside. The registration numbers of the van and that of a smaller van entering and leaving the parade that evening had also been captured and clearly readable. As there were no disturbances on that particular night, the images remained undiscovered. As the family were unaware of the significance, of the recordings they were erased before the police carried out house-to-house enquiries in the area following the link to the shootings with The Bombardier and were irretrievable.

Dutch had no knowledge of this very lucky escape, as if there is any validation in the theory of him having the luxury of having nine lives, he now has one less than he believed as because of its life time implications, his grandmother and he would consider this incident as another lost life, as if the images had been discovered before his departure, he would have spent most, or the rest, of his life incarcerated. As he planned his future, he was unaware that he is now a mere mortal in perilous employment, in dangerous surrounding, with only one life remaining where a life could easily be lost.

In the way of apology for his sudden departure from his friend and employer, Dutch had sent a text message to Jon which read, "Sorry that we left the party so suddenly but we didn't fancy the storm that was expected." Jon, who had not attended any recent function with Melanie or Dutch, understood the hidden meaning.

Shortly after, Dutch received a similar cryptic message from Jon. "As you have an interest in this field, two unpleasant predatory migrating birds flew in recently, looking for scraps. Didn't feed them a crumb so they left to continue their search elsewhere."

Although Dutch did appreciate bird life, he recognised that this was Jon's discreet way of informing him that he had been visited by gang members of the cartel that he had part destroyed. He knew from Melanie that the police now suspected him of causing the deaths, but how this crew had identified and traced him to his previous employer was a mystery, but large criminal organisations, such as these, had the means and resources to obtain anything they wished, as he remembered the words of warning that Jorge had told him that they had eyes and ears everywhere. Was it possible that they had got to Jorge so soon? But even if they had, Jorge didn't have a clue who he was. If they had traced him, he thought it highly unlikely that he would still be alive, or did they have some kind of informant within the police? He would now need to be twice as guarded—not only in his new environment with its associated responsibilities but also from this new far reaching threat—especially if and when he returned home as such people had long memories and would make a point of showing what becomes of those who transgress against them.

His one remaining life looked in imminent jeopardy as danger was now lurking on many fronts.

As Dutch and his companions travelled on yet another perilous journey, his mind wandered as to how his extraordinary life and near-death experiences would make a good book in which each chapter could be named with a significant popular song title, followed by a film sequel, and in his head, he was contemplating the title music of such a blockbuster movie, completely unaware that through previous surveillance a group of criminals were positioned around a minor crossroads which was necessary for the convoy to travel before being able to vary their route to their intended destination. As they approached the junction the cross hairs of a telescopic sight of a powerful assault rifle was firmly focused on his head. Once the sniper received the signal that his colleagues were in position and considered his aim to be true, he gently pulled the trigger and the sound of a shot rang out.

About the Author
Paperback Writer (1966)
Artist: The Beatles
Writer: John Lennon/ Paul McCartney

Having lived and worked in Sussex all of his sixty-seven years, this is his first novel. Married to Carla for forty-four years, they have three children and four grandchildren.

He 'coincidentally' shares many traits with his main character: a lifetime runner, as a former police officer of thirty-three years who too feels he may have lost a few lives on the way and also finds himself nominating titles of popular songs to certain situations and nicknames to certain characters.